Echoes of Pia

By
Lermit Ramon Diaz-Salazar

Copyright

El Eco de Pia © 2025 Lermit Díaz Salazar.

Registration Number: TXu 2-474-685
Effective Date of Registration: February 19, 2025
Registration Decision Date: March 14, 2025

Translated by Maria Eugenia Gavides Cedeno, Jonathan Lomeli Perez, and Lermit Ramon Diaz Salazar

E BOOK: 978-1-968165-17-8

PAPERBACK: 978-1-968165-23-9

HARDCOVER: 978-1-968165-24-6

Dedicated to my beloved wife, Fabiola, and to my daughters, Fabiana and Michelle.

Index

The Bridge to New Horizons   1
Pia's Journal   5

The Silent Wound   6
Under the Spell of the Rain   11
Pia's Journal   18

Maria I   20
Between Two Worlds   22
Pia's Journal   28

Beyond the Wall of Silence   30
Maria II   40
The Cave of Silence   42
The Weight of Memories   53
Shadows of Desire   57
The Light of the Irreplaceable   62
A Place to Return To   69
Pia's Journal   71

The Echo of an Uncertain Kiss   73
The Reverberation of Farewell   81
The Weight of Dreams   88
The Shadows of Santa Maria Novella   96
Love at the Threshold of the Abyss   101
The Pawn on the Board   108
The Silent Farewell   113
Pia's Arrival   115
Loneliness in the City That Never Sleeps   122
Lessons in Exile   131
Rebirth in the Storm   134
Under the Shadows of the Dolomites Towers I   137
Shadows of Jealousy Beneath the Dolomites Peaks I   143
Under the Shadows of the Dolomites Towers II   145
Shadows of Jealousy Beneath the Dolomites Peaks II   153

Under the Shadows of the Dolomites Towers III   155
  Pia's Journal   159

Shadows of Jealousy Beneath the Dolomites Peaks III
                                                                          179
Under the Shadows of the Dolomites Towers IV   184
The Name Written in Water   187
Trilogy of the Soul: Accept, Adapt, Advance   190
  Pia's Journal   197

Umberto   199
Via Tito Livio Burattini   207
The Photograph and Portrait of Giacomo   211
Teresa   217
Aglio, Olio e Peperoncino   219
**Song to the Earth, to Time, and to the Mystery of
Moments That Do Not Return**   221
The Unexpected Visitor   224
Silence Resounded   229
The Edge of Night   233
Under the Crimson Light   238
The Wound of the Soul   242
Alessia   245
  Pia's Journal   248

The Big Apple   250
The Roman Emperor   254
A Winter in New York   258
The Phantom of the Opera   262
  Pia's Journal   270

Echoes of Pia

The Bridge to New Horizons

The fog rose slowly over the deserted streets of Florence, wrapping every corner in a cloak of mystery and nostalgia. In the distance, the bells of Santa Croce announced the arrival of a new day, but for Pia, it was nothing more than the muffled echo of a time that no longer existed. She remained still in the dimness of her apartment, gazing at the half-open door, knowing that beyond those walls, Giacomo would fade into the shadows of his own farewell.

They had once been lovers, in another time, when the world felt less uncertain and promises didn't crumble like sandcastles at the first gust of wind. They had met under the starry sky of a distant spring, and in their gaze, dreams that seemed indestructible had been forged. But life, with its cruel patience and quiet stealth, wears down even the firmest foundations.

Pia had watched him fade little by little, like the flame of a candle fighting not to be extinguished in the darkness. First it was the words that broke, filled with silences that not even love could fill. Then the glances turned distant, and the caresses became gestures devoid of meaning. And so, without either of them noticing, they stopped being Pia and Giacomo, becoming instead two souls searching without finding, trapped in the labyrinth of withered affection.

That morning, when Giacomo looked at her for the last time, Pia saw something in his eyes she never would have imagined: the reflection of her own resignation. There was no hatred or reproach, only a quiet sadness, like the melancholy that overtakes travelers as they say goodbye to a land they know they will never set foot on again.

—Pia…—he whispered, as if his voice belonged to a stranger. But she gently shook her head, closing the distance between them with a firm gaze.

—Don't say anything, Giacomo,— she replied, her tone carrying more tenderness than he deserved. — Some things don't need to be explained. Love doesn't die all at once; it fades away until one day, without warning, we realize that what we feel isn't love but the shadow of what once was.

Giacomo lowered his head, caught between guilt and helplessness. Pia stepped closer and took his hands. She felt the coldness of those fingers that had once made her feel so alive, and with a knot in her throat, she knew she had to be strong. Because to love, sometimes, also means to let go.

—It's time to release, she said in a thread of voice. — To stop fighting an invisible enemy. Love isn't this sadness we carry; it's not this nostalgia that has made us prisoners. Love is freedom, and we lost the key to this cage long ago.—

Giacomo looked up, surprised by the determination in her words. She looked at him sweetly, with that ancient affection still beating somewhere in the corners of her soul. But it wasn't enough. It couldn't be.

—And what do we do now?— he asked, as if there was still a flicker of hope left.

—Nothing,— Pia murmured, and as she said it, she felt herself shedding a weight that had bound her for far too long. — We're going to let silence do what we didn't know how to. Accept that some paths, no matter how often they cross, aren't meant to walk together.—

Then, she let go, allowing his hands to slip from hers like sand through her fingers. Giacomo looked at her one last time, trying to memorize every detail of her face, every curve of her lips. Yet he knew, just as she did, that those images would fade with time, replaced by other shadows, other memories.

With a sigh that tore at his soul, he turned and walked to the door. There were no goodbyes, no promises. Only the sound of his footsteps retreating down the hallway, echoing like the heartbeat of a heart that no longer belonged to her. When the door closed behind him, Pia was left alone, surrounded by the silence of her empty home.

In that moment, she understood that endings don't always represent the conclusion we imagine. Some linger in the air, like notes lost on the last page of an unfinished score. But she also understood that within that absence, in that imperfection, lay true freedom: the possibility to rewrite, to reinvent oneself, and maybe, one day, find a love she wouldn't have to let go.

Ultimately, she thought as the morning light filtered through the window, the battle was not against the other, but against oneself. And she had chosen the wisest path: that of stillness. The peace that blooms when we accept that sometimes, the boldest and bravest act is to surrender or walk away.

Pia picked up her journal with trembling hands, as one might caress a past that both hurts and comforts. With every word she inscribed on the pages, the ink seemed to come alive, capturing the echoes of a sleepless night and a farewell she hadn't yet fully processed. She wrote without hurry, letting herself be carried by the weight of her thoughts, as if each line were an exorcism, an attempt to tear from her chest the sadness that still held her captive. But by the time she reached the end, weariness enveloped her with the same softness as the fog that covered the city. She closed the journal, set down the pen, and in a whisper of resignation and relief, let herself fall into the bed of memory. And so, between dreams of lost love and broken promises, she fell asleep.

Pia's Journal

Saturday, March 19, 2022.

In the labyrinth of my existence, I have encountered crossroads where the wisest path is that of stillness. To let be what no longer is, to rid myself of what no longer exists, to detach from hands that no longer connect with mine, to distance myself from echoes that no longer vibrate in my soul. Sometimes, the battle is nothing more than a mirage in the desert; the word, a song for deaf ears; the plea, an offering before an empty altar.

Endings, like books, are not always concluded with the elegance or neatness that I desire. They leave blank pages, unfinished chapters, lingering questions, unanswered inquiries, or a bitter taste in memory. However, in that imperfection, in that lack of finality, I find a profound lesson: my life is not evaluated by what happens around me but by what thrives within me.

The task of cultivating my inner garden consists of sowing the seeds of peace and nurturing the soil of tranquility. Thus, from that oasis, I will transform myself into a beacon in the storm, a call to serenity. And if my surroundings prefer chaos or disorder, a grateful goodbye will be my most valuable compass; it will be the bridge toward new horizons.

Because in the end, the true journey is not the one I chart on maps but the one I undertake toward myself.

Until next time.

The Silent Wound

Twenty years ago, Giacomo couldn't remember the last time he had felt peace in his own home. That place, once a refuge where the walls echoed with laughter and whispered promises between him and his mother, had become a prison. The echoes of arguments, the clinking of empty bottles hitting the floor, and the screams that tore through the silence had become his only company.

He had once been an ordinary child, with simple dreams and a deep love for his father, Franco. He saw him as a hero—a large, strong man who came home from work tired, yet always managed to offer a smile, a gentle gesture that made little Giacomo feel safe. But those days of safety had vanished like the smoke trailing from the cigarette butts in Franco's trembling hands.

One afternoon, Giacomo had stood at the doorway, watching his father hunched over the dining table with a half-empty bottle. His mother, María, stood nearby, her hands shaking, her lips tight, trying to calm a storm she no longer knew how to contain. Giacomo was barely twelve, but he already knew that something had broken inside his father. The man who once tossed him in the air, making him laugh until his stomach hurt, had turned into a stranger.

—You're good for nothing!— Franco's voice was a hoarse growl, loaded with hatred and disappointment. — You're just like the rest of them!—

The words flew like sharp knives, slicing through the air with surgical precision. But they weren't enough. They didn't carry the weight needed to quench the rage burning in Franco's face. Giacomo barely had time to process it, to understand that something was terribly wrong. The sound of his father's hand cutting through the air was like the crack of a whip, a thunderclap about to break in the storm already looming over them.

The impact was brutal, almost cinematic. The blow landed with a dry, echoing thud, like someone had thrown a rock through a glass window—only this time, it was his mother collapsing to the ground. Time seemed to slow. Giacomo's eyes locked on the strands of her hair flying in all directions, like a curtain shredded by the wind, before she crashed heavily onto the cold marble floor.

The punch had been precise, right to the jaw. Franco had knocked her down as effortlessly as a boxer flooring his opponent— but this wasn't a fair fight. This was an execution. The sound of her body hitting the ground echoed hollowly, reverberating in Giacomo's chest like a slow-motion explosion. He watched blood drip from her split lip, a crimson bloom spreading across the floor like a scarlet flower.

Franco kept yelling, his voice a hammer shattering every corner of the room. His words had become incomprehensible, a savage blend of shouts and howls that rang in Giacomo's ears like a detuned radio. Fear gripped him, paralyzing him. It wasn't just fear of his father—it was the visceral horror of seeing the person he loved most in the world reduced to a helpless figure on the ground.

Giacomo stood frozen, as if forced to witness a macabre spectacle. Every second felt like an eternity, a string of harrowing images etched into his memory forever. Franco's ragged breathing, the sour stench of alcohol in the air, and his mother's trembling hands trying—failing—to rise. And then, as if the universe itself had stopped, Giacomo saw his father raise his hand again, threatening to replay the scene.

The bond Giacomo had forged with his mother was the most tangible expression of that tragic awareness of existence that lies deep within every human being. In his case, that bond, more than a support, was a fragile thread—strained by an environment where every scream from Franco was another crack threatening to snap it. Giacomo lived with the certainty that his world was suspended by the delicate presence of his mother—should that presence break, he would be set adrift. It wasn't just fear of physical harm; it was dread of the void, of absolute desolation, of being cast without shelter into a world that had suddenly become hostile and foreign.

What he would later come to know as attachment theory was nothing more than the rationalization of a truth lived in flesh and blood: the ever-conflicted coexistence between the longing to be protected and the visceral fear of abandonment. Young Giacomo, though still unaware, was already tangled in an ontological dilemma. In his need for closeness to his mother, he found an anchor that clashed violently with the terror sparked by his father's very presence. Thus, caught between affection and dread, the child fell into a perpetual state of doubt: Would love be enough to hold him up? Or would he drown, pulled under by the destructive force of Franco? That experience, engraved deep within him, would shape the way he tried to relate to the world as an adult—forever oscillating between the search for security and the relentless fear of loss.

Franco's words were like sharpened daggers, each leaving invisible scars on Giacomo's mind. The echo of his voice lingered inside—not because of its volume, but because of the way it corroded his understanding of the world.

Giacomo watched the scene from the threshold, feeling each second become more unreal, as though the air itself was turning heavy, suffocating.

The blow wasn't only physical—it was an earthquake that shattered the very foundations of what Giacomo believed. Seeing his mother on the floor, her face contorted in pain and despair, made him feel like something inside him had broken. Fear held him in place, but the worst part wasn't the paralysis—it was knowing, with crushing certainty, that his world would never be the same.

Franco kept shouting, but Giacomo no longer heard the words. Everything had become a buzz, a fog clouding his mind, isolating him from immediate reality. The emotional impact of watching his hero morph into his executioner was what left the deepest scars. In that moment, Giacomo understood something terrible: the person who was supposed to protect him had not only betrayed him—he had destroyed any chance at safety or genuine love.

From that day on, something in Giacomo shifted. The attachment he once felt toward his father crumbled every time he heard the creak of the door, every time he saw Franco's glassy eyes filled with a rage that seemed endless. Giacomo began avoiding his gaze, tiptoeing through the house, terrified that any small sound might awaken the beast now living inside his father.

Violence became a daily presence—a silent monster lurking in every corner. It wasn't just physical; it was emotional, like a slow-acting poison seeping into the air they breathed. In his desperate attempt to understand why his hero had betrayed him, Giacomo began retreating into himself. He developed a constant fear of abandonment, a wound that would follow him for life. Every relationship, every bond he tried to build, was stained by the same question: Am I enough?

Will I be abandoned again?

The last night Franco was in the house felt strange. There were no screams, no fights—just a dense, almost unreal silence blanketing every corner. Giacomo watched him with the same tense, wary look as always, but something had shifted in the air, as if everything was moving in slow motion. Franco walked with a disturbing calm, fixing a piercing gaze on his son, barely blinking.

The house seemed to hold its breath, as if even the walls knew something irreversible was happening. Giacomo watched him in silence, feeling a weight lift from his chest. In that moment, something inside him broke too—as though the child he once was had faded into the darkness Franco left behind.

At dawn the next day, the first rays of sunlight timidly slipped through the curtains, but Giacomo was already awake. In his mind, a flicker of hope sparked, imagining it had all been a nightmare, and he rose with the faint desire to resume routine as he stepped through his bedroom door. But with that first step, the harsh reality hit him like a cold, impenetrable wall.

Under the Spell of the Rain

The rain lashed against the windows with fury, a symphony of droplets crashing onto the asphalt, sweeping away the last traces of a gray afternoon. Florence's streets, usually buzzing with life, had turned into a sea of umbrellas and shadows sliding swiftly in search of shelter. Pia and Alessia looked at each other through the veil of water separating them from the bar they'd planned to visit, but their steps were drawn instead toward a small restaurant that seemed to beckon from the corner, wrapped in warm lights and irresistible aromas.

They entered the restaurant like two castaways finding a safe harbor. The trattoria, with its low ceilings and exposed stone walls, radiated the welcoming charm of places where time seems to stand still. The open kitchen was the heart of the place, where the chef—a jovial figure with a cheerful face—oversaw each dish like a conductor, ensuring that every gastronomic note was in perfect harmony.

—To start, I'll have the tagliatelle with porcini mushrooms,— said Pia, her voice soft yet sure. She knew exactly what she wanted—a dish that brought back memories of childhood, of damp mushroom forests and warm kitchens. Alessia, smiling, chose the pappardelle with wild boar ragu, a Tuscan classic that spoke of long nights and deep conversations.

With a knowing wink, the chef sent over a tray of antipasti: aged pecorino cheeses, plump olives, and cured meats that seemed to tell tales from distant hills. A prosecco from Alto Adige arrived at the table, its light bubbles rising in spirals inside the crystal glasses, as if trying to capture the laughter beginning to flow between the two friends. Then came a Nobile di Montepulciano, deep and velvety, promising to ignite a conversation that still lingered in whispers.

The chef approached with hands full of culinary promises, and when the tagliatelle with porcini mushrooms reached the table, the air filled with an aroma of damp earth and deep forest. The tagliatelle, handmade with the delicacy of someone who understands the art of pasta, curled around Pia's fork like fine golden ribbons. The porcini lay atop the pasta like little treasures, their edges browned to perfection, releasing a perfume that evoked autumn walks through woods where the wind carried the echoes of fallen leaves. The first bite was a balance of textures and flavors, where the earthy tone of the mushrooms blended with the silky smoothness of the pasta, while a hint of extra virgin olive oil and a whisper of garlic elevated the natural flavors without overpowering them. Each bite was a celebration of autumn in Tuscany, a dance between the simple and the sublime.

Alessia's dish, the pappardelle with wild boar ragu, told a different story—one of strength and character. The wide, generous pappardelle seemed made to embrace the boldness of the sauce. The wild boar ragu, slow-cooked for hours, was a dark red hue and carried an aroma that spoke of ancestral secrets kept in rustic kitchens. The wild boar, shredded to the point of melting, had been infused with red wine, Tuscan herbs, and a touch of tomato that rounded the flavor with a subtle acidity. The taste was deep, almost primal, yet refined by the precision of the chef, who had struck a balance between the wild strength of the meat and the elegance of the pasta. Every bite was an explosion of bold yet balanced flavors, like a symphony where every instrument played in harmony under the baton of an invisible maestro.

Pia couldn't help but notice the man watching them from the kitchen. Tomasso, with his calm demeanor and that gaze that seemed to unveil secrets. Their exchange of glances was brief but enough to ignite something inside her. It was a different look than Giacomo's—more serene, but with a mystery she couldn't ignore.

The conversation between Pia and Alessia soon drifted to the inevitable: the lessons left behind by past loves. Alessia, always direct, wasted no time asking about Giacomo.

—How are you feeling now?— Alessia asked, lowering her voice as she saw Pia gaze into her wine glass.

Pia sighed, but not out of sadness—out of relief. She had come a long way from the days of emotional chaos.

—I never forced anyone to choose me,— Pia began, her voice firm and clear, reflecting the strength she had found in her own heart. —If you think you can find something more meaningful somewhere else, go ahead; I won't stop you. Life is too short to trust someone who isn't committed to staying.

The trattoria's hum continued around them, but in that moment, Pia could hear only the beat of her own truth.

—I believe in freedom and in the authenticity of emotions,— she continued, her eyes shining with conviction. —If you choose to stay, let it be because your heart tells you your place is by my side, not because I ask you to. I want to be a choice, not a fallback option in anyone's life.

Alessia nodded slowly, sipping her wine. Pia, still speaking, radiated a serenity that only comes from learning to value oneself.

—I deserve someone who sees my worth,— Pia said with a quiet smile. —I don't want someone who stays out of fear of loneliness or out of habit. I want someone who stays because they can't imagine life without me.

There was something almost poetic in the way she spoke, as if each word was another piece of her new identity. The Pia sitting in that trattoria was a woman reborn from her own ashes: stronger, wiser, and above all, freer.

—The door is always open; you can leave whenever you want,— she concluded, raising her glass in a silent toast to life. — Meanwhile, I'll keep building my own life, creating harmony, peace, passion, and joy. My joy doesn't depend on others, but on my ability to grow, to evolve, and to keep moving forward every day.

Alessia, with an admiring smile, raised her glass too.

—To you, Pia. And to this new version of yourself that inspires me so much—

The two women toasted, their glasses clinking in the air as the trattoria buzzed with the echo of Tuscan life. Outside, the rain continued to fall just as heavily, but inside the restaurant, the warmth of wine, food, and friendship filled every corner, enveloping Pia in a sense of wholeness that depended on no one but herself.

Their conversation flowed easily, full of laughter and toasts, but Tomasso's presence remained palpable. From his spot in the kitchen, just a few steps from their table, he moved with the same finesse as before, yet his eyes occasionally drifted toward her. It was a gaze that didn't intrude but invited—an invisible bridge only Pia could cross, if she so desired.

Alessia, ever perceptive, was quick to notice the exchange of looks. With a mischievous smile, she lifted her glass.

—Looks like someone's quite interested,— she whispered playfully, gesturing toward Tomasso with her eyes.

Pia lowered her gaze with a shy smile, unable to stop the soft warmth spreading across her skin. It wasn't the kind of immediate, burning connection she had once had with Giacomo, but something different, deeper—charged with possibilities that had only just begun to surface.

When the chef approached their table to ensure everything was to their liking, it was Tomasso who followed with a glass in hand. He leaned slightly toward them with relaxed courtesy and placed a small bottle of liqueur on the table to accompany their dessert.

—A gift from the house,— he said with a smile, but his eyes met Pia's, and in that instant, words felt unnecessary.

The silence that followed was not awkward but filled with endless possibilities. Tomasso gave a slight nod, as if recognizing something in Pia, and returned to the kitchen— but not before leaving something more than just a bottle on the table. Pia noticed a small card beside it, written in elegant, confident handwriting:

—Hope to see you again. Tomasso.—

Alessia picked up the card with a gentle laugh.

—Looks like you won't have to look far for a second encounter.—

Pia smiled, this time with a sense of certainty that surprised her. She was no longer the woman who doubted, who clung to what she couldn't have. Now, she knew she was ready for something more—something built on newer, stronger, more conscious foundations.

The rain still poured outside, but it didn't matter anymore. Pia felt something had begun—something that might change her life again, but this time, it would be on her own terms.

—I think I'm ready now,— Pia said softly, more to herself than to Alessia, as she tucked the card into her purse, casting one last glance toward Tomasso, who was watching her from afar, eyes filled with promise.

And so, fate offered them both a new opportunity— one that Pia now felt ready to embrace.

The rain had stopped when Pia and Alessia said goodbye in front of the trattoria, the warmth of the evening still glowing in their smiles. They stepped together onto Via della Condotta, their footsteps echoing over the wet cobblestones that reflected the golden glow of the flickering streetlamps. The city, still damp from the recent storm, exuded that earthy, fresh scent that only follows a hard rain—petrichor filling the air with its nostalgic touch.

At the end of the street, where their paths would part, Alessia smiled and offered a warm farewell. She turned toward Via San Miniato, the road that would lead her home to San Niccolò, while Pia continued on toward Via dei

Leoni, in the direction of Via Bufalini, where she lived. They walked away in opposite directions, each wrapped in her own thoughts, carrying with them the memories of the night.

Pia moved through the deserted streets, letting the silence of the city wrap around her, though something in the air unsettled her. In the distance, she could hear an echo— soft but steady—like the measured rhythm of footsteps following her own. She stopped for a moment, and the sound ceased. She looked back but saw only long shadows cast across the empty sidewalks. The echo of her own steps rang in her mind, but the quickening beat of her heart told her she wasn't alone.

She kept walking, faster now, as the wind swept the last raindrops from the rooftops. She felt a presence— something she couldn't explain but which pressed against her chest. The air was saturated with the petrichor of the recent storm, that mix of nostalgia and loneliness the city always left behind after each rainfall.

It wasn't until she reached the entrance of her building on Via Bufalini that she felt the slightest relief. The sound of the footsteps had vanished, but the feeling that someone had followed her lingered on her skin like an invisible trace. Only when she closed the door behind her, the muffled echo of the city left outside, was she finally able to breathe freely.

Pia's Journal

Thursday, October 13, 2022.

This morning, I woke up with the feeling that something inside me had changed. I could still hear the echo of the rain on the streets, but what truly lingered was that gaze. Tomasso's gaze—one that seemed to pierce through me in that trattoria, as if he had known every hidden corner of my being without even exchanging a word. His card—I've read it over and over, almost obsessively, captivated by the gesture.

I always believed that love, true love, didn't arrive with the speed of lightning but with the slow pace of understanding—with the patience of mutual knowing. Yet, when I looked at Tomasso, I felt something different, something I hadn't experienced before. It wasn't simply attraction—it was an instant understanding, as if our souls had recognized each other in that fleeting moment. His voice, deep and resonant, still echoes in my mind. And those clear, profound eyes, partly concealed by a beard that suggests a long-standing grudge against razors, left me speechless.

Fromm once wrote that to love is not merely a feeling but an art that requires practice, discipline, and devotion. But isn't there something about love that defies logic? Something that makes us feel, in a single encounter, the possibility of sharing our life with someone—not out of need or habit, but from the certainty that this person awakens something dormant and forgotten within us.

Tomasso looked at me in a way that made me question everything I thought I knew about love. Fromm would say that real love is born of freedom, of not depending on someone else for our happiness. Yet in those few seconds, I felt that there was something in his gaze that called me to discover him—to learn his contours, his light and shadows. His presence doesn't intimidate me. On the contrary, it invites me to be more—to be authentic.

I don't know if what I felt was love at first sight, but I do know that there's something in him that draws me in—something that perhaps is meant to change me, to lead me toward a new kind of love. One that, as Fromm says, is born from the shared effort to grow together. Maybe love isn't only a matter of time but of willingness—of being open to the unexpected.

Tomasso is everything I didn't know I needed to see in a man. And yet, there's something about him that feels familiar, as if that deep voice, that thick beard, and that velvet gaze had already existed in my life in another form, in another time. Is this what they call destiny? I don't know. But I'm willing to find out.

Maria I

María, originally from Austria, was a homemaker whose sweetness and charisma stood in stark contrast to the harshness of her husband, Franco. They had met in college and, from that moment on, built a bond that seemed unbreakable. Franco, shaped by the shadow of his father—a World War II veteran who had unleashed the fury of his post-traumatic stress disorder on him—found in María a safe haven. She, with infinite patience, knew how to navigate the storms that raged within her husband.

For years, María and Franco's home was a haven of peace. However, fortune is fickle, and the last few years brought financial hardship to Franco's business. The pressure from banks and creditors pushed him toward the abyss of alcohol, and with each drink, his violence grew more intense. María, in her effort to preserve harmony, endured it in silence, hoping that the man she had once fallen in love with would return from the shadows.

One night, the silence in the house was so thick it felt almost tangible. Franco, under the influence of alcohol, became enraged. María tried to calm him, but her words were futile. Franco's fury exploded—he swept the food and dinner plates off the table with his forearm, and in a fit of rage, struck her with such force that she collapsed, her body crashing onto the shards of broken glass. Giacomo, their son, witnessed the scene from the doorway, frozen in terror. María gestured for him to leave to spare him from seeing the rest of the violence. Time seemed to freeze as rage overtook their home.

With her lip split open, María tried to stop the bleeding by pressing the tip of her tongue against the wound, tasting the sharp, metallic tang of fresh blood. Franco grabbed her by the hair, yanking her face close to his, and shouted with a voice full of fury:

—Look at what you've done! —

Tears filled her eyes, and with a trembling voice, she pleaded:

—Please, Franco, calm down. Look at Giacomo—I beg you, for the love of God.

The tension in the air was suffocating as María tried to appeal to the humanity that still remained in her husband, desperate to shield her son from the violence surrounding them.

Between Two Worlds

Pia couldn't stop thinking about Tomasso. There was something about him, about his presence, that unsettled her in a strange way. It wasn't just attraction; it was something deeper—a subtle calling she couldn't ignore. Since that night at the trattoria, when their eyes met in a glance that seemed to contain promises, Pia had counted the days until she could see him again. That Saturday, she had decided to go alone. She needed to confirm whether the feeling Tomasso evoked in her was real or just a mirage woven by her imagination.

But in the early hours of that very Saturday, October 15, something unexpected happened. A message from her father disrupted the calm of her sleep. It was unusual—her father rarely wrote to her. He had been sick for years, battling a lung disease that, while leaving him frail, never seemed to break his spirit. Yet that morning, the letter she received changed everything.

—Dear Pia,

No one taught me how to be a father, just as no one prepared you to face the countless trials life had in store for you... —

Her father's words echoed from afar, filled with wisdom and the kind of melancholy that only comes with the nearness of death. Pia read the letter again and again, unable to stop a tear from slipping down her cheek. Her father's voice echoed in her mind as if he were right in front of her, as if he were there, speaking to her from an unfathomable distance. Each word weighed on her chest, a mixture of love and farewell that wrapped her in a wave of urgency and longing.

Images from her childhood began to surface, mingling with her father's words. She remembered the days when the world revolved around small, joyful moments: a walk in the park, the carefree laughter of a little girl who had yet to discover the shadows life would cast. Now, it all felt so far away, as if those days belonged to another life, to another person.

—I love you, Pia. You will never be alone. Even when the night seems endless, there will always be a flickering light in the distance, the letter concluded.

Pia closed her phone and sat in silence. That Saturday, which she had longed for to reunite with Tomasso, suddenly seemed unimportant. Her father's words changed everything, and deep in her heart, she knew what she had to do. The train to Padua would depart in a few hours. She had to see him. She had to be there.

The train to Padua moved with the steady rhythm of the rails, but Pia's mind was elsewhere, split between two worlds. On one side, her father—her home, the pull of blood, and unconditional love; on the other, Tomasso—a man who had awakened something in her that she still couldn't name. She wondered if he would be at the trattoria that weekend, waiting for her, watching her from the kitchen with those clear eyes that seemed to guard secrets.

What would he think when she didn't show up? Would he really be waiting, or was it all just her imagination playing tricks on her?

Pia leaned her head against the train window and let the morning light wash over her face. Life, she thought, was a sum of presences and absences—a delicate balance between what we have and what we lose. Her father was dying, and though his spirit remained strong, she knew there wasn't much time left. The illness had taken so much already, and now it was taking what remained. Still, amid that certainty, Tomasso lingered in her thoughts like a shadow refusing to fade.

The train passed through Ferrara, a town that seemed drawn from another era, with its narrow, winding streets; medieval and Renaissance palaces rising with imposing grace; and small houses with red-tiled roofs and smoking chimneys. Every detail hinted at a quieter, simpler life, where worries were limited to daily concerns, not the existential dilemmas tormenting her. Pia watched as the first light of day illuminated the rooftops, and for a moment, she wished to be inside one of those homes, living a predictable, peaceful life far removed from the turbulence of her thoughts. But that wasn't her life. Her path lay in the complexities of emotion—between love and duty, between the yearning for an uncertain future and the demands of a present she couldn't ignore.

When she finally arrived in Padua on Sunday morning, October 16, the crisp air struck her face, snapping her out of her thoughts. Time moved slower there, and the city seemed to doze under the pale morning sun. Pia stepped off the train and took a deep breath. She knew her father was waiting, and the words they would exchange would be few but meaningful. Life, as he had said in his letter, was a solitary journey one had to choose to embark upon, but she also knew that, at least for now, she was not alone. She was surrounded by love—in her father's words and in Tomasso's gaze, though she didn't know when she would see him again.

As she walked toward her father's house, the echo of the letter's words still rang in her mind. She knew that moment would mark a before and after in her life, and although the future was uncertain, she was ready to face it.

Her father's letter was a reminder of how fragile life was, but also of how powerful love could be. Pia knew the choices ahead wouldn't be easy. Love was a balance between what we want and what we must do, and she stood right in the middle of that delicate tension.

Pia began reading the letter again, this time aloud. Her voice was barely a whisper, trembling, as each word echoed through the air with deep weight. At first, her voice was restrained, gentle, but with every sentence, she felt it crack, emotions long held at bay rising to the surface. The words embraced her and wounded her all at once, reminding her of the magnitude of the man who had raised and loved her unconditionally.

With each line, her voice broke more, and finally, she gave in to her tears. In that moment, amid her sobs, like an echo in her mind, her father's hoarse voice began to resonate. It was a ghostly whisper—warm, familiar, an intangible but deeply real presence. It was as if he were there, reading the words he had written for her, wrapping her in one final goodbye.

—Dear Pia...— began her father's voice in a soft murmur as she closed her eyes and let that echo envelop her soul. Each word transported her, and she felt Lucien as if he were sitting beside her, speaking every line with the love and wisdom only he could offer. Pia, broken but at peace, listened to her father's voice in the shadows of her thoughts, and for a moment, the pain gave way to a warmth that comforted her.

When the voice reached the end, Pia opened her eyes, and a strange silence filled the room. It wasn't a silence of sadness, but of gratitude and love. She knew that farewell, though painful, would remain with her always as a beacon, just as her father had promised. In that moment, she understood that his presence would never fully disappear, that his words would be the home she could always return to, no matter where life would take her.

—Dear Pia,

No one taught me how to be a father, just as no one prepared you to face the countless trials life had in store. And yet, you have faced them with a courage that leaves me in awe—like someone who, when standing before an endless labyrinth, chooses to walk forward. You have fought the monsters that lurk in the shadows of dark days, and despite the invisible wounds etched in your soul, here you are— strong and radiant, with your head held high and eyes full of stories you will one day tell.

Here you are, shaped into a woman by the relentless flow of time, bearing the invisible scars that only years and experience can leave behind. I think of the thread that weaves our past together, of the days of your childhood that flowed with the peaceful continuity of dreams, and I wonder: if you could return for a moment to that original place, to that starting point, what would you say to the little girl who had yet to know the weight of her choices or the pain of inevitable defeats?

With the privilege of distance, I would tell her not to give up her essence for the sake of pleasing others. Not to sacrifice herself at the altar of others' approval, because each of her wishes, her dreams, and her hopes is a small flame that keeps her alive. I would tell her to guard that flame as one would guard a treasure. Not to waste her time and soul trying to fill the emptiness of those who don't wish to be happy, because fulfillment, after all, is a solitary journey that each person must undertake by their own will. Because joy, like eternity, is a choice, not a discovery.

But now, as I look at you, I wouldn't say any of this. I wouldn't give warnings. I wouldn't try to edit the past. Because everything you are, everything you've learned, has come from those uncertain roads, from the cliffs you had to skirt without a map, from those falls that made you rise stronger. And I prefer you this way—with your scars and your triumphs, with your silences and your laughter. Everything you are today, you learned because you didn't know it, and you discovered it on your own.

That's why I only want you to know that I love you. That I am infinitely proud of every step, every silence, and every word you've spoken in this unfathomable journey. Being your father has been the most fascinating and mysterious task of my life—the one that demanded the most from me and the one that fulfilled me the most.

I want you to know that you will never be alone. Even when the night feels endless, there will always be a flickering light in the distance—a beacon, even if lost in the fog of years, that will keep pointing to the safe harbor of my unconditional love.

If ever you feel lost in the absurd geometry of life, remember that I will be here, waiting with the patience that only fathers and dreams can have. Because a true home is not a place, not even a memory—it is the heart of the one who waits for you without time or conditions.

With all my love and certainty, Dad —

Pia's Journal

Saturday, October 15, 2022

Today, when I least expected it, life reminded me how fragile and fleeting everything is. For days, my thoughts have revolved around Tomasso—that strange connection we've barely begun to explore but that has left me yearning for something more, something I still don't know how to name. I had been looking forward to Saturday, preparing to see him again, to discover whether that gaze of his held the answers I've been longing for. And then my father's letter arrived.

His words were a soft but deep blow, as if each sentence reminded me of what truly matters—of what I've been neglecting while losing myself in the illusions of the new. I wasn't expecting it. He rarely writes, and certainly not in that tone... that tone that speaks of farewells, of a love that is eternal yet nearing its end.

As I read, I felt the weight of every one of his memories—his pride, his pain, his love for me. How did I get to this point without realizing how much I've grown, how much we've changed? For so long, my father has been a solid figure, someone who was always there, even if his words were few. Today, though, I feel that he has become vulnerable—and with that vulnerability, something inside me has cracked too.

He tells me not to change the past, not to try to fix what's already been lived, because it's thanks to those wounds, to those falls, that I've become who I am. And yet, as I read, I couldn't help but think how much I'd give to protect him now—to be the one who takes care of him, the way he cared for me for so many years. What would I do if I lost him? The mere thought pulls me into a darkness I'm not sure I'd know how to escape from.

But at the same time, he speaks of moving forward, of staying true to my desires, of guarding that —fire— that keeps me alive. And what am I supposed to do with that fire now? I wanted to see him—Tomasso. I wanted to find out if there was something more between us, something real. But today, everything feels different. Right now, all I want is to get to Padua, to be with my father, to hold his hand, and to make sure he knows that I will always be by his side.

Love… I wonder if love is what's teaching me now. Love isn't always what we expect—it isn't always that overwhelming emotion we feel in our chest when we look at someone new. Sometimes, it's that subtle connection that ties us to those who have always been there, like my father. Perhaps what hurts most about this letter is realizing that he's come to understand things I still haven't fully grasped and that, despite everything, he has always been watching over me, guiding me in silence.

Tomorrow, I will see him. And I don't know whether I'll speak about what I've felt, or if I'll simply be there in silence, the way he so often was. But what I know for sure is that this moment has changed something inside me. Sometimes, we look for answers in all the wrong places, and maybe what I need most now is to be on that train to Padua—getting closer not only to my father but to the part of me that's still searching for where it truly belongs.

Beyond the Wall of Silence

At fifteen, Giacomo still didn't understand what depression was. To him, his mother had simply stopped being the woman he used to know. María, who had once been a warm and steady presence, was now crumbling before his eyes. She wouldn't get out of bed; the house had become a mess that mirrored her own inner chaos, and she had stopped taking care of herself. Her eyes, once full of life, were now an empty reflection of the sadness that consumed her.

Giacomo couldn't understand why his mother was no longer capable of doing things that seemed so normal and everyday, like keeping the house tidy or making sure he had clean clothes. But what troubled him most was not the physical mess but the emotional distance that grew between them. Although Giacomo, in his confused way, tried to approach her, to seek her comfort and her presence, fear also compelled him to pull away. He was a child lost in his own home, desperately seeking the affection of a mother who could no longer give it but not knowing how to deal with the fear this caused him.

One day, coming home from school, he found his house surrounded by police, onlookers, and neighbors. A bittersweet feeling washed over him: he knew that the only thing he had left was suddenly gone. His mother, María, had died after a long struggle with depression, although the details of her passing were never revealed to him. In his young heart, the void grew like an abyss—a loss he couldn't fully grasp but which left an indelible mark on him. Shortly after, Giacomo was transferred to a boarding school for orphaned children. There, a new chapter began; surrounded by other young people in similar situations, he quickly learned to close himself off from the world. His environment was filled with noise and chaos, but he, increasingly reserved, became a shadow in the hallways of the boarding school.

During his first few months, he didn't show his emotions, and his gestures were calculated and cold. However, his intelligence stood out. Giacomo impressed his teachers, especially in subjects like math and physics, but his emotional capacity remained blocked.

It was at this boarding school where he met Professor Sequera, a man who saw in him more than just a brilliant student. Sequera, with his firm character and perceptive gaze, would be the figure who would try to enter that closed world Giacomo had built around himself.

This behavior had isolated him from the rest of his classmates. He was a brilliant boy, but his intellectual abilities did not compensate for his inability to relate emotionally to those around him. No one dared to approach him, and he himself rejected any attempt at connection, as if maintaining a safe distance was his only way to protect himself from a world that had already wounded him too deeply.

Professor Sequera was no ordinary teacher. For him, teaching went beyond textbooks and exams. He firmly believed that in every human being there was latent potential and that a teacher's mission was not simply to transmit knowledge but to seek out that potential and help it blossom. Sequera saw education as an opportunity to transform lives, and in his years of experience, he had learned that some students needed more than a good lesson to achieve it; they needed someone to believe in them, even when they didn't believe in themselves.

When Sequera saw Giacomo for the first time, he knew there was something special about him. It wasn't just his brilliance in math or his natural talent for solving complex problems that caught his attention. It was something deeper, something that went beyond academics. Giacomo came from a sad background, and that was evident to anyone who paid attention, but for Sequera, it was not enough to see the suffering; his mission was to penetrate that armor of isolation and cynicism that the boy had built around himself. He knew it would be difficult, but he was also convinced that, if he managed to gain his trust, Giacomo could unfold his full potential and change his own destiny.

Despite his efforts, Sequera couldn't find any way to enter his circle of trust. Giacomo was an enigma, and every attempt to approach him was met with sarcasm or, worse, an impenetrable silence. However, Sequera was not intimidated by this. He had seen young people like Giacomo before: those who hid their pain behind a facade of coldness and avoidant attachment but who deep down wished to be understood, even if they never admitted it.

However, Sequera continued and was not intimidated by Giacomo's armor. Professor Sequera, a man known for his strong character and firm temperament, had observed Giacomo attentively. Sequera had seen beyond the aggressive behavior and biting words; he recognized in the young man a potential that, if properly molded, could take him far. Despite Giacomo's constant displays of contempt, Sequera was determined to become his mentor and guide him towards something greater than the resentment and loneliness that consumed him.

And so began an arduous, yet purposeful process. Sequera was not a man of soft words but of discipline and character, something that Giacomo, unconsciously, respected. During their months of working together, the professor was able to slowly earn the boy's respect, and though he wouldn't admit it, Giacomo began to see him as more than just a teacher.

But that relationship was about to be tested. Giacomo had always been avoidant when anyone tried to delve into his past. If any teacher or classmate asked an inappropriate question, he would change the subject or respond with a sarcastic remark that shut down any possibility of conversation. But Sequera was not a man who was easily deterred. He had spent months observing Giacomo, watching how he avoided talking about his family, his childhood, and everything he had left behind. He knew there was something more, something that didn't fit into his file.

Professor Sequera had a military career before becoming a teacher, and that experience had endowed him with a sharp intuition. Sequera knew how to recognize when someone was hiding something, and in Giacomo, everything pointed to his story being incomplete. One night, after a particularly difficult training session, Sequera cornered Giacomo in the classroom. It wasn't a violent act but a firm confrontation.

—Something doesn't add up in your file,—Sequera said, with that deep voice that seemed to pierce the silence. —I've read about your family, but there are gaps. There's missing information.

Giacomo looked at him, as he always did, with that mix of defiance and emptiness. But this time he couldn't escape. Sequera, with the determination of someone who had interrogated harder and more experienced men, wasn't going to let Giacomo evade him.

—What really happened?—the professor asked, without looking away. —Don't tell me what the file says; tell me what's not there.—

Giacomo felt something inside him cracking, but he still clung to his silence, to that wall he had built over so many years. Sequera didn't yield; each of his words was a piece of artillery fired with precision.

And that night, under the faint light of the lantern coming through the window, after so many months of accumulated tension, a resistance that wouldn't fade. Giacomo and Sequera stared at each other in silence. Giacomo, his face hardened by years of suffering and emotional armor, had raised his fist, but the professor, instead of backing away, looked him in the eyes and challenged him.

—Do it if you think it's what you need.—

Sequera's words cut through the air, firm, without a trace of fear. Giacomo hesitated for a moment, his hand trembling, but not with rage; it was a mixture of pain and confusion. No one had ever challenged him that way. Sequera, far from showing weakness, held his gaze, waiting.

—I know what happened to you,— the professor finally said, his deep voice echoing in the empty classroom. —I know what you had to face.—

The words fell like a hammer on Giacomo's shoulders. No one had spoken of his past with such knowledge or compassion. The memories of his childhood, of his mother, and of his father returned to him like an unstoppable torrent.

—Tell me, Giacomo,— Sequera asked, his voice now softer, but with the same authority of someone who knows they are touching a wound that needs to be healed. — You are not the only one who has gone through hell, but you can't keep carrying this alone.—

The silence was sepulchral. Giacomo lowered his fist, and his body, tense until then, slumped into the chair. He stared into the void, his eyes fixed on an invisible point, until he finally spoke, as if he were wrenching the words from his soul.

—I saw him hit her again and again,— he said, his voice broken, barely a whisper. —My mother was on the ground, not moving. I didn't... I didn't know what to do. It all happened so fast...—

The images returned to his mind with painful clarity. Giacomo, standing at the kitchen threshold, watched his father, Franco, unleash his fury on Maria, his mother, with a brutality that left him petrified. The first blow made her stagger, the second knocked her to the ground, and each subsequent impact was an echo that resonated in Giacomo's soul.

—I couldn't do anything, not at that moment,— Giacomo continued, swallowing as if each word cost him breath. — The blood... it was all blood. My mother, on the floor, her eyes almost closed. And he... he was coming at her again. —

Franco kept going without stopping. Even though his mother was vulnerable, his father didn't hesitate to raise his hand to hit her again, grabbing her hair, his face distorted with rage. In that instant, something inside Giacomo fractured. He was no longer a terrified observer; he was now a child overflowing with fury, fear, and helplessness.

—There was a knife on the table...— Giacomo lowered his gaze, as if the shame and horror of what he had done still haunted him. — I didn't think; I just took it. And when he raised his hand again... I... I...—

The first stab was precise, sinking into Franco's side. His eyes widened enormously, more from surprise than pain. But Giacomo didn't stop; the knife repeatedly pierced his flesh as his father's body collapsed. His mother's voice broke into the scene, filled with despair:

—No, Giacomo, please, don't!— Maria screamed, her voice shattered with horror.

For Giacomo, everything happened in a deafening silence, broken only by his ragged breathing and the wet sound of the knife tearing through skin. He lost track of how many times he stabbed him until his hands and arms were covered in warm blood.

Franco stared at him; it was a piercing gaze, difficult to decipher, laden with anger or perhaps sadness. He tried to crawl towards his son, struggling to fill his lungs with air, emitting a guttural sound that Giacomo would never forget. In that instant, he dropped the knife, and the clash of metal against the tile echoed as a final sound in the room.

—I never stopped to think. I don't know how many times I did it... I only know that, when I stopped, he was already dead.—

Sequera, still seated across from Giacomo, said nothing at first. The weight of the confession hung in the air, crushing. Finally, Sequera leaned forward, his hands firm on the table.

—You were just a child, Giacomo,— he said, his voice deep but without judgment. —You did what you thought you had to do. Now, you must learn to forgive yourself for surviving. Silence fell again, but this time it was not an impenetrable barrier. It was the kind of silence that precedes a new understanding, an opening that, though painful, was necessary.

And that night, in that empty classroom, Giacomo knew that for the first time someone had truly listened to him.

The next day, the sun had barely begun to filter through the curtains, but Giacomo was already awake. In his mind, the hope that it had all been a nightmare sustained him for a moment, a fleeting illusion that pushed him to get up with the longing to find normalcy on the other side of his bedroom door. However, upon leaving, reality hit him like a cold, impenetrable wall.

Maria stood at the sink, washing dishes with quick, mechanical movements. Giacomo watched her intently and noticed her face disfigured by the beating, her eyes swollen and purple, and her hair stiff with dried blood. The bruises and abrasions spread like dark shadows across her arms, and her posture reflected a fragility he had never seen in her before. The sight of his mother, broken and wounded, forced him to accept that there was no escape, that what had happened was not a bad dream.

Everything seemed to have returned to normal, at least in appearance. The house, which until then had been a reflection of Maria's internal disorder, was beginning to regain the order it had lost so long ago. But as Giacomo watched in silence, he could not ignore that there was something deeply disturbing in that scene of apparent tranquility.

He didn't know what Maria had done with Franco's body. That was something that was never spoken of, nor would it ever be. The blood, the stabbings, the screams... all of that had disappeared into some dark place of memory, as if the house itself had decided to erase the existence of that night. Neither he nor his mother would ever be the same. He knew it deep in his soul, but he had no words to explain it.

—Mom...— Giacomo said, hesitating as he approached. —Where is he? Where... what did you do with Franco?—

It was difficult for him to pronounce his name, as if by doing so he recognized him in some way. He could no longer call him Dad. That man who had been his father had ceased to exist the night before, along with everything he had once meant to him. Maria stopped washing for a moment but didn't look at him. She remained silent, the water running over her hands, as if searching for a way not to answer.

Finally, she took a breath and, with an empty voice, pronounced:

—He's gone, Giacomo. Let's not speak of this anymore.

Maria knew that Franco's death had to remain a secret. With determination, she cleaned the scene and concealed the body, burying not only her husband but also the years of pain he represented. She instructed Giacomo never to speak of what had happened, creating a pact of silence that would bind them forever. Franco's disappearance was attributed to a voluntary abandonment, and life went on, though the invisible scars remained in the souls of Maria and her son.

And so it was. There were no more words. No more explanations. The silence, always present in their lives, now became deeper, heavier. Giacomo, who had always sought to understand, realized at that moment that there were things not meant to be understood or remembered.

They would never speak of Franco again, nor of that night, nor of what followed. But, though the words did not say it, they both knew that something had died in that house, along with the man they once called father.

Thus, in the labyrinth of her existence, Maria became the guardian of a secret that slowly consumed her, while the world went on its course, oblivious to the drama that unfolded behind the walls of her home.

Maria II

From María's perspective, in that moment, Giacomo—driven by a desperate impulse—grabbed a knife from the table and, with a determination born of fear and the instinct to protect, drove it into his father's side. Franco turned, stunned, and collapsed to the floor, his life fading quickly.

María, horrified, ran to Franco, trying to stop the bleeding with trembling hands. Her tears fell onto his lifeless face as she whispered:

—Franco, no! Please, don't leave me!—

Giacomo, still holding the bloodied knife, stood in shock and confusion. María, looking up at her son, saw the terror in his eyes and understood that, despite everything, he had acted to protect her.

With a resolve born of maternal love, María stood and embraced Giacomo, whispering in his ear:

—Don't worry, my love. Everything will be alright.

That night, María worked in silence to hide Franco's body and erase any trace of what had happened. The weight of her actions bound them in a silent pact—a burden they would carry together for the rest of their lives.

By dawn, the house was back in order, as if nothing had occurred. With a forced calm, María made breakfast and called Giacomo to the table. As they ate in silence, both knew their lives had changed forever — but also that, together, they could face whatever adversity fate had in store.

María, trapped in a cycle of violence and submission, embodied the paradox of the victim who, even while suffering, tries to preserve the family's unity. Her passive resistance and her desire to maintain harmony reflected a resigned acceptance of her fate—a kind of complicity with her own tormentor. This attitude, far from mere submission, was her way of confronting the absurdity of her existence—a silent struggle to find meaning in the midst of chaos.

Giacomo, a witness to the brutality inflicted on his mother, was torn between hatred for his father and confusion over María's behavior. His mother's apparent passivity in the face of violence left him bewildered, generating deep emotional conflict. This family dynamic—marked by violence and submission—plunged Giacomo into an absurd reality, where actions lacked logic and emotions twisted into an indecipherable tangle.

In this absurd universe, María and Giacomo were castaways searching for a lifeline. She clung to the hope of her husband's redemption; he struggled to make sense of a world that seemed incoherent and cruel. In their shared solitude, they embodied the human condition, confronting the meaninglessness of existence—fighting to find a reason to go on amid the despair.

The Cave of Silence

Tomasso didn't understand what had happened, but something inside him had started to quietly fade. The unanswered messages, the calls that vanished into the unknown, and the waiting at the trattoria—each detail piled up in his mind like a repetitive and painful echo. Without any explanation, Pia had disappeared from his life just when he was beginning to believe in something deeper, in the possibility of something real.

For someone like Tomasso, silence had always been both a refuge and a defense. He had learned that when you're hurt, sometimes the best remedy is silence—not raising your voice, not assigning blame, just stepping away. Staying kind, even when sadness threatens to consume you from within. This time was no different. He felt that, without truly knowing how or why, a part of him was falling apart. There were no scenes, no accusations—just an increasingly dense silence that surrounded him.

As the days passed, the idea of distancing himself from Pia began to take root. Outwardly, he remained the same man: smiling, courteous — but inside, something was breaking beyond repair. He knew he could keep going, pretending everything was fine but his soul longed for something else. The distance, the silence, the failed attempts—everything pointed to a painful revelation.

—Why does this keep happening?— Tomasso asked himself in moments of solitude. He knew there were many reasons to feel this way, but none of them made complete sense. He was tired of offering so many chances; he had waited, he had believed, and yet he always seemed to be left alone in the end. In time, he felt life was giving him a silent but powerful lesson: it was time to set boundaries, to choose his own well-being over unfinished promises.

Walking away wouldn't be an escape; for him, it was an act of self-preservation. It was an act of courage and self-respect. He could have stayed, could have waited again—but at what cost? He decided that his self-love could not flourish if he remained tied to a silence that offered no answers. And so, quietly, he began to let go of the feeling.

Without saying much, Tomasso slowly stepped away from the bond that had just begun to form. He knew how easy it would have been to stay, to give in to the possibility of a future, to the hope that everything had been a misunderstanding. But not this time. This time, walking away was an act of love—for himself.

He remembered Joseph Campbell's quote and thought of his own journey, of that cave he had always been afraid to enter. Maybe the treasure he was looking for wasn't in someone else, but in himself—in learning to set boundaries, in accepting pain without being consumed by it. With a final sigh, Tomasso let the echo of his decision wash over him with unexpected calm. His heart, though hurting, understood that sometimes, the hardest love to find is self-love.

That Sunday, the late morning sun filtered between the old facades of Florence's city center, illuminating every corner with golden warmth. Alessia walked leisurely down Via Roma, her steps echoing over the stone slabs that had witnessed centuries of history. As she turned the corner toward Piazza della Repubblica, the vibrant heart of the city enveloped her—the laughter and chatter of tourists and Florentines mingling in the air. It wasn't a new place for her, but every visit to the center brought renewed emotion, as if

Florence itself were a living work of art, changing shades with each ray of sunlight.

Right beside a bookstore stacked to the ceiling and a century-old pasticceria, Alessia spotted a quaint café with red-and-white striped awnings and wrought-iron tables that looked like they belonged on a vintage postcard. The place offered a splendid view of the piazza, framing in the distance the elegant Arch of Triumph, standing as a silent guardian of the past. At nearby tables, people sipped their coffee while soaking in the vibrant pulse of the streets.

It was there she saw Tomasso, seated near a window, his gaze lost in his coffee cup. Bathed in morning light, he seemed like a melancholic brushstroke in the city's vibrant canvas. When he noticed Alessia, he looked up and offered a soft smile—the kind that makes time slow. She smiled back and walked over, feeling a small rush of excitement.

—Mind if I join you?— Alessia asked, her expression a playful blend of innocence and charm.

Tomasso nodded, and she sat across from him. She ordered a latte macchiato; Tomasso already had a foamy cappuccino, its rich aroma filling the space between them. The waiter brought a brioche to share. The setting was perfect: the serenity of the morning, the hum of Italian conversation, and the intoxicating scent of roasted coffee.

Alessia took a sip of her drink and let her gaze settle on Tomasso. The way she looked at him left little doubt— there was flirtation in her eyes, in the slight tilt of her head as she spoke.

—So, Tomasso...— she said, playing with her spoon, —Always this pensive on a Sunday morning?—

Tomasso let out a soft laugh, but Alessia could tell his eyes remained distant, as if a shadow still lingered. But she wasn't giving up so easily. She gave him a teasing smile and leaned in a little closer, closing the space between them.

—Florence is a city meant to be lived, not to get lost in thought,— she murmured, her words filled with warm enthusiasm. —Especially when you've got good company.—

Tomasso smiled, though his eyes were still caught in some battle he couldn't name. Yet Alessia had a way of filling the silence, of making even the heaviest moments feel lighter. Her energy gave him a brief escape from the weight he carried—even if just for a while.

Around them, Florence breathed with life: the distant rumble of trams, children laughing in the piazza, and carefree conversations floating through the air, wrapping the two in a fleeting bubble of normalcy. Alessia sipped the last of her coffee and gave him a flirty glance, letting him know she was enjoying the morning far more than he might have guessed.

Sensing his withdrawn expression, Alessia let out a light, slightly ironic laugh.

—What's with you today, Tomasso?—she asked, crossing her arms and looking him over. —It's a beautiful day, and you've got that long face. Where's the lively guy from Thursday night? —

Tomasso tried to smile, but worry still clouded his eyes. Alessia sighed, and before he could make excuses, she took his hand with quiet resolve.

—Come on, no gloomy faces. Today's a day to enjoy, not waste on gray thoughts. Let's take a walk—what do you say?

He nodded, almost out of obligation, letting her guide him aimlessly. Alessia led him through cobbled streets on a journey that slowly became a tour of the city's most iconic corners. They moved along Via dei Calzaiuoli, where shops and cafés buzzed with tourists and locals, and ancient facades cast long shadows on the stone pavement. Alessia kept talking—joking, teasing, and trying to draw out a real smile.

Soon, they turned a corner, and the majestic profile of the Cathedral of Santa Maria del Fiore rose before them. Brunelleschi's dome, grand and commanding, loomed above the skyline, radiating the kind of magnificence only Florence could offer. Alessia paused, watching to see if the architectural wonder could pull Tomasso from his thoughts.

—Look at this city, Tomasso. How can you stay so silent with all this beauty around you?—she asked, gesturing at the cathedral with a sweeping motion.

He smiled faintly, and they continued on. They wandered narrow streets where buildings leaned toward one another like old friends sharing secrets until they reached the Ponte Vecchio. The bridge, lined with jewelry shops whose windows reflected sunlight in golden bursts, bustled with tourists and locals admiring the calm flow of the Arno River and the old buildings mirrored on its surface.

Alessia took the opportunity to loop her arm through his, drawing slightly closer than usual. She kept talking— sometimes in a soft voice, sometimes with laughter that rang in the air—telling him stories of the city, anecdotes about friends, and bits of her own adventures. Her voice and energy filled the space, as if determined to occupy every corner of the silence he refused to break.

Eventually, their walk brought them to Piazzale Michelangelo. From there, Florence stretched out below them—a panoramic view of red rooftops, ancient towers, and domes fading into the horizon. Alessia breathed in deeply, savoring the fresh air and the view.

—See?—she said, nudging him gently. —Told you. A day like this shouldn't be wasted on dark thoughts. Florence always brings you back to life—even when you least expect it.

Tomasso, though still burdened by emotion, couldn't help but smile a little more genuinely. The view, the air, and Alessia's unrelenting energy began to soothe his mind.

Throughout their journey, Alessia never stopped flirting—casting glances and laughing freely, never letting the weight of his silence define the atmosphere. She filled every pause with words, and though he didn't respond much, she didn't seem to need it. Alessia was her own show, moving to her own rhythm, as if the world were an extension of her radiant energy.

Finally, as Tomasso looked out over the city, Alessia gave him a mischievous smile and said, half joking, half serious:

—You know, Tomasso, if I didn't have to do everything myself, I think I'd have already won you over.—

Tomasso laughed—and this time, the smile was real.

It seemed Alessia had everything figured out. As they descended the hills from Piazzale Michelangelo, she guided him with a natural ease, as though every corner of that part of Florence was an extension of her own home. The autumn sun painted the streets in warm tones, and the crisp breeze carried the scent of cypress trees and damp earth from the recent rains.

They made their way down Via di San Miniato, a narrow street winding between moss-covered stone walls, while golden leaves drifted from the trees lining the path. Rounding a bend, they entered Via San Niccolò, a charming street filled with old buildings—wrought-iron balconies and wooden shutters bearing layers of time. In the distance, small artisan shops and galleries beckoned, drawing in locals and curious travelers alike.

Eventually, they reached a small bar nestled beside a medieval gate that marked the entrance to the neighborhood. It was unpretentious yet exuded a welcoming charm. With its exposed brick walls and well-worn wooden tables, the place was frequented by locals chatting animatedly over Spritz and late afternoon aperitifs.

They both ordered Aperol Spritz. Alessia, full of her usual energy, encouraged Tomasso to unwind and savor the moment. After a while, stretching with a playful smile, she remarked that the walk to Piazzale Michelangelo had left her feet aching—and nothing sounded better than relaxing at home.

Using that as her excuse, delivered with a wink, she invited him to her apartment, just a few steps away, in one of those timeless buildings with ivy-covered facades that swayed gently in the breeze.

Alessia's apartment was a studio styled with impeccable taste—a space where every object seemed chosen with care. As Tomasso stepped inside, he was greeted by a large window framing a stunning view of the city: Florence's red rooftops, the majestic cathedral dome, and, in the distance, the Arno winding quietly through it all.

The studio had a minimalist elegance, bathed in soft, warm tones that created an intimate ambiance. A cream-colored sofa, plush with linen and velvet pillows, rested in a corner near the window, inviting him to sit and lose himself in the view.

A dark wooden coffee table stood in front of the sofa, holding a few art books, a scented candle, and a half-finished glass of wine—details that lent the room a comforting sense of presence. On one side, a small open kitchen was perfectly arranged, with shelves displaying hand-thrown ceramic mugs and neatly labeled jars of spices. A tall bookshelf filled with books and black-and-white photos dominated one wall, revealing Alessia's eclectic mind.

But the apartment's true jewel was the narrow balcony accessed through a glass door beside the window. Alessia stepped outside with a glass of Conegliano prosecco in hand, gazing out over the city just as the sun began to set, casting golden and amber hues across the skyline.

—This place has its own kind of magic, don't you think?— she said, shooting Tomasso an insinuating look. — A place like this, with the right view, can make you forget any sadness.—

She gave him a warm smile and gestured toward the sofa.

—Give me just a minute, okay?— she added in a soft, almost whispered voice. —I want to freshen up after our walk. But please—make yourself at home. She paused and pointed to a small bar in the corner, its shelf lined with carefully curated bottles.

—You're free to pour yourself whatever you'd like. It's a small bar, but well-stocked. A little of everything—and only the best,— she said with a wink.

Then she disappeared behind a door, leaving him alone in the glow of the space she had so effortlessly made her own. Almost without thinking, Tomasso let his gaze wander. He absorbed the details and the atmosphere and felt how intimately the room reflected the essence of Alessia.

She returned as if emerging from the shadows that surrounded her, with a presence that carried both mystery and self-assurance—like something out of a Caribbean legend.

Her skin, golden as the sunset, seemed to contain the sun itself, radiating a warmth that transformed the small apartment into a space suspended in time. Her every movement held a calm grace, as though she were entirely at ease in her body, aware of the quiet admiration her presence evoked.

Her eyes, a deep and serene green, were like reflections of unexplored jungles—full of secrets, inviting you to get lost without promise of return. There was an eternal mischief in her gaze, as if she knew life was a story in constant evolution, and she—with her green eyes and radiant smile—was the heroine. Framed by long black lashes, her eyes seemed to see beyond the visible, as if they could read thoughts or peer into the soul's quietest corners.

Her hair, an ebony cascade falling in soft waves to her chest, absorbed light in a dance of shadow and glow, like a starless night where secrets slept. Each strand seemed to hold its own story, brushing against her cinnamon-toned skin in a contrast that echoed time itself, as if all seasons and ages resided within her.

Alessia was grace laced with wild freedom, with curves that spoke the language of nature—like palm trees swaying in a gentle breeze. Her breasts, perfect in their simplicity, seemed sculpted by the Caribbean wind itself. Her flat, toned stomach carried the promise of youth and strength, in perfect harmony with her rounded hips that whispered of warm lands and deep seas.

Every part of her body was soft and smooth, like the finest sand—crafted, it seemed, by the earth itself with patient precision. At the center of that golden skin, her rosy nipples stood out like the blush of a tropical flower at dawn—alive and hidden, waiting for the right moment.

Alessia was a woman shaped in dreams and shifting sands, in sun and shadow. Her beauty carried the promise of untold stories and secrets shared only in whispers beneath the stars. She was the embodiment of elegance and passion—a living vision of nature in its most sensual and purest state. Her slow smile, when she saw Tomasso, was the key to a deeper world—one where time lost its grip, and only the moment remained, whispered and present, as her presence filled the entire room.

As Alessia moved forward with the confidence of someone who knew her body was a masterpiece, every line and every curve spoke in its own language—rich in sensuality and mystery. Her belly, smooth and sculpted, was flawless, untouched by shadow or blemish, as if the Caribbean breeze had shaped it to perfection. Her skin—sun-kissed and silken—seemed made to be touched, polished like the fine sand of a deserted beach. That impeccable surface added a natural elegance to her figure, accentuating the grace and freedom that defined her. Alessia was a woman who cared for every detail, and her flawless belly was the symbol of the harmony between her outer beauty and the confidence she radiated from within.

The Weight of Memories

The train had stopped, and dawn was just breaking. Pia stepped off in silence, letting the fresh air of Padua wash over her. Each step she took toward her parents' house was a journey into the past, a reminder of the life she once had and the strength she now needed. The house stood unchanged, faithful to her memories, its white walls worn by time and ivy climbing up to the windows, as if trying to embrace what remained inside.

It was her mother, Nicoletta, who opened the door. The weight of the years showed on her face, yet there was a serenity only the deepest love can bestow. Nicoletta looked at her, and in that instant there were no words, only the whisper of an unbreakable bond, of a shared history told without the need for voices. Pia simply murmured:

—Mom.—

And in that instant they merged in an embrace that seemed to defy time.

Nicoletta's arms wrapped around her tenderly. Her hands, rough and weary, traced her daughter's back, as if wanting to erase the distance that time and life had put between them. They hugged tightly, exchanging silent tears, and for those seconds, time truly seemed to stand still. Pia wished, with all her heart, that this stillness would last forever, that nothing would pull her away from that moment when her mother's peace and comfort were enough to banish any sadness.

But reality returned with a question Pia almost feared to ask, as if voicing it would break the spell of their embrace.

—Dad?—she whispered, her voice trembling.

Nicoletta sighed, an exhale carrying the weight of her worries, her sleepless nights, and her deepest fears. She forced a smile, and her tone was gentle but heavy with a resignation Pia felt to her core.

—He's there, holding his own, like always,— she replied, trying to keep her voice steady. —He doesn't say it, but I know he's not well.—

They looked at each other, knowing that in that simple statement lay a painful truth neither of them was ready to face. Lucien's fragility—the man who had been their anchor and guide—was becoming a palpable presence in the house, a shadow that seemed to stretch across every corner. Nicoletta explained she had been preparing food because many would come to see her father that day, to offer the comfort of their presence and celebrate the life he stubbornly held onto.

Pia walked through the rooms like someone visiting a museum of her own childhood, observing the memories still hanging on the walls: photographs of happy moments, trophies and diplomas, and small traces of the lives they had shared under that roof. But that day, even those memories seemed muted, as if they knew a cycle was about to close.

Among the visitors, Antonella, Pia's sister, who was traveling from New York to be with him, was also expected. This gathering, which at other times would have been a celebration, now seemed shrouded in a melancholy no words could dispel.

Lucien was a doctor, a pediatrician used to diagnosing, observing symptoms, and foreseeing the inevitable. He knew the course of his illness very well and had faced that reality with silent dignity, without burdening his loved ones with the extent of his pain. But however much he tried to hide it, Nicoletta and Pia sensed something indefinable in the air, a shift, as if the house itself were getting ready to say goodbye.

Pia's home, which for so long had been a refuge, now felt different. There was something in the light filtering through the windows, in the smell of the family meals Nicoletta prepared—something suggesting a last supper, a final embrace. The shadows seemed to lengthen, and every corner of the house was filled with a tense stillness, the kind of calm before a storm that life stubbornly chooses to ignore.

Nicoletta, meanwhile, returned to the kitchen, where the aroma of the food filled the air like a silent tribute to the life they cherished. The sound of pots and boiling water seemed like a sad melody, a song telling stories of love and loss. Pia's mother worked with the serenity of someone who understands that life is found in small gestures, in the daily rituals that, though they seem insignificant, have the power to unite people and etch memories onto the soul.

—We always celebrate my birthday around this time, Nicoletta said, without taking her eyes off the pot she was stirring. —But this year...— She paused, letting the words dissolve in the air, heavy with a sorrow that needed no explanation.

Pia felt a lump in her throat—a mixture of sadness and gratitude. She knew that moment, however brief, would be etched into her memory. Her mother's presence, the aroma of the food, the house full of familiar echoes... All of it wrapped her in a feeling of farewell. Nothing seemed to have changed, but everything was different. And deep down, they both understood that, no matter how much

Lucien tried to make things seem normal, the air was filled with a silent goodbye.

At that moment, the doorbell rang, breaking the spell. Pia looked at her mother, and they shared a final glance, as if communicating what words couldn't express. Nicoletta went to the door, and Pia followed, preparing to receive the visitors who, like them, had come to pay homage to Lucien, to be with him in his final battle.

And although that day would pass like others—with hugs, with laughter, and with tears—they both knew that time had not stopped. They were together, yes, but under the weight of an inescapable certainty: farewell was coming, and with it, a void no meal, no ritual, no word could fill.

Shadows of Desire

The kiss deepened. Alessia's tongue explored Tomasso's mouth with an urgency he couldn't match. Her hands, quick and sure, fumbled with his belt while he remained passive, his mind miles away. Despite the passion she radiated, a shadow of doubt settled in his heart. Their lips moved with a practiced rhythm, but something was missing: the spark that ignited his blood, the connection that made them one.

He let her lead him, like a puppet in the hands of a skilled puppeteer. They stumbled across the room, their bodies tangled in an awkward, hurried dance. The furniture, silent witnesses to their encounter, seemed to watch with silent judgment. Reaching the bedroom, he pulled her onto the bed with a suddenness that took her by surprise. Alessia, breathless, desire burning in her eyes, welcomed him with open arms. But instead of responding to her passion, he just stared at her with an unreadable look.

—Tomasso,— she whispered, her voice heavy with wanting and a hint of doubt. He blinked, as if waking from a dream, and leaned over her. He kissed her again, harder this time, but the distance remained—an invisible wall between them. His hands eagerly explored her body, but his mind drifted elsewhere, tormented by memories and doubts he couldn't quiet.

After they made love, he took her to the shower, hoping the cold water would put out the fire burning inside him. Under the spray, they kissed desperately, clinging to each other like a burning ember. Steam fogged the mirrors, reflecting a distorted image of their passion. But not even the icy water could cool the storm raging within him.

While Alessia surrendered to the pleasure of the moment, her moans filling the air, Tomasso felt increasingly detached, like a spectator of his own life. His body answered desire, but his soul was elsewhere, lost in a maze of conflicting feelings.

They stepped out of the shower, skin flushed, hair wet. Alessia, wrapped in a towel, went to the closet for clean clothes. Tomasso, though, dropped naked onto the bed, his eyes fixed on the ceiling. He watched her move with that feline grace that drew him in, but a pang of guilt tightened his chest. He couldn't give her the surrender she offered; he couldn't fake a passion he didn't feel.

—Tomasso, are you okay?— she asked, concern showing in her green eyes. He forced a smile, trying to push away the lurking shadows.

—Yeah, I'm fine,— he lied.

Alessia wasn't convinced. She sat beside him, gently stroking his cheek.

—What's wrong? You seem far away.—

He looked away, unable to meet her eyes.

—It's nothing. Just tired.—

She held him close, resting her head on his chest.

—Rest then,— she murmured, kissing his hair. Tomasso closed his eyes, breathing in the scent of flowers and sea from her skin. For a moment, he let the warmth of her embrace carry him, wishing he could forget everything else. But the ghosts of the past relentlessly haunted him, reminding him of his mistakes, his fears, and his doubts.

He pulled away from her abruptly, getting out of bed.

—I need some air,— he said, heading for the balcony.

Alessia watched him go, confused and hurt. She saw him lean against the railing, looking out at the city spread below. The nightlights shimmered like a sea of stars, but he saw only the darkness closing in around him.

—What is it, Tomasso?—she pressed, walking up to him.

He looked at her, his eyes filled with a sadness she didn't understand.

—I can't,— he whispered, his voice breaking.

—You can't what?—

—I can't be with you.—

His words hit like cold water, chilling the air between them. Alessia stared, her face pale, her eyes wide with disbelief.

—What are you talking about?—

—I'm sorry, Alessia,— he said, his voice thick with regret. —I can't give you what you need. I can't give you what you deserve.—

She shook her head, unable to take it in.

—But... why?—

—Because I'm not ready. Because I'm not the man you think I am.— He turned away, his back to her. —Please, just leave.—

Alessia stood, frozen by the pain. Tears welled up, tracing paths down her cheeks like sad rivers. She looked at Tomasso, her heart aching, her hope shattered. Then, without a word, she turned and left, leaving him alone with his demons.

Alessia, alone in her apartment, felt sadness and frustration twisting in her chest, squeezing tight. The echo of Tomasso's words still rang in her mind, as cold as the distance she'd felt between them. She knew, deep down, it wasn't just about the sudden goodbye; it was something more, something that demanded she look inward. For a moment, her reflection in the mirror showed her an image she'd tried to avoid: a woman who, even confident and radiant, had chosen to use her body as the key to open doors that wanted to stay closed.

She recalled a thought that had surfaced another lonely night, when the city lights pulsed and the silence became a mirror to her worries: "You attract what you use to impress." It was a truth as simple as it was powerful. If she had sought attention through seduction, it made sense that those drawn to her were guided only by desire. But Alessia knew in her heart she yearned for something deeper—more real, more lasting. And that yearning pushed her to examine her choices.

The thought led her to the ideas of Jean-Paul Sartre, who proposed that existence comes before essence—meaning we aren't born with a set nature but create it through our actions and choices. Alessia then understood she'd been trying to fill an emptiness with actions that didn't show her true self but a front she'd built for instant acceptance. That was the trap Sartre warned against: choosing to live falsely, taking on roles that aren't truly ours, and lying to ourselves to avoid the responsibility of being genuine.

Alessia realized that by using her body to draw others in, she'd chosen an easy but empty path. It brought her temporary attention, but not the deep connection she craved. In a world where being authentic felt increasingly like an act of rebellion, she understood she had to move past the surface—she had to start showing more of her true self: her intelligence, her passion, and her vulnerability.

The issue, Alessia reflected, wasn't about generations or the nature of men and women. The issue lay in what she, and so many others, chose to reveal. And in that choice—in the responsibility to show yourself as you are—was the key to attracting people who valued her true essence, not just how she looked.

Alessia knew then she had to be intentional. Every action and every word mattered because they shaped the direction of her life.

Looking in the mirror, her skin still damp from the shower and hair messy, Alessia offered a sad smile. She'd failed, yes, but she had also learned. She understood it wasn't too late to change, to be more true to the person she really wanted to become. The choice to start showing her genuine self, instead of the mask she'd worn so many times, was her first act of freedom—a step toward a new beginning.

The Light of the Irreplaceable

Pia opened the heavy door of the family home and froze at the sight of Davide. He wore a smile that radiated confidence—that relaxed expression he had perfected over the years. His stocky figure, shaped by time and hard-earned successes, stood outlined beneath a dark overcoat. His thick, wavy chestnut hair still fell in a tousled cascade to his shoulders, and his honey-colored eyes, deep and bright, seemed to absorb every detail, every flicker of emotion on Pia's face.

She didn't know what to say. The sound of her mother Nicoletta's footsteps echoed down the hallway, slowly approaching. Pia instinctively tried to pull the door closed, as if she could hide Davide's presence— but Nicoletta had already appeared, wearing that calm, wise smile, the look that seemed to understand everything without needing words.

—Pia, it's alright. Let him in,— she said, nodding gently, granting her permission.

Davide, amused, arched an eyebrow and chuckled, —I thought you were going to leave me out here at the mercy of the wind.—

Still confused and a little flustered, Pia opened the door fully, allowing Davide to step inside. With a ceremonious gesture, she swept her arm in a mock bow, inviting him in. At her feet, her suitcase and bag still lay scattered at the entrance—witnesses to a long and rushed journey.

The house, like its inhabitants, held a deep, ancient peace, infused with Nicoletta's characteristic simplicity and elegance. The walls were a soft ivory, adorned with vintage landscapes and family portraits. The polished wooden floors creaked gently underfoot. The entryway led directly into a cozy sitting room, where light filtered softly through the windows, illuminating old bookshelves lined with stories and mementos. There, in the living room, sat Davide, thumbing through a newspaper—perhaps from yesterday or the day before—while sipping a red Grodino, the bitter aperitif Milena, Nicoletta's housekeeper, always served on special occasions. Beside him, a dish of plump, glistening olives seasoned to perfection completed the scene.

Without saying a word, Pia hurried upstairs. At the master bedroom door, her eyes met her father's in the mirror. Lucien, his face marked by illness, smiled at her with the same warmth that once had been contagious. Wanting to return the gesture, Pia managed only a faint smile, fighting back tears that threatened to spill.

She approached and hugged him, noticing the frailty of his body, the way each motion drained him. His shallow breaths echoed softly in the room—a subtle reminder of all that time had taken.

Gently, Pia finished buttoning his shirt. Lucien, a glimmer of humor in his tired eyes, quipped, —Now it's your turn to button me up.—

Pulmonary fibrosis had slowly consumed him, but his mind remained sharp, his spirit intact. They spoke in hushed tones about life and its meaning, about what lasts and what inevitably fades. From the kitchen drifted the scent of Nicoletta's cooking, filling the air with the promise of comfort, stirring both their appetites.

Before leaving the room, Pia asked the question that had been pressing on her mind.

The Light of the Irreplaceable

—Dad, what's Davide doing here?—

Lucien looked at her with tenderness and nodded, as if he had been expecting it.

—I've made peace with Davide,— he said softly. — He'll tell you the rest. I hope you'll understand.—

As they descended the stairs, Lucien leaned on the railing, moving slowly but steadily. When they entered the living room, Davide stood and approached with respect, greeting Lucien with the warmth of old times.

—Good morning, Doctor. How are you feeling?—

Lucien, his voice calm and firm, smiled and replied, —Like an oak tree.—

It wasn't an answer grounded in reality but rather in how he wished things to be.

Nicoletta's kitchen was modest but full of life. The walls were lined with warm-toned antique tiles, steeped in decades of lovingly prepared meals. On the large wooden table, polished by years of use, lay the dishes: a hearty beef stew releasing deep, spiced aromas, and a delicate, savory quail ragù—both ready to be ladled over creamy, golden polenta. As sides, a mix of mushrooms sautéed with garlic and parsley completed the spread. At one end of the table, a selection of salamis, paper-thin slices of prosciutto, and chunks of Piave Vecchio—the region's signature cheese— waited to be savored.

Milena had carefully set the table, placing each glass and plate as if it had a designated role in this quiet ritual of farewell. For the aperitivo, she served a bubbly, crisp Prosecco, the perfect prelude for the meal. Alongside the meats, two bold red wines stood ready: a Valpolicella Ripasso, laced with cherry and spice, and a brooding Amarone della Valpolicella, dark and intense enough to match the depth of the stew and ragù. For the rebellious few, there was also a white wine—a Soave Classico, light and refreshing, a gentle breath amid the richness of the reds.

As everyone gathered in the living room, the air took on a nostalgic tone, as though every corner of the house knew this moment's importance.

From the shadows, Davide watched Lucien and Nicoletta with respect—and something more, something only he could name. Meanwhile, Pia couldn't shake the sense that this reunion, this family gathering, was really a quiet goodbye, cloaked in smiles and shared glances.

Antonella's arrival filled the house with commanding energy. She was a woman impossible to overlook. Tall and striking, with an elegant demeanor and imposing beauty, she had carved out a career in New York as an attorney in one of the world's top law firms. Her presence was as powerful as her voice—always clear, always strong. Antonella didn't beat around the bush. Her confidence and force of character could be intimidating.

Though she had a good relationship with her sister, long hours and the intensity of her job had created distance—a weight felt in moments like these. She had rushed home after reading her father's letter, knowing that no matter how rare her visits were, there would always be a place for her in this house. People said her strong personality scared men away, but in truth, it was her devotion to work that left little room for romance.

Attilio, Lucien's brother, arrived shortly after. He had a kind face and a calm demeanor, the presence of someone who had lived without rushing, savoring every moment. The bond between Lucien and Attilio went beyond brotherhood—they were friends, confidants, and shared a deep passion for music and cinema. With a conspiratorial smile, Attilio hugged his brother, exchanging a look filled with years of shared memories and unspoken understanding.

The house, now filled with more than twenty guests between family and friends, took on a special atmosphere. The soft clinking of glasses and the murmur of overlapping voices mixed with laughter, creating a scene almost festive. Lucien, showing an unusual vitality for someone in his condition, moved among his loved ones, spreading a contagious joy that turned the gathering into a celebration of life. For a fleeting moment, illness and time seemed to pause, allowing everyone to bask in a rare, unburdened happiness.

It was a moment suspended in time—as if the memories, the unsaid words, and the restrained emotions filled every corner of that home. And as they gathered around the table, with the aroma of food and wine surrounding them, each person knew they were sharing more than just a meal. They were sharing the weight of memory, the story of a family, of love, and of a farewell that would remain etched in their hearts forever. The dining room table dominated the room with a majestic presence. It was an immense piece of solid oak, hand-polished to reveal the rich depth of its grain. There were only chairs at the ends, which were high-backed and upholstered in dark leather, while, on the sides, two large benches of the same wood allowed family and friends to settle in with ease. It could comfortably accommodate thirty diners, a detail that Lucien had planned with the hope that his daughters, Antonella and Pia, would one day fill the house with grandchildren and prolong their family's legacy in gargantuan feasts.

The tableware, of a vibrant Delft blue, had arrived from the Netherlands; its delicate designs of flowers and landscapes seemed to dance on the gleaming white of the plates. They contrasted perfectly with the white linen tablecloth, woven with the precision and mastery that only the artisans of Venice knew how to provide. The edges were adorned with intricate lace, a touch of subtle opulence that spoke of Nicoletta's refined taste. The silver cutlery, bought in Toledo, Spain, gleamed under the warm light of the antique chandeliers that hung from the ceiling, illuminating every corner of the room and reflecting a soft and elegant shine in each utensil. It seemed that each piece, each detail, had been chosen with love and dedication, as if the table itself were a work of art that paid homage to the generations of her family.

The dining room was spacious and welcoming, with walls in warm tones and paintings of Italian rural landscapes strategically hung, evoking the simplicity and beauty of life in the countryside. Shelves with well-selected bottles of wine lined one of the walls, and the aromas of the freshly served food—the beef stew and the quail ragout, the polenta served with the mixture of mushrooms sautéed with garlic and parsley—filled the air, inviting everyone present to enjoy that unique moment. There was something ceremonial in each dish that arrived at the table, a celebration of good food, but, above all, of shared time.

As the hours passed, when the dishes had been cleared and the last sip of Amarone della Valpolicella had been savored, Attilio stood up with a smile, took his guitar, and began to strum the strings gently. A nostalgic note floated in the air, and one by one, all present joined in an impromptu song, performing the melodies of Lucio Dalla, Battisti, and Adriano Celentano. The songs filled the room with a contagious joy, and the pain that dwelt in their hearts seemed to dissipate, as if the music momentarily anesthetized the sadness.

Laughter and love for Lucien transformed the atmosphere. The farewell began to take on a different light: it was not the painful and somber goodbye they had feared, but a celebration of the life he had lived, of the shared moments, and of the love he had sown in each one of them.

A Place to Return To

Monday's dawn lit the horizon with a serenity that stood in stark contrast to the night before—a cruel reminder that the world, indifferent to the joys and sorrows of mortals, always continues its course. Lucien's house, which just hours earlier had been a refuge of laughter, music, and love, now lingered in a suspended stillness only the early morning could emphasize. Cities awakened, life marched on, and clocks marked time with indifference, leaving behind those unable to keep up.

Lucien, still filled with an almost mystical energy, had led the guests in singing —Happy Birthday— to Nicoletta—a song now heavy with emotion, echoing with an unfamiliar tenderness. As the first rays of sunlight poured through the windows, guests began to say their goodbyes, leaving behind a flicker of hope: that they might see Lucien once more. The echoes of the final laughter still floated in the air when Milena arrived to help Nicoletta tend to the remnants of the evening's feast.

In the intimacy of the home, Lucien embraced his daughters and kissed his wife with a love that seemed boundless. Taking her hand and offering a slight bow, he pulled a small red velvet box from his pocket and placed it in her hands. Inside, a pendant bearing the symbol of infinity glowed in the soft morning light—a reminder of his eternal promise.

—Nico, I've been the most fortunate man in the world. I wouldn't be who I am without you by my side. Thank you, endlessly, for being my companion, my strength, and my love. If there is life after this one, I want it to be with you.—

Nicoletta's face lit up, and in that moment, the house filled with a blend of love and resignation—as if everyone, deep down, knew that this gesture was a goodbye disguised as a celebration. Lucien told them he wanted to take a nap, and Nicoletta, along with Pia and Antonella—exhausted—retired to their rooms to rest.

But before lying down, the two sisters decided to peek into the master bedroom. They opened the door and found their father lying down, his eyes closed, a soft smile on his face, as though his soul had recognized their presence. Nicoletta, lying beside him, gently stroked his silky white hair—a gesture steeped in love and tenderness beyond the realm of words.

It was at noon when Nicoletta heard what would be Lucien's final breath. He, who had given so much without ever asking for anything in return, had departed in silence—with the same peace he had cultivated throughout his life.

Nicoletta woke her daughters with a trembling voice and pain etched into every movement.

—Papa is gone,—she said—and those words, though expected, pierced their hearts with the force of the inevitable.

Pia's Journal

Monday, October 17, 2022

There is an unfathomable mystery in the fact that you chose—or perhaps it was never your choice—to leave on October 17, the very day of Mom's birthday. As in Borges' stories, time unfolds like a labyrinth of possibilities, and the end—though inevitable—always arrives as a blow that catches me off guard. Life offers no guarantees, no verdicts. No one enters this world with a label that says —you have seventy years— or —you'll make it to eighty-five.— All it grants us is the certainty of existence, and in that uncertainty lies its tragic beauty.

Time with you, Dad, was a paradox: fleeting, yet profound. Only now do I begin to grasp its true worth—the richness of those moments that, though ephemeral, are eternal in my memory. Life has taught me, through more than a few stumbles, that love—like everything else in this absurd world—evolves. And even so, who can truly say someone ever dies? I held you in the flesh, embraced you, lived you—and though you're no longer physically here, your essence still lives within me. Like the characters of Camus, you defied the apparent meaninglessness of existence and, in that defiance, turned shadows into light. You protected us from your own tragedies, showing me that true happiness is a choice—a rebellious act in the face of the inevitable.

You were an alchemist of the everyday—a simple man who found joy in the innocence of small things, who lived without luxury or the burdens of others' expectations. You understood that what mattered most was the now, the wise stewardship of emotions and passions. That was your true legacy—the one still alive in those of us lucky enough to have known you.

Dad, as Carl Jung taught, you were faithful to your purpose—and that faithfulness was your greatest triumph: —The privilege of a lifetime is to become who you truly are.— Your love for pediatrics and for us—your family— was your compass, the center that gave meaning to it all. And for that reason, your departure is not just a loss; it's a lesson in what it means to live with authenticity and unconditional love.

And yes, Chaplin was right: —Sing, laugh, dance, cry, and live every moment of your life before the curtain falls and the play ends without applause.—

With love—and with the certainty that your legacy still beats within me—I say goodbye, Dad. Because even though the curtain has fallen for you today, your presence will forever be the silent applause that echoes through our lives.

I love you, Pia.

The Echo of an Uncertain Kiss

The spring sun shimmered over the waters of Lake Braies, reflecting the majestic peaks of the Croda del Becco as if they were guardians from an ancient tale. Tourists from around the world marveled at the view: a group of Austrians with strong Viennese accents chatted animatedly, a Japanese couple walked in silence, admiring the landscape, and a Sicilian woman, speaking in her rich Palermo dialect, exclaimed about the beauty of the place, gesturing passionately with her hands.

Pia and Davide, thrilled and filled with that youthful curiosity, had walked nearly the entire circuit of the lake, following the Seerundwanderweg—the circular trail that led them farther and farther away. The panoramic staircase that should have guided them back to the group was now behind them, and without realizing it, they had strayed. In the distance, the Hotel Lago di Braies stood with its wooden facade, inviting rest. For a moment, they thought they could swim across to reach it but knew they had to turn back.

On their way back, the sound of the Cascata Ghiacciata di Braies broke the silence with a refreshing echo. The mist sprayed in the air made the breeze feel colder, and their shared laughter mingled with the murmur of rushing water. It was then that Pia, stepping onto a slick rock, lost her footing and fell. A stifled cry escaped her lips as pain made her clench her eyes shut.

—Pia!— Davide immediately dropped to his knees beside her, concern flooding his eyes.

She tried to hold back tears as he carefully removed her hiking boot and sock, revealing a red, swollen ankle.

Davide couldn't help but notice the fragility of her foot—small and perfect—a reflection of the same delicacy he always saw in Pia.

—We'll have to go back. You can't walk like this,—he said firmly.

Pia nodded, still biting her lip to keep from crying. Davide offered his back and, without hesitation, carried her. His strong arms held her gently, and he felt each step under the shared weight of their bodies. The return path became a challenge beneath a sky now streaked with shades of orange and pink. Tourists passed them—among them, the Sicilian woman and the Japanese couple—watching with surprise and smiling in admiration. It took more than thirty minutes before they spotted the school group, who had already begun to grow anxious over their absence.

As Davide carried Pia, those around them couldn't help but pause and take in the scene. The Sicilian woman, her head wrapped in a brightly colored scarf, exclaimed with her thick Palermo accent:

—*Ma guarda, che ragazzo coraggioso! Chistu sì ca è un vero gentiluomo!* — she said, a blend of admiration and pride in her voice while her hands made an emphatic gesture that underscored her words. [1]

---

[1] **Sicilian Woman's Comment:**—*Ma guarda, che ragazzo coraggioso! Chistu si ca è un vero gentiluomo!*— —Look, what a brave lad! He is indeed a true gentleman!—
Comments from the Austrians: —Schau, er trägt sie wie ein Held! Solche Dinge sieht man selten heutzutage. ——Look, he carries her like a hero! You rarely see such things nowadays.—
—Ein junger Mann mit Herz, das muss man ihm lassen. ——A young man with heart, one has to give him that.—

A group of Austrians, with distinct Viennese accents and curious eyes, murmured amongst themselves:

—Schau, er trägt sie wie ein Held! Solche Dinge sieht man selten heutzutage,— one of the men remarked, impressed, as another nodded in agreement, adding:

—Ein junger Mann mit Herz, das muss man ihm lassen.—

The Japanese couple, discreet but observant, exchanged words with tender tones. The woman, with a soft smile, whispered in her native tongue:

—Subarashii desu ne. Wakai ai no chikara wa donna konnan mo norikoerare yo ni miemasu.—

Her partner nodded, eyes gleaming at the touching scene before them, and replied:

—Hontō ni, kokoro ga atatamarimasu.—

The words of admiration floated in the air like echoes, accompanying Davide with each increasingly difficult step. And though sweat beaded on his brow and his arms strained with the effort, a quiet determination propelled him forward. Pia, feeling all of Davide's warmth and strength, gently squeezed his shoulder in a silent gesture

---

Comments from the Japanese Couple: —素晴らしいですね。若い愛の力はどんな困難も乗り越えられるように見えます。(Subarashii desu ne. Wakai ai no chikara wa donna konnan mo norikoerare yō ni miemasu.) ——It's wonderful, isn't it? The power of young love seems capable of overcoming any difficulty.—
—本当に、心が温まります。(Hontō ni, kokoro ga atatamarimasu.) —— Indeed, it warms the heart.—

of gratitude, while the surrounding landscape filled with golden hues, and the admiration of the onlookers became a backdrop to his heroic march. The exertion left Davide's arms numb, but he did not utter a single complaint. When they finally arrived, the teachers' gazes were a mixture of concern and relief. Pia was taken to rest, and her ankle was examined more thoroughly, while Davide collapsed onto a bench, exhausted but wearing a smile of satisfaction for having brought her back.

The next morning, the group's activity was a rowboat outing. The teachers, in order to avoid another adventure, decided to separate Pia and Davide. Pia, despite limping slightly, insisted on participating. From his boat, Davide watched her, their gazes meeting occasionally, filled with a complicity that words could not explain. Pino, Davide's rowing partner, noticed his distraction and nudged him.

—Still thinking about your heroine from yesterday, eh?— he joked, expecting no reply.

Pia, seated across the lake, also searched for Davide among the water's reflections, her heart beating in rhythm with the oars cutting through the surface. Though they were in separate boats, they shared something deeper than proximity: the adventure, the innocence, and a bond beginning to form with the invisible threads of youth and spring.

When Davide and Pino's boats began rowing in the opposite direction of Professor Tolo's instructions and ended up nearly parallel, just a couple of meters apart, the group watched with anticipation. Laughter and whispers rippled through the students, all eyes drawn to the small rebellion of the two friends. Suddenly, Pino, with his usual humor and a grin lighting up his face, shouted toward Pia:

—Roxane, your Christian is coming—guided by the real Cyrano!—he cried, pointing at Davide with his oar and striking a theatrical pose, as if he were performing on stage.

Laughter erupted among their classmates, filling the lake's crisp air with carefree joy. Even Pia, who still felt a twinge in her foot, couldn't help but laugh at Pino's antics. Davide, on the other hand, felt a blush creep up his cheeks— slightly embarrassed to be compared to Cyrano, the romantic hero and poet who wrote love letters in secret for another man.

Professor Tolo, who had been watching the scene with a mix of exasperation and amusement, let his stern expression soften upon hearing the literary reference. A lover of great works, he couldn't suppress a small smile tugging at the corners of his mouth.

Pino, now fully committed to his role as an improvised romantic lead, continued to recite with exaggerated drama, raising his arms to the sky like Cyrano himself:

—'Yes, I have loved you always! I love you still!'—

Davide, trying to cover Pino's mouth before he could go any further, leaned too far toward him. The boat wobbled dangerously, rocking from side to side as the other students widened their eyes in alarm. Laughter rippled across the lake, and a few meters away, Professor Tolo, watching in disbelief and mild despair, shouted:

—That's enough, boys! You're going to dump us all into the lake!—

Pino and Davide, now overtaken by laughter that made them shake, ignored the warning. Suddenly, with a mischievous smile and a gleam in his eyes, Davide leapt through the air in a staged combat move and tackled Pino. Both of them plunged into the lake with a huge splash, water flying in all directions as a roar of laughter erupted from the boat.

Tolo's face shifted from concern to horror in an instant, his mouth open in a silent scream as he watched the two boys resurface, laughing uncontrollably. His terrified expression, combined with the constant swaying of the boat, only made the rest of the students laugh even harder. Whatever seriousness he had tried to maintain dissolved in the hilarity of the moment as he struggled to stay balanced.

Nearby boats drifted closer, drawn by the commotion and the laughter echoing across the lake. Tourists passing by watched the scene with amused smiles—some even applauding the boys' antics.

—Pino, I never imagined you quoting Rostand,— said Tolo, nodding with a trace of approval, while the students erupted into even more laughter. The moment was sealed with laughter and jokes—a fragment of pure joy etched into their memories, beneath the clear blue sky of the Dolomites.

It was Sunday morning when Professor Tolo gathered the students in front of the Capella Lago di Braies. The soft light of dawn bathed the chapel and the surroundings in a golden glow, while the crisp air carried the whisper of the lake and the scent of nearby pines. The chapel, humble yet solemn, stood like a timeless sentinel in the heart of the Dolomites—a silent witness to stories lost in the mist of history.

Tolo, with his signature deep tone and passion for history, began to speak as the students formed a semicircle around him.

—This chapel,—he said, pausing with gravity,—has seen more than it seems. In 1945, during the final days of World War II, this region became an unexpected stage for a little-known chapter of history. A German commander of the Schutzstaffel—the feared SS—brought a group of prominent prisoners here. His plan was to use them as bargaining chips if the war turned against Germany.

Silence settled over the group as Tolo spoke. Pia and Davide, standing side by side, felt the weight of the moment—as if the stones of the chapel themselves held echoes of that era.

—The commander— Tolo continued—was a man torn between loyalty to the regime and the burden of his conscience. On a cold April night, as Germany's defeat became inevitable and the Allies drew near, he made a decision that would change the fate of everyone there: he released the prisoners and resigned his post. Some say he spent that final night sitting before the lake, staring into the water, waiting for dawn, and accepting whatever came next.

The first rays of sun lit the lake's surface, casting sparkles that made the waters seem to whisper secrets from the past. Tolo's voice carried a subtle echo, as if history itself were reaffirming its presence.

—This chapel, dear students, is a reminder that even in the deepest darkness, the human soul can find a glimmer of redemption. Here, in this corner of the world, war took a pause, and one man, in his final act, left behind a legacy of hope.

The group remained silent, letting the story settle over them like morning dew on grass. Davide looked at Pia, and she returned his gaze with a soft nod, both acknowledging that memory, regret, and redemption were as profound and enigmatic as the lake surrounding them.

That Sunday afternoon was tinged with the soft melancholy of a day coming to an end. Pia and Davide sat together on the bus, their bodies barely separated by the narrow seat. Their hands met naturally and intertwined, sharing a silent gesture that spoke of deep affection and complicity.

As the bus pulled away and merged onto the highway toward Padua, the students began singing "Baciami Ancora" by Jovanotti, their young, carefree voices filling the space with vibrant, easy joy.

Pia and Davide looked into each other's eyes, laughter and music wrapping around them like an invisible blanket. In that gaze—wordless and full—lurked a promise, a silent invitation to a first kiss they had yet to share but already felt inevitable. It was as if their hearts had already taken that step, intertwined in the rhythm of the song, in the notes and emotions floating through the air.

The bus rolled on, the landscape blurring with speed—but in that moment, the whole world seemed to stop just for the two of them.

The Reverberation of Farewell

Lucien was mourned the following day with a solemnity that seemed to stretch beyond the hall's walls, as if time itself had paused to mark the moment. The burial, set for Wednesday, October 19, drew a crowd that surpassed all expectations: notable figures from the region, relatives who had traveled great distances, childhood friends, and colleagues. Acquaintances from university and even high school showed up, as though Lucien's life unfolded in an unseen tapestry of shared memories.

The ceremony was held in the majestic Basilica of Saint Anthony of Padua, a place that seemed to resonate with echoes of the eternal. The basilica is a fusion of styles reflecting centuries of history: the solid, humble Romanesque that gives a sense of depth and weight; the pointed arches and high Gothic vaults lifting the gaze heavenward, bestowing an air of infinite spirituality; the Renaissance details bringing harmony and balance; and finally, the Baroque ornaments—rich, overflowing with detail—capturing the energy and drama of human life. It was a place where the architecture seemed to tell the stories of generations' struggles, hopes, and devotions.

Entering the main nave, attendees found it imposing and grand, with light streaming through stained glass windows, creating a play of colors that danced softly on the marble floor. In the background, the monumental organ stood silent, as if honoring the moment's solemnity. Its pipes rose in formation, an army of pewter and gold that could, with the slightest touch, fill the space with sounds vibrating the basilica walls and stirring the soul's deepest fibers. For many, it felt as though Lucien's spirit merged with every part of the church in a final act of presence.

Outside the basilica, surrounding streets like Via del Santo and Via Cesarotti filled with people who, unable to enter, gathered in a gesture of respect and admiration. Among the crowd, several colleagues from the Faculty of Philosophy and Letters at the University of Florence tried to get closer to the entrance, hoping to go inside to pay their respects. Though he belonged to the Faculty of Information Technology, Giacomo, an old family acquaintance, was also there, observing with his usual reserved gaze.

Alessia, who wasn't from the university but shared deep ties with some of those present, was also nearby. Hidden in a column's shadow, looking thoughtful, she avoided being seen by Giacomo, keeping her distance. Her presence was a quiet echo of past feelings and shared secrets—one more figure in the tapestry of intertwined lives honoring Lucien that day.

The moment's solemnity extended even to the Piazza del Santo, where groups stood in silence or murmured among themselves, remembering Lucien with expressions of nostalgia and affection. Faces varied from the oldest, seeming to carry a lifetime of memories, to young medical students who saw Lucien as a role model.

It was a farewell that, due to its magnitude and emotional weight, felt like a reverberation, a wave that extended not only through the streets of Padua but also in the memory of all those who had known him.

In the dim church light, where column shadows seemed to whisper ancient secrets, Pia received condolences from those who came to honor her father. It was a procession of repeated words and looks filled with respect and sadness. It had been incredibly difficult for Davide to reach Pia; each step was a challenge, an act of courage pushing through the crowd and the weight of his own feelings. As he made his way through people, he stumbled, accidentally stepping on Giacomo's foot. Giacomo reacted instantly with indignation, his face flushed with contained anger. Davide, keeping his composure, smiled and brought his palms together in a gesture of apology and peace, murmuring apologies to others as he continued to move forward.

Giacomo, unable to process the moment, felt completely detached from the solemnity. He knew about Davide from Pia's words but couldn't identify him. Yet, feeling Davide's apology wasn't enough, he filled with rage and began following him through the crowd, expecting a more formal response. He watched with suspicion as Davide advanced with determination, as if the brief apology was too little for the insult Giacomo felt.

Suddenly, Giacomo stopped. He saw that Davide had reached Nicoletta and her daughters, Antonella and Pia. Davide's gaze, moments before calm and focused, softened with respect as he stood before them. In that instant, Giacomo understood, though only partly, that he was out of place—disconnected from a scene he couldn't fully grasp. He chose then to melt into the crowd, blending with the murmur and sway of those waiting their turn to offer respects, rather than approaching the family directly.

From a distance, Alessia watched part of the scene, struggling against the tide of people that made it hard to see clearly. She wondered why Giacomo, so close, didn't approach Pia or offer condolences to the family. Confusion and curiosity washed over her as she kept her distance, staying hidden from Giacomo in the throng.

Davide moved forward with firm but respectful steps toward Nicoletta, his face marked by genuine sadness. Seeing him, Nicoletta set aside any past hard feelings and welcomed him with an embrace holding years of history, shared memories, and unspoken reconciliation. Her eyes filled with tears as Davide whispered his heartfelt condolences.

—I'm so sorry, Mrs. Nicoletta,— he said softly, his voice a contrast to his usual easygoing tone.

Nicoletta nodded in silent gratitude, saying nothing more; the gesture said it all.

Antonella, ever watchful, was next to receive him. Though her relationship with Davide had been more distant, she embraced him with the same warmth. She hugged him sincerely and warmly, and Davide felt that, for that moment at least, the barriers of years and biases dissolved.

—Thank you, Davide,— Antonella said, her expression showing respect. —We know how much he meant to you too.—

Pia watched from a few steps away, surprised by her family's familiarity with Davide. Something about the scene felt strange, like a small crack opened in time, an echo of what once was. She quickly pushed the feeling away; there were too many emotions already, and she simply wanted a moment's relief from her worries.

Finally, Davide approached her, his gaze a mix of tenderness and pain.

—Good morning, Pia. How are you holding up?— he began, his voice low and measured. —Please accept my condolences. I am so sorry for your loss.—

Pia, worn out and still caught in the whirlwind of emotions, looked at him with a faint, grateful smile. She didn't know what to say or how to bear the weight of words just then. But just having him there, offering silent support, was enough.

Pia spoke softly, barely a whisper she alone could hear, —What are your immediate plans?—

She looked up, eyes clouded with fatigue and sorrow, and paused before answering. In that stillness, the world seemed to shrink, as if all the weight of memories and emotions focused in that space between them.

—All I know is I want to sleep, Davide,— she replied, her voice tinged with a weariness that felt not just physical, but spiritual. —Sleep and not wake up, at least until the weekend.—

Davide lowered his gaze, understanding the depth of her words. He swallowed, trying to form an answer that wouldn't come.

—I understand,—he finally said, nodding slightly. —I'd like to talk to you before you leave.—

Pia's lips tightened in a slight grimace, and she shook her head—a gesture of both refusal and plea.

—Let's just leave it, Davide. Not now.—

The echoes of her words settled in the church's silence—a silence heavy with all that was left unsaid. Davide, skilled at reading looks and gestures, nodded again, this time with a touch of resignation. He stepped back and withdrew, leaving Pia alone on the edge of a grief she didn't yet fully grasp. The church, smelling of wax and history, seemed to hold them both, a silent witness to stories even time wouldn't dare forget.

As Davide stepped back with slow, controlled movements, Giacomo remained in place, barely visible. From the shadows, his eyes tracked Davide's every move with a mix of suspicion and unease. Something about the way the family had received him sparked a nagging doubt.

He watched Nicoletta and Antonella hug him with a familiarity that unnerved Giacomo, and Pia's coolness toward Davide only sharpened his curiosity.

Who was this man? Giacomo wondered, his mind spinning theories, each more unsettling than the last. He'd recognized a distinct tone in Pia, a guardedness—something only someone who knew her well would notice. He knew when Pia avoided prolonged contact, it was because she held complex feelings, perhaps unresolved resentments.

Intrigue consumed him. Changing tactics, he decided to blend in with the attendees still in the church. His goal was clear: find out who this man was, treated so warmly by Lucien's family, yet met with such distance by Pia. He wasn't just any friend; the family's eyes confirmed that.

Without anyone noticing, Giacomo approached acquaintances in the church hall, listening to hushed conversations, catching fragments of words. His anxious mind seized on any hint confirming his suspicions, like a hunter silently stalking prey, alert to every detail. Anxiety burned hotter inside him, as if the truth was about to break through any second. But Giacomo wasn't the only one observing.

Alessia, who had followed his movements from a distance, noticed how he avoided approaching Pia's family. His sudden retreat after being so close, his furtive way of following Davide—it all sparked a flicker of unease. She knew Giacomo well enough to know he was plotting something, and her gut told her this might lead him into dangerous territory. She remembered the few times Pia had mentioned Davide, always with a veiled discomfort, like someone referencing a closed chapter of her life. Alessia wondered what Giacomo was searching for and why he was so fixated on a man who, though a stranger to them, seemed to carry echoes of a past Pia didn't want to remember.

The Weight of Dreams

The trip back from the Dolomites marked a turning point in Pia and Davide's lives. Those days by the lake, sharing laughter and stolen glances, where their hands intertwined and their hearts beat as one—they were etched into memory with an intensity only first love can offer. It was as if, in those moments of pure innocence and adventure, the entire world had paused just for them.

From that trip on, the love between Pia and Davide blossomed with an intensity worthy of the novels Pia cherished. Their relationship felt like a chapter pulled from a book, narrating love in its purest, most untamed form: a love free of burdens or responsibilities, where days felt endless and the future was in no hurry to arrive. They were two young souls discovering every part of each other, lost in that bubble where only they existed.

Davide, with his contagious laugh and spark for life, became the center of Pia's world. He made her laugh like no one else, with his carefree nature and a natural intelligence that overflowed with creativity, even if he rarely fit neatly into school. Pia loved him precisely for that—for his genuineness, his rebellion, and the freedom that seemed to flow from him like a river refusing to be held back. By his side, Pia experienced life in ways she'd never imagined, laughing freely under the sun, sharing secrets beneath the stars, and dreaming together of a future that felt eternal.

But as love bloomed in their hearts, worries began to sprout in Pia's home. Lucien and Nicoletta, her parents, watched with growing unease as the enthusiasm and drive Pia had always shown for her future started to fade. Lucien, protective and concerned, remembered with longing the days his daughter spoke passionately about studying literature and philosophy at the University of Milan, where she dreamt of unraveling the great works of literature and philosophy. But now, that spark in her eyes seemed slowly dimming, and conversations about the future grew increasingly evasive.

Davide's influence, though undoubtedly full of love, also brought a shadow of nonchalance that began to color Pia's dreams. Lucien saw Davide as a bright young man but directionless—someone whose lack of commitment and clear plans could steer his daughter down an uncertain road. As charming and fun as Davide was, Lucien feared the love they shared would become an anchor, holding Pia back from her true potential.

Nicoletta, for her part, observed the situation with quiet sorrow, feeling the bond with her daughter become a tug-of-war between the present and the future. In her heart, she understood Pia and Davide's love, but it hurt her to see her daughter, who once dreamt of soaring high, seeming more and more caught in the moment, setting aside the dreams that had once guided her.

Tensions in Pia's home rose with each passing day. Arguments with her parents became frequent, especially when Lucien, with his desperate love, tried to warn her about the dangers of giving herself completely to someone without a clear purpose. To Pia, these warnings made no sense, as if her parents couldn't see what she saw in Davide—that innate freedom, that unbridled joy that made her feel truly alive. The more they tried to pull her away, the tighter she clung to his love, as if defying her parents was a test of her feelings' strength.

Davide's relationship with Pia's family quickly fell apart. Awkward silences and disapproving looks turned into doors shut between them.

Finally, Lucien and Nicoletta decided Davide was no longer welcome in their home. But this ban, far from separating them, only strengthened the bond between Pia and Davide, uniting them in a quiet pact of defiant love. Davide, though hurt by the rejection, remained true to himself—the carefree young man, his laughter always ready to chase away any worry.

However, Pia began sensing something shifting within herself. At first, she let herself be swept away by Davide's carefree spirit—his wild nature that seemed to float above the world's troubles. But inside, a silent unease began to surface. That spark of ambition that once drove her toward a bright future struggled to reignite. Her dreams of Milan, her university plans, became a distant echo, a faint melody still lingering in some part of her heart.

The love between Pia and Davide remained strong and passionate, but reality started seeping into their perfect moments. The edges of adolescence—a time when mistakes felt forgivable and decisions reversible—began showing their first cracks. Pia knew it, felt it deep inside, in those quiet moments when the weight of her own desires and her love for Davide collided like opposing forces.

One afternoon, walking together under the starry sky, Pia confessed her doubts, her fears, to Davide. He listened, trying to understand, but their worlds, though bound by love, began showing their differences. Davide couldn't grasp why Pia still held onto dreams of studying and a future beyond their small world. For him, the present was enough; the now, with her beside him, made him whole.

Pia, on the other hand, was starting to see life differently. Her love for Davide was intense and real, but life whispered other paths, other possibilities she couldn't ignore. And in the dim light of that night, beneath the starry blanket that had once united them, Pia understood that love, however powerful, wasn't always enough to silence the voice of her own being.

Pia and Davide's story, in that chapter of their lives, was beautiful and fervent, but also brief—like sparks flying from a bonfire in the dark. The young woman, caught between the love consuming her and the dream of a future fading before her, found herself at a crossroads. She knew one day she'd have to choose, that her life couldn't forever be a carefree dance under the sun and moon.

Davide, his soft voice carrying that charmingly easygoing tone that so disarmed Pia, began recounting memories of their trips—not just a simple retelling, but a declaration of everything they had experienced, trying to keep her tied to their shared past.

—Remember Salzburg, Pia?— Davide said, as if unearthing a treasure from time's folds— That city that seemed lifted from an old fairy tale, with its medieval facades and the air of mystery lingering everywhere. We walked along Getreidegasse street, where even the signs looked like art. I saw you in front of Mozart's house, eyes shining with feeling, and I thought that city—with its history, its music—was made for you. You took me to Hellbrunn Palace, where we had fun like kids among the surprise fountains—and that laugh of yours... I can still hear it. We tried the palatschinken together, those soft crepes melting in your mouth, and then the Mozartkugeln, which you translated as 'Mozart balls.' I tried to be serious, but the double meaning of that translation made it impossible, and we ended up laughing like two kids in the middle of that magical moment.

Pia looked at him with a mix of nostalgia and tenderness as he continued, mapping their memories with words.

—And Munich...— Davide went on, with a playful smile. —That Gothic square that seemed made for legendary heroes, Marienplatz, towers reaching for the sky. I remember you spellbound, like you were living in a chapter of one of your books. We sat in the market, on those wooden benches, eating hot pretzels and bratwurst while people toasted around us, and for a moment, it felt like we were part of that lively, timeless energy. That memory, under the Bavarian stars, will always be ours, Pia. The world belonged to us that night.—

Pia closed her eyes for a moment, letting Davide's words carry her, while he watched her with pride and devotion, wanting to assure her those memories were real— as real as his love.

—And Paris?—he continued, as if unveiling the most precious part of a story.

—The city you love so much... We got lost in Montmartre, among the echoes of artists and dreamers, where you imagined the spirits of Picasso and Toulouse-Lautrec still lingered. And when we sat by the Seine, facing the Louvre, sharing a simple baguette with camembert and grapes, it felt like the whole city conspired to make us feel at the center of something eternal. I listened to you talk about Notre Dame, and in that moment, Pia, you were the poetry of Paris. Every word was a verse, and I was happy to be the reader in that book.—

Davide intertwined his fingers with Pia's, squeezing gently, then continued, his voice a whisper, as if afraid the memories might escape if he spoke too loud.

—Then we went to Barcelona, remember? We wandered into the colorful chaos of Park Güell, and it felt like we were walking inside a dream Gaudí created just for us. We laughed and marveled as if time didn't exist. Then, on La Rambla, we tried Iberian ham tapas, and I, who never knew much about food, felt everything in that moment made sense. The Sagrada Familia rose above us—a reminder that some things take a lifetime and are still worth it. That's how my love for you was, Pia: something neither time nor distance could erase.—

Pia felt each of Davide's words wrap around her and wondered if any future memory could compare to what he described, to what she'd shared with him.

—Dubrovnik, Pia... that city that seemed hidden from the world, suspended between sky and sea. We walked those ancient walls, looking out at the Adriatic, and I remember joking I was a medieval knight. We laughed until the sun began to set. In that small restaurant, we shared seafood peka. I looked at you, and there was no doubt in my heart. You were there, with me, and I needed nothing else. It was as if the sunset knew we were that city's best-kept secret.—

Davide paused, looking at the sky as if he could see those days reflected in the clouds.

—And Lucerne, with its wooden bridge, the Kapellbrücke, where we stopped to see the lake, mountains mirrored in the water, reminding us how small we are compared to the world. We tried fondue, and you said that cheese tasted like a perfect moment. And I... I stayed quiet because I knew you were right. It was perfect, Pia. Everything was perfect because you were there, because we were together.

Davide leaned in slightly, eyes fixed on hers, and continued softly:

—Each of those cities, each of those moments... they taught me that love, true love, is the kind we share in the simplest places and also in the most magnificent ones. And Pia, even though the world is vast and full of possibilities, I know the only one I want to explore it with is you. Don't let the weight of the dreams others have for you make you forget what we really want, what we really are. We aren't just memories or promises. We're the sum of all those laughs, of every glance and every moment where we knew that this— what we have—is the most real thing we have.—

Pia, moved, felt the walls of her doubts crumble before Davide's words. Their love, in that moment, was as tangible as the air they breathed. And as night closed in, she knew that, at least for now, she didn't need answers, because he was the only certainty she desired.

Watching Pia in that moment of vulnerability, he felt a weight he hadn't wanted to face. His love for her was deep and real, but deep down, Davide knew something had to change. The carefree way they lived, the bubble where they hid, was starting to show cracks. And he, though he tried to hold onto the simplicity of their days, felt something undefined pushing him toward the reality he was trying to avoid.

In his pocket, the weight of an unanswered message felt like it was burning. Days ago, Lucien, Pia's father, had sent an unexpected text: *"Davide, we need to talk. Alone. Pia can't and shouldn't know about this message."* Since then, those words had been a constant whisper in his mind—a warning mixed with the ache of knowing his love for Pia, immense as it was, might not be enough to shield her from everything.

Davide looked at Pia, who seemed lost in memories of their travels, eyes nostalgic, a smile still soft on her lips. He loved her. He loved her with everything he had, and every word he'd spoken was true. Yet he knew the conversation he'd put off couldn't wait much longer. Lucien wanted to see him alone, and though facing her father worried him, Davide was beginning to understand that meeting was perhaps unavoidable.

He squeezed Pia's hand, as if to reaffirm his promise of love, of those perfect moments shared. But deep down, a whisper of doubt stayed with him. Could he protect their love from the realities closing in? Or was Lucien's message a sign that everything was about to change?

And so, while love still bloomed, the first shadows of farewell began to fall across their path.

The Shadows of Santa Maria Novella

In the bustling Santa Maria Novella neighborhood, where the train station drew a constant stream of travelers and the echo of footsteps blurred among the alleys and the rumble of motorcycles, Alessia walked with a mix of nerves and anticipation. She'd planned this visit carefully; she had dropped a friend at the main station and, using the excuse of feeling uneasy crossing streets filled with swindlers and pickpockets alone, asked Giacomo to meet her. —I know you live nearby,— she'd added, with a smile and a tone hinting at a subtle request. When he agreed, she noticed the spark in her voice and felt her plan unfolding just as it should.

Walking along Viale Francesco Redi, Alessia commented on the Santa Maria Novella area with feigned innocence, asking about the side streets and the crowds. Then, without beating around the bush, she admitted, — Actually, Giacomo, I'm curious to see your apartment.— Surprised by her directness, he gave her an ambiguous smile, as if he'd expected something like that. Without hesitation, he invited her in, joking that the place was a bit of a mess.

It wasn't the kind of place Alessia was used to. She came from a well-off family, living behind a facade of opulence she'd rarely questioned. Yet, there was something captivating about this neighborhood that seemed to have a life of its own, its swindlers and pickpockets moving like shadows among the throng. Every corner held a story in its worn walls and graffiti. For Alessia, going to Giacomo's apartment was like opening a door to a world she didn't belong to but felt drawn to in some way. Following his quick pace down Via delle Ghiacciaie, her gaze drifted into the depths of a dark alley, where her footsteps' echo mixed with the nearby train station's noise and the constant flow of passersby.

Crossing the building's threshold, the smell of dampness and old tobacco greeted her, and she climbed the stairs to the small second-floor studio. Giacomo's apartment mirrored his personality: cluttered, mysterious, and chaotic, but with a dark charm Alessia found irresistible. With deliberate movements, she dropped her bag in a corner, letting her eyes slowly scan the room, taking in every detail: the carelessly stacked books, a crooked picture frame, and a window overlooking an indistinct, gray urban view.

Alessia, skilled in the art of seduction, found herself caught in a forbidden dance with Giacomo, her friend Pia's partner. A game that stirred in her the same fascination a snake holds over a bird—a blend of attraction and fear.

Was Giacomo the true object of her desire, or was it Pia, with her shadow of rivalry, fueling this tightrope walk?

Their first encounter unfolded in an apartment bathed in twilight, where words weren't needed. Alessia, fluent in the language of silence, cast her spell with speaking glances and promising gestures. Giacomo, caught in the ambiguity of her game, wrestled with regret and temptation, like a sailor lured by a siren's song.

Each meeting in Santa Maria Novella was a ritual where lines blurred. Alessia and Giacomo became shadows seeking and avoiding each other in a maze of wants and secrets. But the fear of being found out lurked like a tiger, and Alessia worried Giacomo might become her undoing.

Betrayal—that mirror showing Alessia her own twisted face—consumed her. She admired her power to seduce, but at the same time, she loathed herself for it. Giacomo wasn't just a man; he was a symbol of her insecurities, an echo of her deepest fears.

In the Santa Maria Novella apartment, Alessia and Giacomo explored the dark corners of their identities. But each encounter left Alessia feeling she had lost a piece of herself. The real betrayal, she realized, was to herself, and Giacomo reflected the inner emptiness threatening to swallow her whole.

That Saturday afternoon, March 19, twilight settled over the Santa Maria Novella neighborhood, heavy, almost like a premonition. Alessia arrived at Giacomo's apartment after his call—his voice sounding more urgent and needy than usual. He hadn't explained much, just insisted it was important and she had to come right away.

Entering, she saw a mix of anxiety and determination in his eyes. Without hesitating, Giacomo stepped toward her, gripping her shoulders, as if the news was a blow he needed to share physically to lighten his own burden.

—It's over with Pia,— he whispered, as though that confession offered some release, some opportunity. His words hung in the air, expectant, perhaps waiting for an eager response from Alessia—a promise that now they were free, without secrets, without walls. But nothing could have been further from the truth.

As Giacomo spoke, Alessia felt something inside her go numb. His words, full of anticipation and desire, sounded hollow. She looked at him without feeling, without the initial fire that had led her to walk the edge of the forbidden with him. Deep down, she knew it; what had attracted her was the danger, the thrill of breaking rules, not Giacomo himself.

He, not sensing the coldness in her gaze, moved even closer, trying to kiss her, to pull her into his emotion. But Alessia pulled back, dodging him, and then, almost without thinking, a feeling of contempt took root in her chest. Disgust, like a spreading coldness, enveloped her until Giacomo's touch became unbearable.

—What's wrong, Alessia?— Giacomo said, frowning, his voice laced with disbelief and jealousy. —Did you tell Pia anything about us?— he demanded, his eyes glinting with accusation and rage.

Alessia denied it firmly, forcefully, but her tone felt more like a final declaration than a defense.

—I didn't tell Pia anything. This thing between us...— Alessia hesitated, then found her voice. —This is over, Giacomo. What we had was never real; it was just a mistake.

But Giacomo wouldn't accept her rejection. Desperate, with a fervor bordering on violence, he grabbed her arms, pulling her close, intensely claiming possession. Alessia felt the strength of his grip, and for a second, fear flashed across her face.

She tried to break free, but Giacomo held tight, his lips nearing hers for a forceful kiss—a show of power that no longer held sway.

—Giacomo, let me go!—Alessia said, her voice sharp, filled with a rage she'd never known.

The struggle was short but brutal. Alessia, in a last effort to free herself, struck him with a loud slap that echoed in the small studio like a final verdict.

Giacomo, stunned and his pride wounded, released her. In that second of shock, Alessia backed away quickly, breathing hard, her blouse torn, bra broken, breasts exposed—a stark image of a lost battle, yet one fought with dignity.

Without a look back, Alessia fled the apartment, running down the stairs as if escaping a dark pit about to swallow her. She felt the weight of rejection and guilt, but also freedom—a sudden clarity that danger and forbidden attraction had lost all their appeal.

Reaching the street, the cold breeze hit her face, and for the first time in a long while, she felt she could breathe. Behind her, she left Giacomo, the mistake, and the thirst for transgression. She didn't know if she could face Pia or if she'd ever confess what happened, but in that moment, the only thing certain was that something inside her had shifted, as if she finally understood the price of her own choices.

Love at the Threshold of the Abyss

Davide arrived at the small bar next to the hospital, where Lucien awaited him with the patience of someone who's lived long enough to understand time's importance. It was a discreet spot, with warm lights and dark wooden chairs worn smooth by years of conversations. In one corner, a couple of men talked quietly while the waiter dried glasses with the focus of someone who knows his trade. The walls were lined with old photographs of Padua, and a shelf behind the bar displayed bottles of wine and local liqueurs, lined up like soldiers in formation.

Lucien watched him from a corner table, his Grodino in hand, and raised his other hand slightly so Davide could see him. When Davide approached, his smile was wide and easygoing—the same smile that had won Pia's heart and that Lucien knew so well. He sat down across from Lucien, still looking relaxed, but in his eyes, there was a hint of unease.

After a few minutes of polite conversation, Lucien, calm as ever, broke the ice without beating around the bush.

—Davide, I wanted to talk to you alone because there's something you need to understand about Pia... and about the love you say you feel for her.—

Davide's smile faded a little, and he looked at Lucien closely, sensing this meeting carried a weight he didn't fully grasp yet.

—You know, Davide? Since she was little, Pia was different. I remember how she'd lose herself in books, how she explored the world with her imagination before she could do it with her feet. Words were always her refuge and her guide. She dreamt of unraveling the world's mysteries, of understanding the depth of human nature. And in those dreams, I saw a girl who already knew her life was meant for something bigger than herself. That purpose gives her life meaning, Davide. There's nothing more important for a person than knowing their purpose and pursuing it, even if the road is hard.—

Davide nodded, feeling genuine respect for Lucien's view of his daughter. Yet, deep down, a quiet unease began to settle. He knew Pia had a special brightness, an inner fire that had always drawn him in, but now he understood that fire could consume anything in its path—even him.

Lucien sipped his drink, then looked at him with the intensity of someone who had thought long and hard about his words.

—Love, Davide...— he continued, his voice seeming to carry echoes of past experiences. — In the absurdity of our relationships, what harms them most isn't what the other person does, but the fantasy, the ideal we create of what we expect them to do. We build an idealized love, demanding the other person be, have, or give something… And in doing so, we cut it, we fragment it, and we turn it into a reflection of our own expectations. We refuse to see them completely, in their complex and beautiful individuality. We fall into the absurdity of seeking perfection in an imperfect world.

Davide lowered his gaze, his hands fidgeting with the edge of his glass. Each of Lucien's words sank deep—a revelation he hadn't asked for but needed to hear.

—Let's let go of the comfort of conformity, the illusion that someone will come to complete us— Lucien went on, his tone soft but firm. — We aren't puzzle pieces, but whole universes, with our own shadows and depths. To love isn't to demand, Davide—it's to accept. Accept the other's freedom, their right to be authentic, to contradict our fantasies. To love is to embrace the darkness along with the light, rejecting the romantic idealization of love.

Lucien's words seemed to fill the small bar. Unable to answer, Davide looked at him, feeling each idea seep into his mind like the echo of a truth he'd never considered. Lucien continued with an almost philosophical air:

—Let's build a free love, where negotiation is the language of authenticity. A love where individuality is respected, where vulnerability is welcomed, and no one pretends to be the other's savior. From that freedom, we can create a dynamic balance: supporting, accompanying, giving and receiving, finding peace in silence and closeness, arguing without hurting, forgiving, and growing together. Connecting and disconnecting, without stopping being who we are, without demanding the other be who they're not—

Davide closed his eyes for a moment, processing the weight of those words, which went against everything he'd believed about love. It was a vision that challenged him— an idea of love without possession, without empty promises.

Lucien leaned in slightly, lowering his voice, as if sharing a secret:

—In an absurd world, where searching for meaning often leads to frustration, loving another completely is an act of rebellion. It's defying logic, embracing contradiction, and finding beauty in imperfection. It's an affirmation of life— a way to create our own meaning amid chaos. A free, conscious, authentic love. A love that thrives in the acceptance of the absurd.—

The silence that followed was heavy, full of unspoken meaning. Lucien watched him with a calm gaze, but in his eyes, there was something more—something like compassion.

—If you truly love Pia, Davide,—he said finally, his voice thick with contained emotion,—stay away from her and let her be.—

The statement landed like a sentence. Davide felt each word pierce his chest—an unexpected blow that stole his breath. The plea in Lucien's voice, so deep and genuine, completely disarmed him. He had never considered that his love, perhaps, wasn't the best thing for Pia. The possibility of staying away from her was an abyss he had never been willing to face.

—Work on your future, Davide,— Lucien added gently. — Adolescence—that time that forgives mistakes and bad choices—is falling away. It's time for you to think about what you're going to do, about what you need to build your life. Think about what you can offer... and what you need to be for her, for any family you might have someday.—

Davide could barely meet Lucien's gaze, feeling small, and vulnerable, as though the strength that had driven him was crumbling. He knew Lucien's words were a call to grow, to face reality with a maturity he'd avoided. In his heart, he loved Pia intensely, a love he'd thought unbreakable. But now, he wondered if that love was enough, if it was fair to her.

Finally, he nodded, unable to find the right words. The weight of that message, as foreseen as it was unexpected, had stripped away the certainty of his feelings, leaving him alone with an overwhelming truth.

Lucien watched him in silence, understanding the impact, and with a last look of compassion, stood up, took a step, and placed his hand on Davide's shoulder.

—Remember, Davide,—he said with a sad smile,—true love doesn't bind. And if one day you decide to return, come back as the man Pia deserves.—

Lucien nodded goodbye to the waiter by name, left a ten-euro bill, and walked out.

Davide left the bar, unsure which way to go on Via Gattamelata, the weight of Lucien's words now heavy in his chest, as if an invisible shadow followed him. The night air, cool and damp, touched his face but couldn't lift the unease consuming him. For the first time, Davide, the perpetual optimist, faced an abyss he hadn't seen coming: the future.

Each step echoed on the cobblestones, amplifying their conversation. Lucien's words lingered, repeating like a relentless echo: *"Adolescence, that stage that forgives bad choices, is falling away."* Simple as they were, those words carried immense weight—a reminder that time, which he'd always felt was an ally, now seemed to turn against him.

Lucien's lessons weren't just about love but about life. —True love doesn't bind,— he'd said with a calm only someone who deeply understood existence could convey. Davide knew those words weren't a judgment, but an invitation to think, to grow. Yet the message was clear: if he truly loved Pia, he had to let her be—even if that meant stepping out of her life.

He stopped when he reached Via Ospedale Civile, looking at the streetlights casting their warm glow on the stone walls. There, dreams filled his mind. He thought of that summer when he and Pia would travel across America from New York to San Francisco. He knew the excitement of that trip would mark every mile. Everything would be perfect because they'd live in the moment, without worrying about tomorrow.

But, for the first time, Davide understood what he'd avoided seeing. His love for Pia had been a series of beautiful but temporary moments. While she'd always had a clear purpose guiding her, he'd drifted aimlessly, holding onto the idea that the present was enough.

Walking toward Piazza Eremitani, Lucien's words sank deeper. —When a relationship's foundation rests on what I want, need, or demand the other person be, have, or give me, we're cutting it into little pieces.— Davide paused by the lit windows of a nearby building. Had he done that to Pia? Had he shaped her to fit his wants, ignoring who she really was?

For the first time, he questioned the basis of their relationship. He remembered the beginning—the intense passion, the certainty that Pia was his missing piece. But now, under the dim lights, burdened by Lucien's words, he understood he had never truly seen Pia in all her depth. He'd seen her as an extension of his own needs.

He continued down Via Altinate, a quiet street holding centuries of untold stories. His steps were slow, as if measuring himself against the questions haunting him. Finally, he arrived at Prato della Valle—a square he'd always felt was infinite, but that night seemed small compared to his vast uncertainty.

Facing the moon's reflection in the canal water, Davide paused. Had he truly allowed Pia to be free? The answer hit him hard, almost making him stumble. His love was deep but also selfish. He hadn't understood what it meant to let her fly, to be who she was meant to become.

The square's silence wrapped around him, and with a sigh, Davide made a decision. He would move up his trip to America. He knew if he stayed in Padua, or even Italy, he'd end up looking for Pia, unable to resist clinging to what they shared. But it wasn't about what he wanted anymore; it was about giving Pia the freedom she deserved.

He didn't have the courage to tell Pia their relationship had to end. Lucien's words still weighed on him like a promise: *"Don't tell Pia anything about this meeting."* Out of respect for Lucien and the love he felt for Pia, he would keep that promise.

At dawn, Davide boarded a flight to New York. As the plane climbed, he looked out the window, watching Italy shrink below the clouds. For the first time, he felt not excitement, but a deep sadness. He knew this trip wouldn't be like the others. It wouldn't be an adventure—it would be a confrontation with himself. The carefree Davide was gone. Now he faced an uncertain future, far from Pia, but perhaps closer to finding his real purpose.

The Pawn on the Board

Worn down by his own anxiety, Giacomo had finally uncovered what had tormented him: the man he'd bumped into was none other than the infamous Davide—the name that had surfaced so often in Pia's words and silences. The revelation knocked the wind out of him—not just because he now knew this was the man from Pia's past, but because his paranoia had found a new focus. With the ceremony drawing to a close, Giacomo decided it was time to act. Without much thought, he moved toward the family to offer his condolences, but with a deeper intent: to get close to Pia and confirm his suspicions.

As he approached Nicoletta and Antonella, he was met with an unexpected presence. Alessia, standing beside the two women, locked eyes with him—a sharp, piercing gaze full of warning. It was an electrifying moment, a silent exchange where they both acknowledged the secret they shared but refused to speak aloud. The air between them grew heavy with tension, and though not a single word passed between them, they knew this encounter was an invisible battlefield where fears and guilt collided.

Giacomo, regaining his composure, offered his condolences in a measured, respectful voice. He spoke first to Nicoletta and Antonella, who responded with polite formality. But when it was Pia's turn, the atmosphere shifted. Giacomo, trying to sound casual, said,—Pia, I'm very sorry for your loss. I'd like to talk to you sometime, when you have a moment. —

Pia, physically and emotionally drained, responded softly:

—Thank you, Giacomo. Maybe when I return to Florence, we can talk. For now, I have to stay here and help my mother.

The invitation, though seemingly innocent, did not go unnoticed by Alessia. As if some internal alarm had been triggered, she pinched Giacomo subtly as she listened. She couldn't help but wonder what he really intended with that conversation—what secrets he might be digging up or what hidden motives lay behind his cordial demeanor.

As the moment to close the casket and proceed to the cemetery approached, the family began moving among the attendees. Taking advantage of the brief chaos, Alessia decided to leave with Giacomo. She couldn't miss the opportunity to confront him—and to make sure whatever he planned to say to Pia wouldn't endanger her own secret.

Alone, in a quiet corner of the church, Alessia stopped him, her voice cold and calculated:

—Giacomo, I don't know what you're planning with Pia, but you'd better not do anything that complicates things—for you.—

Giacomo looked at her, a mix of disbelief and defiance in his eyes, but Alessia went on, her smile thin and sharp:

—I know enough about you to say this: don't play games with me. I might not know all the details about what happened with your father... —her voice dropped to a whisper—but I know enough to make your life hell. So it's in your best interest to tell me exactly what you plan to say to Pia.

Giacomo's gaze hardened. For a moment, he looked ready to respond, but something in Alessia's eyes stopped him. They were the eyes of someone willing to use whatever weapon necessary to protect herself—someone who understood the power of blackmail and wouldn't hesitate to wield it. Realizing the delicate ground he was standing on, Giacomo stayed quiet, measuring every word.

—What I say to Pia is none of your business,— he finally said, with more firmness than he truly felt.

Alessia let out a short, sarcastic laugh.

—Maybe not now, but make sure it stays that way. You don't want the secrets you've worked so hard to bury to come to light, do you?—

Their exchange ended in a tense silence. They stood facing each other like rivals in a chess match. Alessia turned and walked away first, head held high, knowing she'd planted a seed of doubt in Giacomo's mind. He remained still, his heart pounding, fully aware that Alessia was not an opponent easily dismissed. His intentions toward Pia were now under the watchful eye of someone with as much to lose as he did.

Before leaving, Alessia paused and glanced back at Giacomo. Her eyes were sharp with both disdain and warning.

—What you say to Pia, from now on, is my concern. Don't get it twisted, Giacomo—I'm always one step ahead.

Without waiting for a reply, she scanned him from head to toe, as if assessing his position in a game she already considered won. That final look shrank him, made him feel smaller, more vulnerable. Alessia knew she held the upper hand, and Giacomo was trapped in his own web of anxiety and regret.

As Alessia began to walk away, her heels echoing against the marble floor of the church, Giacomo, in a burst of desperation, raised his voice—a mix of pleading and resolve:

—I just want to ask Pia to come back to me!—

Alessia didn't stop. She didn't turn. Her stride remained steady, her gaze locked on the horizon, but a barely-there smile flickered on her lips. Inside, she relished the moment, knowing she held control.

—I've got you, idiot,— she thought, sensing the chessboard shifting in her favor.

Giacomo stood frozen, his eyes fixed on the floor. The words he'd just uttered still echoed in his mind, but Alessia's response—or rather, her silence—left him hollow. It was as if the full weight of his past had crystallized in that moment, a specter that wouldn't let him go.

The ghost of his father, awakened by Alessia's mere whisper, took center stage again in his thoughts. Giacomo felt enveloped by the past—like a dark, suffocating labyrinth where every exit was sealed. The memory of Franco—his explosive temper, the night that changed everything—now mingled with the fear of losing Pia and Alessia's veiled threat.

He pressed his hands to his head, trying to calm the storm of thoughts overtaking him. But it was no use. Alessia hadn't just touched a raw wound—she'd wielded his anxiety like a scalpel. Giacomo felt trapped, unable to act, as if the words he longed to say and the steps he wanted to take were bound by invisible knots.

The echo of Alessia's heels faded into the distance, leaving Giacomo alone in the church's shadowed corner. The solitude struck him like a blow, and for a moment, the silence was louder than any word Alessia might have spoken. —What am I doing?—he asked himself, feeling every choice push him closer to the edge.

And yet—even in that emotional paralysis—one desire refused to extinguish: the need to win Pia back. He didn't know how, or even if it was possible, but the idea clung to him like a weak flame struggling to survive.

What he couldn't yet see was that his greatest obstacle wasn't Alessia—or even the past. It was he himself.

Giacomo inhaled deeply, trying to regain some semblance of composure. He knew he had to make a choice, but deep down he also knew the path forward would not be easy. For now, the only thing he could do was take one step—any step—out of the chaos that kept him prisoner.

As night fell over Padua and the church lights dimmed one by one, Giacomo stepped into the cold air, feeling the city—indifferent to his inner storm—carry on as if nothing had changed. With no destination in mind, he began to walk, searching the shadows of the streets for some glimmer of clarity, some sign to guide him back to himself.

The Silent Farewell

Davide had vanished without a trace, leaving behind a void filled with questions and anguish. In his haste to leave, he didn't even take his cell phone, as if wanting to erase all ties to the world he had left behind. The only proof of his departure was a hurried note addressed to his mother, Paola:

—Mom, I've moved up my summer trip to the United States. Don't worry about me; I'm fine. As soon as I can, I'll get in touch with you. I love you. See you in the fall. —

What worried Paola most was Davide's phone. The broken screen made it hard for her to read, but she managed to notice dozens of text messages and missed calls from Pia. There was urgency in them—short words, but full of desperation:

—Davide, please answer me.—
—Where are you?—
—Call me; I'm worried.—

Now, with the phone out of battery and a note that answered none of the questions piling up in her mind, Paola felt completely lost.

Paola had reread those words several times since she found them that morning. Every time she reread them, her bad feeling grew stronger. She remembered how the night before Davide had arrived late, without his usual Vespa, and with a somber air that was not typical of him. He had barely exchanged words with her before locking himself in his room. Now, uncertainty and fear filled the spaces of the house.

Paola was a middle-aged woman with a kind face and brown eyes that had lost some of their sparkle over the years. Her long, slightly wavy hair was beginning to show streaks of silver, but she wore it with dignity. She had always been a dedicated mother—firm but loving—who understood Davide better than anyone. Her husband, Giorgio, was a respected lawyer, a former public prosecutor, known for his analytical mind and his commitment to justice. Although he had left his position in the ministry to dedicate himself to private practice, his meticulous personality and his strong sense of ethics remained intact.

Giorgio had a distant but cordial relationship with Davide. Although he loved him deeply, his pragmatic approach to life often clashed with his son's dreamy nature. Their conversations often revolved around responsibility and expectations, which made Davide feel misunderstood and, at times, judged. Giorgio, however, always saw in Davide a potential he had not yet discovered.

The family home, located in Città Giardino, was an elegant but modest dwelling, with details that reflected Paola's refined taste and Giorgio's methodical order. In Giorgio's office, next to the main living room, the shelves were filled with law books, well-organized files, and a small collection of classic Italian films—his only indulgence outside of work. In contrast, Davide's room was a creative chaos: posters of rock bands and maps of places he dreamed of visiting covered the walls, while a cluttered bookshelf housed travel books, notebooks full of annotations, and souvenirs from his adventures with Pia.

It was a space that screamed youth and freedom—a reflection of his carefree personality.

Pia's Arrival

Night was advancing quickly as Pia, astride her Vespa, sped toward Davide's house. The wind lashed her face as she raced through the streets of Padua, from Arcella to Città Giardino. Anxiety pushed her forward recklessly, ignoring traffic signs and honking horns demanding her attention. With every kilometer that brought her closer to her destination, the anguish grew heavier, and her mind spun with scenarios to explain Davide's silence.

At last, she reached the house. Without cutting the engine, she leaned on the horn several times. Paola appeared at the door almost immediately, her face a mixture of surprise and worry. Before she could speak, Pia rushed inside, calling Davide's name as she climbed the stairs.

—Davide!—she shouted. —Where are you?! Answer me!—

Paola, close behind, tried to explain what little she knew.

—Pia, please, listen to me for a moment. Come, I'll make you some tea,— she said, her voice calm but firm.

Pia, on the verge of breaking down, stopped in the hallway and turned to face her.

—Where is he? What happened?— she asked, her voice cracking.

Paola led her into the kitchen and began to prepare the tea, trying to gather her thoughts.

—Yesterday afternoon he left, said he was meeting someone. He told me he'd be back for dinner, but he never returned. I called him several times, but he didn't answer. I kept his favorite lasagna in the oven, thinking he'd come back late like he sometimes did.—

Pia listened in silence, her hands trembling. Paola went on:

—I heard him come in, but I didn't see him. This morning, when I woke up, he was gone. At first I thought it was his brother Armando who had left early, but then I noticed all the photos of you two had been put away, and his phone—turned off—was sitting on his desk. And I found this…—

Paola pulled out the note Davide had left and handed it to Pia. She read it quickly, her eyes filling with tears.

—No… this can't be,— she whispered, letting the note fall to the floor.

She collapsed onto the edge of Davide's bed, unable to hold back the sobs.

—He left me…—she said between cries. —He didn't tell me anything. I can't believe this. —

Paola stood in the doorway, watching her with sadness. She wanted to comfort her but knew that no words would be enough in that moment.

—Pia, Davide has a restless spirit, but I know he cares for you deeply. Maybe he needed time to figure things out.

Pia looked up, her face streaked with tears.

—Why didn't he tell me? Why didn't he trust me?—

Paola walked over slowly and sat beside her.

—I don't have the answers, dear. But I'm certain this isn't about you. Davide is searching for something… something he may not even understand himself.—

They fell into silence, sharing a moment of grief and understanding. Davide's room, filled with his memories and dreams, now felt empty—a mirror of the absence he'd left in their lives.

As Pia's tears continued to fall, Paola embraced her gently, trying to offer a sliver of calm.

—He'll come back, Pia. I know he will. But until then, we have to be strong.—

Davide's Note:

—*Mom,*

I've moved up my trip. Don't worry, I'm okay. This summer will be different, and I need this time for myself. Take care of everyone. We'll see each other in the fall. Love you.

Davide—

Pia collapsed onto Davide's bed, desperately searching for something that could still connect her to him. She buried her face in his pillow, breathing in deeply, trying to find his scent. Her mind refused to accept his absence, as if she could still feel him nearby—how many times had they made love between those sheets? Now the laughter, the promises, echoed faintly in a space that had once been full of life. Curling into a fetal position, she clutched the pillow, eyes shut tightly as tears spilled freely down her cheeks.

Paola stood silently at the door, her heart torn between compassion for Pia and worry for her son. She couldn't shake the image of all the missed calls and messages she'd seen on Davide's phone. She walked to the kitchen and picked up the phone, dialing the number of Pia's parents.

—Nicoletta, it's Paola,— she said, her voice tired but steady. —I need to speak with you and Lucien.—

On the other end, Nicoletta called Lucien, who was in the study reviewing documents. They both listened closely as Paola explained what had happened.

—Davide is gone. He left ahead of the trip he was supposed to take with Pia. He left a note saying he was going to America. Nothing more. Pia's here... she's devastated. I think it would be better if she stayed the night with me. I don't want her to be alone right now.

Lucien and Nicoletta exchanged a knowing glance, one layered with emotion: sadness for their daughter's heartbreak, but also a subtle relief. A part of them hoped this might be a turning point—a way for Pia to find her path again, the one they felt she'd left behind by following Davide's carefree rhythm. Yet, they also understood that young love was beyond their control. They had interfered in a way that now felt intrusive, and despite their intentions, they couldn't escape a twinge of guilt.

—Of course, Paola. Let Pia stay with you tonight, Nicoletta said in a calm, almost maternal tone. —Tell her we're here for whatever she needs.—

Lucien, listening to the call, couldn't help the shadow of doubt that passed over him. He had insisted on speaking to Davide, convinced that his relationship with Pia was pulling her away from her dreams. Not because Davide was a bad person, but because his lack of direction risked dragging her into uncertainty. But now, seeing the fallout of his words, he questioned whether he had gone too far.

After hanging up, Lucien returned to his chair in the library. The warm glow of the lamp lit the shelves of books he'd collected over the years, but tonight, they offered no comfort. For the first time in a long while, he felt empty, as though even the wisdom of all those pages had gone silent.

—Did I do the right thing?— he murmured, not expecting an answer.

Nicoletta entered with two cups of tea, her expression soft.

—You did what you thought was best for her. Pia is young, Lucien. And love at her age burns bright—but it passes too.—

Lucien sighed, sipping his tea.

—I'm not so sure. Davide isn't a bad boy. Maybe I was too hard on him.—

Nicoletta held his gaze, letting his words settle.

—Lucien, we can't make their choices for them. Pia and Davide have to find their own way—even if it means making mistakes.

Meanwhile, back at Davide's house, Pia couldn't sleep. Her mind replayed the past few days on a loop, searching for signs that could've warned her. She remembered the way Davide looked at her when they talked about their dreams—that mix of admiration... and something else. Something she now recognized as fear. He had felt he wasn't enough for her, and that thought shattered her.

From the hallway, Paola listened to Pia's quiet sobs. She knew there wasn't much she could do to ease the pain, but she stayed close, a silent, comforting presence. Sitting in a chair just outside Davide's room, she whispered a quiet prayer—asking that her son would find what he was searching for, but also that he would not forget the way home.

Lucien's intervention, though born of the best intentions, now loomed as an act of control over a relationship that was never his to govern. His concern for Pia's future—a weight he carried always like a silent burden—had led him to act in a way that, unintentionally, undermined the autonomy of the young couple. Confronting Davide, his words, loaded with authority, seemed to push the boy toward an abrupt decision—one born from a feeling of inadequacy and guilt.

Nicoletta, for her part, walked a gentler line, though her concern mirrored her husband's. She too had seen the relationship with Davide as a potential obstacle to their daughter's dreams—a bond filled with love, yes, but one that appeared to pull Pia off the path she and Lucien had always envisioned for her. Their decisions, though grounded in love and protection, now sketched a fragile boundary—one that might fracture the trust between parents and daughter and, in the worst case, sow resentment not easily mended.

In contrast, Paola took a more neutral stance, torn between worry and understanding—the kind of understanding only a mother could offer. Her approach wasn't to interfere or redirect the relationship but to support both Davide and Pia amid the emotional chaos that engulfed them. Despite the ache of not fully grasping why her son had left, Paola remained a calm, empathetic presence. Her willingness to console Pia, to offer her shelter in the storm, reflected a more balanced, less invasive outlook—one that placed the emotional well-being of both young hearts above any desire to control their journey.

Loneliness in the City That Never Sleeps

Davide arrived at JFK Airport with a backpack full of clothes, books, and memories—but with a heart empty of certainties. The vastness of New York welcomed him with a clamor that clashed with the deafening silence of his thoughts. His English, rudimentary and tinged with a heavy Italian accent, was his only tool for navigating a transit system that seemed like an endless maze. Yet his smile, faint as it was, managed to stir empathy from several passersby—airport workers, subway employees, and police officers alike.

The first challenge was finding the AirTrain, the monorail that connects JFK's terminals to the city's subway and train stations. Davide studied the signs with a mix of focus and anxiety, trying to decipher the maps using the few English words he knew. At last, a kind airport employee pointed him toward the correct platform. He boarded the AirTrain with a small sense of accomplishment, watching the industrial landscape unfold around him as he made his way to Jamaica Station.

At Jamaica Station, his next step was to transfer to the E subway line, which would take him toward Manhattan. Buying a MetroCard involved a series of gestures and pointing, but he finally managed. He descended the stairs into the heart of New York City's underground—a chaotic world of constant motion, indifferent faces, and the ceaseless arrival and departure of trains.

The subway car was packed, and Davide, backpack still strapped on, did his best not to disturb anyone while he studied the line map on the wall. The plan was simple: take the E train toward the World Trade Center and get off at Canal Street to transfer to the J line. But the stops flew by, and the English signs were riddles he had to solve on the fly. An older woman, noticing his look of confusion, approached and kindly gestured when it was time for him to get off.

At Canal Street, Davide followed the signs to the J line, climbing and descending stairs with a backpack that seemed to grow heavier with each step. He boarded the train toward Essex Street, and as the car moved through bridges and tunnels connecting Manhattan to Brooklyn, he allowed himself a moment to breathe. The subway's flickering lights briefly lit up his tired face, and though sadness still lingered, something in the city's constant motion gave him a sense of direction.

At last, the train pulled into Essex Street. Davide stepped off with a sigh of relief, feeling the crisp night air of New York as he emerged above ground. In front of him, the corner of Rivington and Essex awaited with the promise of a new beginning. The building that would be his temporary home had a worn-out facade, windows that had seen better days, and a faded sign above the door. It wasn't exactly welcoming, but to Davide, it meant shelter in a vast and overwhelming city.

With each step toward the door, Davide understood that this journey would be unlike any other he had taken. Now he was alone, facing a city he didn't know, speaking a language he barely understood, with an itinerary he'd have to rebuild from scratch. But deep down, something in him knew this experience—no matter how difficult—would shape him in ways he couldn't yet grasp. And so, with his backpack still slung over his shoulders and the echo of the train still ringing in his ears, Davide climbed the stairs of the building, ready to face the unknown.

Davide arrived at the corner of Rivington and Essex with his heavy backpack digging into his shoulders and a mixture of fatigue and nervous anticipation on his face. The building's facade, with its peeling paint and scattered graffiti, looked like a relic from better days. On the ground floor was a seedy-looking bar—the kind of place that might intimidate any newcomer at first glance. A flickering neon sign promised cheap beer and stiff drinks, while a jukebox in the corner blared classic rock at nearly deafening volume.

The inside was just as peculiar as its exterior. The tables were covered in plastic checkered cloths, many bearing cigarette burns and stains from years of neglect. The walls were adorned with an eclectic collection of tattered posters—some of forgotten bands, others from cult films of the 1980s. A battered couch with sunken cushions sat beside a warped pool table, its corners worn and its cues splintered from overuse.

The air was thick with the scent of spilled beer and old tobacco, cut by a damp undertone that clung to everything. The few patrons inside seemed as weathered as the place itself, drinking in silence or trading murmurs with the bartender. And yet, there was something oddly welcoming about the chaos. Maybe it was the amber glow of the hanging lamps or the lazy energy that seemed to refuse to be anything other than what it was.

Behind the bar, a handsome man with a warm smile was drying a glass with a rag that had seen better days. His black hair fell in loose strands across his forehead, and his deep brown eyes radiated a kindness that stood in contrast to the rough surroundings. Jack, as he was called, was clearly the soul of the place. His face bore the traces of a life filled with stories, but his open expression and friendly tone seemed to invite anyone in for a drink and a conversation.

When Davide walked through the door, weighed down by his backpack and looking like someone who had crossed not just an ocean but a lifetime, Jack greeted him with a nod.

—Davide?— he asked in clear English, touched by a faint Latin accent that hinted at his roots. Seeing the confused look on Davide's face, he repeated the name with an encouraging nod, adding a smile that had the power to disarm just about anyone.

Grateful for the unexpected warmth, Davide nodded. Jack reached under the counter, pulled out a key, and handed it to him with a wink.

—Your roommate left this for you. Welcome to New York. And if you need anything... well, you know where to find me.

Davide accepted the key, feeling a strange sense of relief amid the chaos inside him. This small act of kindness, in a place as rough as the bar and as vast as New York City, gave him a flicker of hope. Jack—with his easy charm and keen eye for people—was the first friendly face in a city that promised to be as imposing as it was fascinating.

Davide woke at dawn, disoriented by the soft light filtering through the tattered curtains of his new room. For a moment, he didn't know where he was. The distant roar of the city still hummed in the background, but now it was more of a constant whisper than a storm. He sat up slowly, his back sore from the sunken, worn-out mattress. His eyes landed on the photo of Pia he'd placed the night before on the makeshift nightstand. His gaze lingered, and a wave of melancholy surged through him.

He felt caught between two worlds: the one he'd left behind and the one he was only beginning to explore. What had once felt like an act of sacrifice and love—leaving—was beginning to weigh on him like a betrayal, a cowardly escape. He knew he had hurt Pia, but now he was starting to realize how much he had hurt himself.

Needing air, he decided to go for a walk, hoping the morning breeze would help clear his thoughts. He slipped on a light jacket and descended the five floors of the building. Each creaking step of the worn staircase reminded him of the fragility of his new reality. Stepping outside, the chill of the New York morning struck him, flooding his lungs with a mix of smoke, coffee, and the metallic scent of wet pavement.

With no destination in mind, Davide began to wander through the streets of the Lower East Side. The first light of day illuminated the graffiti-tagged walls and shuttered storefronts. He passed a café just opening its doors, the smell of fresh coffee pulling him in like an embrace. At the counter, an older man with white hair and a kind smile welcomed him.

—What can I get you, kid?—the barista asked in a thick New York accent.

—An espresso, please,— Davide replied, trying to hide his Italian accent—though he knew it was no use.

The coffee was strong and bitter, but it gave him just enough energy to keep walking. As he wandered the streets, he thought about Pia—her smile, her dreams, and how he had chosen to remove himself from her life. Lucien's words continued to echo in his mind, reminding him that his departure hadn't been an act of courage but rather a cocktail of fear and uncertainty.

Still, something within Davide was beginning to shift. The vastness of New York—with all its chaos and boundless energy—offered him a new perspective. For the first time, he allowed himself to think beyond Pia's shadow. What did he want to accomplish? What did he truly desire from life? The idea of reinventing himself, of building something of his own, began to take root.

On his way back to the apartment, Davide stopped in front of a small park. He watched a group of kids playing basketball, their laughter echoing through the morning air. He wondered if he would ever feel that lightness again—the carefree joy that seemed lost under the weight of his choices.

When he reached the building, he climbed the stairs slowly, his physical exhaustion mingling with the emotional fatigue he carried. Inside his room, the photo of Pia waited on the makeshift nightstand—a constant reminder of what he had left behind. But this time, instead of sinking into melancholy, he chose to write her a letter. He didn't know if he would send it, but he needed to pour out what was lodged in his heart.

—Dear Pia,

I don't know where to begin, because I'm not even sure how to explain what I've done. All I know is that I feel lost. I left everything behind because I thought it was the right thing to do, but now I realize that I wasn't just running from you—I was running from myself. I wanted to give you freedom, but in the process, I've chained myself to doubt and fear...—

The words flowed as Davide tried to untangle the emotions that consumed him. Writing offered a strange sense of comfort, as if by committing his thoughts to paper he might find clarity in the midst of the chaos.

That night, as Manhattan's lights flickered in the distance and the city's noise seeped through the windows, Davide made a quiet decision: he couldn't keep living in the shadow of what he had left behind. If he truly wanted to be worthy of the love he'd felt for Pia, he would first have to learn how to love himself. And while the path toward that understanding seemed long and uncertain, he was ready to walk it.

Lying once more in bed, Davide stared at the dim light spilling through the window while the hum of New York echoed like a distant drumbeat. In that moment of stillness, his mind returned again and again to Lucien's words—words that had acted like an emotional trigger, setting off a storm of reflection and doubt that had pushed him across an ocean in search of something he still couldn't name.

Leaving had been an act full of contradictions. On one hand, it could be seen as brave—recognizing that his presence might be holding Pia back and understanding that sometimes love means letting go, even if it leads to one's own loneliness. He had wanted to set her free, to let her fly, just as Lucien had implied more than once. But even that gesture bore the heavy trace of cowardice.

He had run. Unable to face the questions and tensions within the relationship, he had chosen to disappear—leaving both of them suspended in uncertainty.
The image of Pia—radiant and full of life—still stared back at him from the photo on the nightstand, a tangible symbol

of all he had left behind. And yet, deep in his mind, a truth he had avoided was beginning to surface: he hadn't just left to protect her. He had left to avoid himself.

Lucien's seemingly wise, calm words had opened up a ruthless mirror, reflecting all of Davide's insecurities—his lack of purpose, the fear of being a burden rather than a partner, and the gnawing feeling of not being enough.

The streets of New York—with their restless rhythm and vibrant disorder—were now the backdrop of his reinvention. Every corner of the city posed a challenge but also a chance. Though his decision had been impulsive and driven by emotion, finding himself alone in such an immense place forced him to confront everything he had been avoiding back in Italy.

But even with the endless possibilities the city offered, Davide could not outrun his emotional dilemma. He had arrived in New York hoping to find a new path, to build something of his own. Yet the melancholy returned each time he thought of Pia. Placing her photo by his bed was an act of love—but also an admission of his inability to let go. Nostalgia had become a silent thread tying him to the life he'd left behind, while the weight of unfulfilled expectations and shared dreams hung above him like a heavy cloud.

Deep down, Davide knew that his departure had been both an act of love and of fear. He loved Pia, but he wasn't ready to be the man she deserved. Lucien hadn't said it outright, but his words had planted the idea that true love isn't just about being present—it's about becoming someone who can stand on their own.

And Davide, in his current state, didn't believe he was that person.

In his small apartment overlooking the intersection of Essex and Delancey, Davide stood at a crossroads. The city offered two paths: to stay, confront himself, and work to become better—or to let nostalgia consume him, surrendering to regret.

He knew this journey, though steeped in solitude, was also a metaphor for growth. New York, with all its chaos and possibility, was not just a place. It was a mirror of his internal struggle.

As he pulled the worn sheets over his shoulders, Davide realized that the road to maturity was more complicated than he had ever imagined. He had tried to protect Pia—but now, he understood he also needed to protect himself. Far from home, far from Pia, and face-to-face with his fears, Davide had to choose: continue running or stay still for once and confront everything that terrified him. The battle between his love for Pia, his longing to be someone better, and his fear of failure would define not only his time in New York but also the man he was meant to become.

Lessons in Exile

In Padua, time moved slowly for Pia. The weeks piled up, and with them, the weight of uncertainty. What had happened to Davide? Their last goodbye had been perfect—one of those memories that remain etched in the heart forever. Why, then, had everything changed so suddenly? The questions tormented her. At night, her mind overflowed with imagined reasons: Had she done something wrong? Had something in her pushed him to make such a drastic decision? The lack of answers was a slow poison that kept her trapped in her sorrow.

Lucien, for his part, couldn't shake the remorse that haunted him. He had acted out of a desire to protect his daughter, but now he watched, heart heavy, as the consequences of his words unfolded. The emptiness in Pia's gaze gnawed at him, and with each passing day, he wondered whether he had made the right choice. Davide, after all, hadn't seemed like a bad boy. Maybe he had misjudged him—maybe he had been too quick to intervene in something that, in hindsight, was not his to control.

One morning, as the summer sun began to soften and the air hinted at autumn, Pia made a decision. She was tired of living among ghosts, of allowing her space to become a shrine to what no longer was. She began redecorating her room, gently removing each object, each photo, and every small relic that reminded her of Davide. She wanted her life back. With resolve, she asked Lucien to help her find a place at the Faculty of Letters and Philosophy at the University of Florence. She needed distance, a fresh beginning in a place where the echo of Davide didn't follow her down every street.

Meanwhile, in New York, Davide faced his own trials. He had found work in a small Venezuelan food joint, where he spent his days frying tequeños—golden, crisp cheese-filled rolls of dough. Over time, he had grown skilled in preparing them, and with every batch he placed into the hot oil, a strange comfort filled the air. It was a modest routine, but it kept him moving forward.

Yet Davide knew he couldn't stay there forever. Life in New York was brutally expensive, and his wages barely covered his essentials. Beyond the lessons of humility his time in America had taught him, he came to realize that his job—while honest—was unsustainable, especially if he ever hoped to start a family. The experience had opened his eyes to something deeper: the need for purpose, for direction, for something more stable than survival. And so, he made a decision—one as unexpected as it was drastic: he would enlist in the military.

For someone like Davide—more persuasive than commanding, more drawn to contemplation than to blind obedience—military life didn't suit his nature. But perhaps that was exactly the reason he chose it. He knew that the structure, the discipline, and the confinement of that life could be the antidote to his weakness—could silence the part of him that longed to run back to Pia. In truth, it was a way of protecting himself from his own heart.

Though the idea of staying in the United States had crossed his mind, Davide knew he didn't have the resources—or the legal footing—to remain. His low-paying job had shown him the raw face of economic survival, and now he understood that staying would only trap him in a cycle of precarity. Enlisting was, in part, a way out of that reality. But it was also something else: an act driven by a deep sense of inadequacy. Deep down, Davide still battled the belief that he wasn't enough for Pia, that his love alone could not build the kind of future she deserved.

That night, after closing up shop, Davide stood at the edge of the sidewalk, looking out over the skyline of New York. The lights shimmered like distant promises, and in their glow, he felt a strange mix of determination and sorrow. He knew the path he was about to take would lead him even further from Pia. But he also knew that if he truly wanted to grow, to become the kind of man who could one day stand beside her without shame, he would have to confront himself in the harshest of ways.

The future stretched before him, uncertain and immense. But so did a faint flicker of hope. Maybe, within the strict walls and merciless order of military life, he would find the clarity he had been chasing across oceans. Maybe there, at last, he would learn how to rebuild himself.

Rebirth in the Storm

Today, Davide stood as a prominent figure in the eyewear industry—a young entrepreneur reshaping the way people saw the world through ingenuity and vision. His enterprise was rooted in the Veneto, a region of Italy that, much like him, carried a legacy of tradition and resilience. He had established his workshop in Belluno, a town recognized as one of the epicenters of Italy's optical industry, where some of the world's most renowned glasses were designed and crafted.

But who could have foreseen it?

In his youth, Davide had been the rebellious kid of the neighborhood—an untamed spirit with a teasing smile and irreverent wit. Brilliantly sharp, he won people over with his intelligence and ironic humor while sidestepping the expectations of a life he deemed too small, and too narrow, too devoid of meaning.

Life, however, had other plans.

During his voluntary military service in the Navy, a stray bullet struck him in the abdomen during a shooting drill. And there—on the cold, unforgiving ground of that training field—began a transformation that would lead him to the depths of his own existence. The months of hospitalization that followed were a constant confrontation with the fragility of life. He left the hospital with a new lens through which to view the world, marked forever by that near-death experience. He had gone in a boy and emerged carrying a weight that would shape his every step.

The military discharge left behind a void—but also an urge to rebuild. He enrolled at Ca' Foscari University in Venice to study marketing and business, as if by understanding the logic of the market, he could also grasp the mysterious forces behind human decisions. At Ca' Foscari, his intellect, intuition, and clarity of vision stunned both classmates and professors alike. It was clear he wasn't a typical student—his insights always stretched beyond the expected, revealing a depth that was both unsettling and fascinating.

After graduation, Davide entered the optical industry as a simple salesman. But his sharp instincts and keen ability to read the unspoken desires of customers propelled him forward. His rise was meteoric—each accomplishment a testament to his transformation from a sardonic, restless youth into a man who, having brushed against the edge of existence, now played by his own rules. That sense of purpose—a quiet, unwavering commitment to life—led him to found his own eyewear brand in Belluno, in the heart of Veneto.

The experience of almost dying had woven itself into the fabric of his life, infusing every action with meaning that others could rarely perceive. His fear of death had dissolved, replaced by a reverent awareness of every fleeting moment.

Davide no longer worked with an empty ambition. Every design, every business decision, was an affirmation of rebirth, an echo of his purpose. He himself was the product of that stray bullet and the thin, trembling line that separates life from death.

In his journey, Davide had found something few ever do: a balance between the hunger to succeed and the peace that comes from no longer fearing failure. For him, business wasn't merely a career—it was a practice of gratitude, a thank-you to the life that, for reasons beyond logic, had given him a second chance. His quiet faith in a divine connection was a whisper that never left him—a feeling that he had been preserved for something more, that life wasn't a meaningless coincidence but a stage where he might leave a trace.

And in every step of his career, in every meeting and every creation, Davide reminded himself of his purpose, cultivating a mindful presence, as though something irreversible hung in the balance of each moment. He had found his treasure in the dark, painful cave of his past—and now, like a true existential entrepreneur, he shaped it into meaning in a world that, deep down, still struck him as absurd.

Under the Shadows of the Dolomites

Towers I

Friday, October 28th dawned with a gentle sun that seemed to caress the fallen leaves scattered across the streets of Belluno with a hint of nostalgia. Davide sat behind his dark wooden desk, his eyes staring blankly at the stack of papers before him. It was Beatrice's voice, crisp and composed, that pulled him from his reverie.

—Davide, I'm sorry, but canceling the meeting with the Japanese clients won't be easy. They won't be pleased—you know how important this deal is. Her tone was firm, though impeccably professional.

Davide, still gazing out the window, answered calmly—but with an uncommon conviction.

—Beatrice, Piero is ready. I trusted him from the moment I hired him. I know he can handle it.

Beatrice frowned, not yet convinced.

—It's not that I doubt Piero, but the clients are expecting to speak with you directly. Meetings like this always carry your signature.—

Turning in his chair, Davide met her concern with a serenity that disarmed any further argument.

—Beatrice, today is different. There's something I've postponed for far too long—something I never resolved. Today, I must. Trust me, please.—

Beatrice studied him, as if trying to decipher the unspoken. At last, she nodded, though her unease remained evident.

—Alright, Davide. I'll make the cancellations. But promise me, if anything goes wrong, you'll answer your phone.—

Davide smiled, picking up the keys to his Porsche Cayman.

—Promise. Though that won't be necessary. Thank you, Beatrice.—

The engine roared as Davide sped down the A27 motorway toward Padua, his hands steady on the wheel, but his thoughts drifting between landscapes and memories. The road wove through the hills of Veneto, where autumn brushed the vineyards and trees in hues of gold, copper, and blood-red. The drive, brief in distance, felt endless in emotion. With every passing kilometer, he drew nearer to Arcella, to the neighborhood where echoes of his past still lingered.

As he left the highway and turned onto Via Venezia toward Padua, the city greeted him with a blend of melancholy and unease. Narrow streets and muted facades stood like guardians of his younger years. He turned down Via Tiziano Aspetti, then headed into Arcella, where modest homes and humble gardens welcomed him back to a place that hadn't changed in a decade.

The Porsche came to a halt in front of Pia's house, its engine purring like a beast resting in unfamiliar territory. Milena, Nicoletta's housekeeper, peeked through the window, and within moments, the news swept through the house.

—It's Davide,— she announced, her voice tinged with curiosity and alarm.

Nicoletta, already busy in the kitchen, heard her just as Pia's voice rang down from the stairs.

—Wait! Don't open the door, Mom. Explain to me what's going on with Davide. Why is he suddenly showing up at this house? You know what that man did to me—and now you're best friends?—

Nicoletta stepped out of the kitchen, drying her hands on her apron, her face wearing the calm expression of someone who had already weighed her options.

—Pia, please. Listen to him. Then we'll decide together what to do. Your father asked you to, remember his words?—

Still fuming, Pia descended the stairs slowly, her expression caught somewhere between confusion and reluctant surrender.

—I remember, Mom. But that doesn't mean I have to accept everything.—

Just then, the doorbell echoed through the house, slicing through the brief silence like a breath held too long.

Pia stood still for a moment, eyes fixed on the kitchen door. At last, she walked toward the entryway, each step deliberate and unhurried—letting him wait, a small punishment for the storm he had caused.

When she opened the door, there he stood—Davide—holding a bouquet of red and white roses.

—Good morning, Pia,— he said softly, almost shyly, extending the flowers toward her.

Pia looked at him with a mixture of disdain and curiosity. Without speaking, she gestured toward the living room with a flick of her arm. Davide stepped inside just as Nicoletta appeared from the kitchen, drying her hands on a towel.

—Thank you, Nicoletta,— Davide said, handing her the bouquet with a smile that seemed to search for her approval.

Nicoletta looked at him with a warmth that contrasted with the tension in the room. —They're beautiful, Davide. Thank you.—

From the kitchen, Milena peeked out discreetly, observing the scene with a mix of curiosity and caution.

Davide turned toward Pia, who remained standing with her arms crossed.

—Pia, I'm asking you with all the humility I have—give me this day. Let me explain something I should've told you years ago. When I'm done, I'll take you home—or anywhere you wish.

Pia's expression shifted between indifference and defiance as she replied, —I'm only doing this out of respect for my father's memory. Let's be clear—I'm not doing it for you.—

Davide nodded, pressing his palms together in quiet gratitude. —Thank you, Pia.—

She sighed, glancing toward Nicoletta before speaking again. —I need to get ready. I've barely gotten out of bed.—

As she trudged up the stairs, she called out over her shoulder from the hallway: —Where are we going?—

—North,— Davide replied. —Wherever the day takes us.—

Pia paused, staring at him from the landing.

—Typical. You still haven't changed.—

Nicoletta stepped in gently—Pia, give him a chance.

She wore a delicate silk robe that flowed over her frame like water, its muted pastels—lavender, beige, and pale mint—lending her an air of quiet elegance. Despite her conflicted face, the robe's long sleeves and cinched waist complemented a pair of pajama pants and a soft, neutral-toned blouse.

Ten years had passed, yet time seemed to have yielded before her. Her fine, straight hair—dark chestnut with golden undertones—cascaded over her shoulders, catching the morning light. Her brown eyes, intense and penetrating, burned that day with the trace of contained fury, a spark that clashed with her otherwise composed demeanor. Her nose, perfectly shaped save for a small, unique notch, and her narrow red lips set her beauty apart with striking distinction.

Her hands and feet, always immaculately cared for, spoke of the meticulous nature that defined her. Her nails, clean and polished in a natural shade, completed the image of a woman who—though weighed down by emotion—still radiated innate grace and unbreakable strength.

Pia said nothing more and continued upstairs, leaving Davide to sip the espresso Milena had placed before him. He sat by the window, watching leaves fall slowly on the other side of the glass as the scent of coffee and memory filled the room.

This day was unlike any other. It was a reckoning with lost time, with words left unsaid, and with guilt and longing that still clung to his soul.

Pia descended the stairs, her steps steady but slow, as if each one marked a shift between past and present. From where he sat, Davide couldn't take his eyes off her. The soft morning light outlined her figure, dressed in a simple yet perfectly seasonal outfit: a fine-knit cream sweater that draped elegantly at the hips, paired with slim-fit trousers in a warm caramel tone. Brown ankle boots with a slight heel completed the ensemble, while a light hazelnut-colored coat rested over her arm. She was a portrait of grace and understated beauty, resisting time and trends with quiet defiance. Never fond of makeup, Pia had only traced her eyes with the faintest liner, and a natural shade of lipstick added a hint of color to her face, which reflected emotions carefully held at bay. To Davide, seeing her like this was like witnessing a painting come to life—an artwork that time had failed to diminish.

Shadows of Jealousy Beneath the Dolomites Peaks I

Giacomo, cloaked in the dimness of early morning, waited in his battered red FIAT 500, hidden among shadows and doubt. Frost from the night had drawn a delicate veil across the windows, while his breath—warm and fleeting—tried in vain to give life to his numbed hands. From his hiding place, his eyes—two abysses of longing and jealousy—remained fixed on the home of Lucien and Nicoletta, waiting for fate to grant him a moment to approach Pia, though he lacked the courage to create it for himself.

Suddenly, a white Porsche, like lightning tearing through the night, streaked down the road and stopped in front of Pia's house. Giacomo recognized Davide instantly, and a storm of rage and unrest erupted within him. Anxiety gnawed at him; every attempt to find an excuse to approach Pia vanished like smoke in the wind. The fear that Davide might steal from him what he considered his own pushed him to step out of the car. He looked like a castaway of time—unkempt beard, greasy hair, and a breath that betrayed sleepless nights.

He shut the car door and began to walk, hesitantly, toward Pia's house. But the roar of the Porsche Cayman's engine—powerful and defiant—froze him in place. That sound, like the cry of a wounded beast, echoed in his chest, reminding him of his own insignificance. Feeling defeated, Giacomo turned back and returned to his car, painfully aware of the chasm that now separated him from Pia.

Heart in his throat, soul burning with jealousy, Giacomo made a fateful decision: to follow the couple. He slipped through the shadows of Padua—a city where the whispers of the past mingle with the murmurs of its canals. The streets, dressed in the cloak of dawn, mirrored on their cobblestones the unrest of a man consumed by envy. In the distance, the Basilica of Saint Anthony rose in solemn majesty, its domes etched against a starlit sky, while the statues of Prato della Valle stood sentinel, unmoved by Giacomo's torment.

The mist rising from the rivers wrapped the city in a cold embrace, deepening the solitude that soaked into his bones. The road from Padua stretched before him like a snake of asphalt, flanked by golden and green fields swaying under the caress of the wind. As he pressed onward, the landscapes of Padua unfolded in his mind's eye: vast fields interrupted by bell towers and ancient villas, rivers and canals that laced through the region, and the gentle hills that cradled the city.

Leaving Padua behind, the highway unwound like a serpent through hushed fields and hills that whispered old stories. Giacomo drove on in a blind pursuit, his neglected, weary FIAT 500 groaning with each passing mile. Every kilometer was a jab of uncertainty, the fuel gauge inching lower as the pressure in his chest climbed higher.

Under the Shadows of the Dolomites Towers II

Inside the car, silence reigned during the first stretch of the journey. Davide drove calmly, heading north. The purring engine and the crunch of dry leaves under the wheels were the only sounds between them. Pia, however, broke the silence with sudden sharpness.

—I want you to know something before we go any further with this madness,— she said, crossing her arms, her gaze fixed on the horizon. —I'm fine, Davide. I've been fine all these years. And I'm not going to let you show up now and stir my life all over again.—

Davide nodded without looking away from the road, his serenity only seeming to irritate her more.

—Pia…— he began, but she cut him off, her voice a cocktail of resolve and pain.

—No. Let me finish. I'm fine. I really am. In fact, I just met someone. I'm excited about him. I don't need you barging in, slowing me down, dragging me back onto this rollercoaster again.

As she said it, something inside her shifted. She realized she had completely forgotten about Tomasso. For a fleeting second, her mind wandered to that relationship, to what she really felt for him. But the image of Davide, beside her, driving toward the mountains, pushed everything else away.

—Go on,— Davide said softly, eyes still on the road.

—'Go on'? That's all you have to say?— she snapped, turning to him. Her voice cracked as she tried to hold herself together. —Do you know how long I waited for you? How many times have I dreamed of you showing up in my room, at my door, in class, at the café, or in the university dining hall? For years, Davide. Years. I used to follow men with your build, with your walk, hoping—hoping it was you. And every time, I ended up with the same

emptiness.—

Davide pressed his lips together, his hands firm on the wheel and gearshift. His calm expression veiled the storm of emotions her words were unleashing.

—You know what was the worst? —she continued, her voice close to breaking. —That I didn't even know what I'd done. What did I do, Davide? What the hell did I do to make you leave me like that, as if I were nothing? Tell me, what could you possibly say today that would erase all these years of pain? Because… because what you did to me doesn't just vanish. It doesn't get forgiven that easily.—

Pia turned toward the window, biting her lip to keep the tears at bay. Davide remained quiet, driving, letting her release everything she had carried for too long. He knew to interrupt would be to ruin everything. He had to listen—absorb every word—before he could say anything.

—Pia,— he said at last, his voice steady and deep. —Do you remember the last time we saw each other?—

She turned sharply, her brown eyes burning with anger and sorrow.

—Of course I remember,— she said, letting out a bitter laugh. —That's the curse with you, Davide. That even if I tried, I could never forget it. Do you know what it's like to live with that memory every day, with that damn image of you walking away without even telling me why? Because if you had died, it wouldn't have hurt this much.—

Davide gripped the wheel tighter, his voice lowering to almost a whisper.

—Pia, I didn't tell you everything that day. Not because I didn't want to—but because I couldn't. That day… your father asked to meet with me. He asked me to speak with him, just the two of us. —

The air in the car suddenly thickened. Pia frowned, bewildered.

—My father?— she asked, her voice laced with disbelief. —What does he have to do with all this?—

Davide swallowed hard, his eyes reflecting guilt and a long-held resolve.

—Pia, he asked me for something that I didn't fully understand at the time, but I agreed because I respected him. He asked me to walk away from you. He told me you had a brilliant future ahead of you, a purpose that couldn't be interrupted. And I… I believed him. I thought that by stepping away, I was setting you free—giving you the chance to become everything you were meant to be.

Pia stared at him, her expression caught somewhere between disbelief and rage.

—Did you ever think to talk to me?— Pia asked, her voice quivering with the ache of old wounds. —To ask me if I wanted you to leave? To give my opinion the slightest importance?—

Davide nodded slowly, his lips trembling slightly as he prepared to confess what he'd buried for so long.

—I did think about it, Pia. But I also thought that if I looked into your eyes, if I heard your voice, I would never be able to go. And I believed you needed me gone to be free—even if that meant losing you forever.

Silence reclaimed the space between them. Pia, eyes now fixed on the mountains rising in the distance, felt her heart tear between fury and painful understanding. The man she had loved had left because he thought it was best for her. But who had given him the right to decide that?

—What you did to me was cruel, Davide,— she said finally, her voice shaking. —And if you think this trip is going to fix everything, you're wrong.—

Davide took a deep breath, gathering the courage to do something he had put off for years. With one steady hand on the wheel, he reached toward the back seat and pulled forward a thick folder, worn and yellowed with time. His movement was measured, but to Pia, still caught between fury and nostalgia, it felt intrusive. She glanced sideways at him, a storm brewing in her eyes.

—Don't you dare touch me, Davide,—she said in a firm voice—almost a warning—as her posture stiffened.

Davide stopped, turned calmly toward her, and spoke with a voice steady but laced with emotion.

—I'm not going to touch you, Pia. I would never do anything you didn't want. I just want to give you something… something I've kept for a long time.—

Gently, he placed the folder on the dashboard between them. It was thick, its pages protruding in messy layers, covered with a thin veil of dust—as though it had lived in some forgotten corner of his past. Pia looked at it with suspicion… and an inevitable flicker of curiosity.

—What is this?—she asked, her voice edged more with irritation than interest.

Davide, eyes back on the road, spoke steadily.

—They're letters, Pia. Over a hundred. I wrote them to you over the past ten years. I never sent them because I didn't know if I had the right… I didn't know if you even wanted to read them. But now… now I think you should have them.

Silence fell again like a blanket. Pia took the folder with trembling hands, her heart pounding. She opened it and saw dates in the top corners of the pages—each marking a different moment during Davide's absence. His handwriting was elegant, almost artistic, and in the very first letter, she found something that took her breath away: the beginning of a monologue that felt eerily familiar.

—What is this?—she repeated, this time softer, almost a whisper.

Davide swallowed hard before answering.

—It's what your father said to me that day. At the bar. Those words have haunted me, Pia. I thought maybe if I wrote them down, I could find peace. But I never did.—

Pia began to read aloud, her voice trembling at first, then gaining strength—like she was casting out ghosts he'd carried into their silence.

—In the absurdity of our relationships, what hurts most is not what the other person does, but the illusion of what we expect them to do. We build idealized versions of love, demanding that the other be, have, or give us something. And by doing so, we cut them down, we fragment them, and we turn them into projections of our own expectations. We refuse to see them in their entirety— in their contradictory, beautiful individuality.

She paused, closing her eyes for a moment.

—Why are you showing me this now, Davide?— she asked, her voice thick with anger and sorrow. —Do you think quoting my father justifies what you did?—

Davide let out a deep sigh, his gaze steady on the road ahead.

—No, Pia. I'm not trying to justify myself. But I want you to understand what was happening in my head back then. Your father told me those words, and I... I took them as a command. As an absolute truth. I didn't see that I was running—not just from you, but from myself.

Pia slammed the folder shut with a gesture that denoted frustration.

—Ten years, Davide. Ten years and over a hundred letters, and you never had the guts to say a single word to me. Do you know what that means to me? It means I was invisible to you. That I didn't matter enough for you to face me.—

Davide nodded slowly, not trying to defend himself.

—You're right, Pia. I was a coward. But each of those letters was a small attempt to make sense of what I did, to understand why I made that choice. And now… now I want you to have them, because they're part of our story—even if that story is full of mistakes.

The car continued its path northward, the autumn landscape unfolding around them, framing the tension and nostalgia that filled the space between them.

Pia, the folder heavy in her lap, stared out the window, trying to process what she had just heard. She knew those letters might hold answers she had been searching for… But she also knew reading them would reopen wounds that had never truly healed.

—I don't know if I'll ever be able to forgive you, Davide,— she finally said, her voice barely audible.

Davide, a knot tightening in his throat, answered without looking at her.

—I don't expect you to, Pia. I just hope that one day you'll understand that everything I did—even the worst of it—was because I loved you in the only way I knew how.—

Silence returned once more, as the car disappeared into the heart of the Dolomites, with a folder of letters resting like a fragile bridge between past and present.

Midday in Agordo brought with it a crisp air that contrasted with the golden warmth of the autumn sun. Fallen leaves adorned the cobbled streets, and the small town looked like a dreamlike postcard. Davide parked the Porsche carefully and, saying little, helped Pia out of the car.

She clutched the folder of letters to her chest—as if it were a shield.

Shadows of Jealousy Beneath the Dolomites Peaks II

By the time Giacomo arrived in Agordo, the gas tank was nearly empty, and his soul felt just as drained. From a distance, he watched as Pia and Davide stepped into a restaurant, its warm interior light casting an inviting glow against the crisp brightness of an autumn day. He noticed Pia was carrying a folder—thick, seemingly filled with documents—which only fanned the flames of his suspicions and fears. There, from his hidden vantage point, Giacomo stood frozen, caught between helplessness and longing, peering into a world that now felt irrevocably closed to him.

Wrapped in a disheveled trench coat and with his beret pulled low over his brow, Giacomo blended with the shadows cast by the leafless autumn trees. The dry leaves beneath his feet crackled with every shift of weight, creating a melancholic soundtrack to his inner unrest. Through the large restaurant window, he watched Pia and Davide—warm and bathed in golden light—while the wind bit at his face and fingers, raw with cold and discontent. Pia, seated by the window, her features lit by a soft mix of sunlight and lamplight, seemed to Giacomo like a distant lighthouse glowing beyond a stormy sea.

The wind whispered through the bare branches above him, carrying with it muffled laughter and the cadence of a conversation he couldn't hear. Giacomo's face was half-hidden behind the raised collar of his coat, and though passersby occasionally glanced at him, none could see the storm that churned within. Every subtle movement from Pia—each tilt of her head toward Davide, each flicker of a smile—was a blade driven deeper into his chest. The folder resting gently in her lap was no longer just paper and ink—

it had become a symbol of shared secrets, of a closeness he would never touch.

In his mind, images flashed like scenes from an inevitable tragedy: Pia drifting farther away, Davide taking the place he had longed to fill. Despair engulfed him, and the cold outside merged with the frost tightening around his soul. Giacomo stood there, motionless, trapped between reality and ghosts, while the world marched on, indifferent to his sorrow. Giacomo remained there, motionless, trapped between reality and his ghosts, while the world, indifferent to his pain, continued on its way.

Under the Shadows of the Dolomites Towers III

The restaurant Davide had chosen embodied the soul of Northern Italy. Housed in an old stone building with dark wooden shutters, it rose with quiet elegance, beckoning guests to step inside. The facade was adorned with pots overflowing with autumn flowers—warm-toned chrysanthemums and crimson leaves that drifted down gracefully. A carved wooden door marked the entrance, opening into a cozy interior lit by the golden glow of hanging lamps.

The air inside was steeped in the intoxicating aroma of fresh herbs, roasted meats, and just-baked bread. The space hummed with the bustle of tourists and locals, the clinking of glasses and plates, and the soft murmur of conversation. The walls bore black-and-white photographs of the village, polished copper kitchen tools, and narrow shelves lined with bottles of carefully selected wines. Tables dressed in immaculate white cloths were each adorned with tiny vases holding wildflowers.

Umberto, the chef and owner, was a broad-shouldered man whose face radiated warmth, his eyes alight with a passion for food. He wore an apron that had seen better days, but his smile alone was enough to welcome anyone who crossed his threshold. When he saw Davide walk in with Pia, his expression brightened instantly. He moved toward them with delight, but Davide gave a subtle gesture behind Pia's back, signaling discretion. Umberto, intuitive by nature and used to reading the mood of his patrons, picked up on it at once.

—Davide!—he greeted, his voice cheerful but tempered. What a surprise to see you here!

—Umberto, old friend, I need a favor —Davide lowered his voice, maintaining a cordial tone as his gaze shifted briefly to Pia, who was eyeing the space with a mix of polite interest and veiled skepticism—. Could you give us a table for two… something away from the noise, if possible?

Umberto nodded, immediately sensing the delicacy of the moment.

—Of course, my friend. Follow me—I have just the place.

He led them through the main dining hall, bustling and lively, until they reached a semi-private corner. Here, the atmosphere shifted. The lighting was gentler, the conversations more distant. The table, nestled beside a window overlooking a small inner garden, had been prepared with great care. The white tablecloth glowed beneath the warm lamplight, and a small vase held sprigs of olive and lavender, evoking an understated charm.

Pia took her seat, setting the folder of letters down on the table, her eyes scanning the details of the room with a blend of curiosity and caution. Umberto, ever attentive, offered them menus, but Davide waved him off with a knowing smile.

—I trust you, Umberto. Surprise us with something special. And please—a red wine, something smooth to accompany the moment.

Umberto dipped his head, clearly pleased by Davide's trust, and left them to the quiet intimacy of their corner. Pia, still wearing her sunglasses, crossed her arms and studied Davide with a neutral expression.

—Do you always make everything this theatrical?— she asked, a trace of sarcasm edging her voice.

—Only when the occasion calls for it —Davide replied, his tone calm as he poured water into their glasses.

—And what occasion would that be? A man trying to redeem himself after ten years of silence? Her tone was sharp, but there was a slight tremble in her voice, betraying the emotional weight she carried.

Davide met her gaze with patience.

—Maybe that. Or maybe it's a man who, after ten years, finally has the courage to face his mistakes. I'm not expecting forgiveness, Pia. I only want you to listen.

Pia leaned back in her chair, letting out a sigh. The aroma of food drifting from the kitchen filled the air—a quiet reminder of the simple beauty that still lingered, even in tense moments.

—You talk as if it were all so simple, Davide. As if these letters could erase what you did —She placed the folder in front of him, her fingers tapping rhythmically on the cover, mirroring her unease.

Before Davide could answer, Umberto returned with two glasses of wine and a plate of antipasti to start: a selection of local cheeses, cured hams, and bruschetta drizzled with olive oil. He set it down with a discreet smile.

—Enjoy, my friends. I have a feeling this is exactly what you need.

As Umberto walked away, Pia lifted her glass, her eyes locked on Davide's with a mix of defiance and melancholy.

—To the memories, Davide—and to the answers I expect to hear today.

Davide raised his glass too, knowing this toast marked not just the start of a meal but the beginning of a conversation that would shape the rest of their lives.

Pia opened the folder with trembling hands, and the first lines of Davide's letters surged into her like an overflowing river. Her eyes skimmed the words cautiously, as if afraid they might awaken something in her too painful to face. But soon the flood of emotions became unstoppable, and tears began to roll silently down her cheeks. She made no effort to wipe them away. They were tears held back for years—tears that carried the weight of absence, of grief, and perhaps of shattered hope.

Without a word, Pia removed her sunglasses, reached into her purse, and pulled out her journal. It was an intimate object, its pages worn with time, a place where she had poured the feelings she could never speak aloud. As she opened it, words began to spill out with the ease of someone who had long found refuge in writing.

Davide watched her quietly, not daring to interrupt. Pia began to write:

Pia's Journal

Friday, October 28, 2022

They've told us we must choose between the mind—that labyrinth of precise ideas—and the heart, that mirror reflecting the soul's passions. They have condemned us to duality, to the eternal fork in the road.

But I tell you this: the mind and the heart are two wings of the same bird, two faces of the same god. They are the two halves of the labyrinth we must travel to truly find ourselves.

The mind, with its hunger to bring order to chaos, offers us a map of the universe—a cartography of reality. But that map is only a shadow of the truth, a fragmented image in the mirror of reason. The heart, with its intuitive wisdom, leads us to the center of the labyrinth, to the very essence of being. But without the mind, the heart gets lost in the endless hallways of emotion, without compass or destination.

True wisdom lies in the union of these two opposites, in the reconciliation of reason and intuition. It is not about silencing the heart so that the mind may reign, nor about letting emotions carry us adrift. It is about integration, about fusion, about creating harmony—where the mind becomes the library that nourishes the heart, and the heart becomes the key that unlocks the secrets of the mind.

In that meeting point, in that fusion of opposites, lies liberation. The freedom to be, to create, to love without the chains of duality. A path that leads us, through the winding labyrinths of selfhood, toward the lost unity— toward the center of the universe that lives within us.

When she finished writing, Pia closed her journal with a deep sigh, placing her hands on it as if to seal the emotions she had just poured onto the pages.

Davide remained motionless across from her, feeling the weight of the moment, fully aware that any word he uttered could shatter the fragile balance that surrounded them.

At last, Pia lifted her gaze and looked straight at him, a blend of vulnerability and strength shining in her eyes.

—You know what hurts, Davide?—she said, her voice barely holding together. That after all this time, after all the nights I asked myself what I did wrong… it turns out it wasn't me. It was you. You and your fears, your selfish decisions dressed up as sacrifice. And now you show up with your letters and your words, hoping they'll fix something you shattered long ago.

Davide nodded, lowering his eyes, as if every one of Pia's words was a deserved blow. In a calm tone, he replied,

—You're right, Pia. There's no excuse for what I did. I didn't write those letters to justify myself but to try to understand who I was. Every word in them is a desperate attempt to make sense of my own cowardice. And though I know I can't undo the harm, I at least wanted to show you that you never left this place —he touched his chest, where his heart beat with force— you were there, in every thought, in every choice I made.

Pia held his gaze for a moment, trying to discern whether there was truth in his words or if they were just another attempt to manipulate her. Then she turned her eyes to the folder of letters, as if searching for answers there rather than in him.

—I don't know if I want to read them all, Davide —she said honestly. I don't know if I want to relive all that pain.

—You don't have to, Pia —he replied gently. I just wanted you to have them, to know that I didn't leave without thinking of you, without missing you, without regretting it.

The silence that followed was long and heavy, broken only by the soft murmur of other diners and the hush of the leaves rustling beyond the window. Pia reached for her glass and took a sip of wine, granting herself a brief pause before speaking again.

—I don't know if this changes anything, Davide. But at least now I know that —for the first time—you're here, looking me in the eyes and facing what you left behind. And that, at the very least, is a beginning.

—When I look back —Davide said, his voice slow and measured, as if each word emerged carefully from deep within — everything comes down to a dilemma that shaped every decision I made in those years. I was caught between my need to grow and my fear of facing my own insecurities.

Pia remained silent, her gaze fixed on Davide's gestures as he spoke.

—Running… —he continued, letting the word hover in the air for a moment— running was my way of escaping the expectations you and Lucien placed on me. But it was also —though I didn't realize it then— an opportunity, however painful, to redefine who I was, to understand what I truly wanted for my future.

—The only expectation I ever had was that you'd keep loving me —Pia interrupted, almost in a whisper.

Davide paused, his hands pressed tightly against the table as if trying to anchor his thoughts. His gaze wandered to the restaurant's window, where autumn leaves danced to the rhythm of the wind.

—That journey, which at first seemed like an act of desperation, became something much greater —he said, turning back to face her. It became a metaphor for my path to maturity. I forced myself to face challenges I'd never imagined —not just the external ones, like living in a foreign country without even a decent grasp of the language, in a city that threatened to swallow me whole— but the internal ones too… He paused, searching for the right words. The ones I couldn't escape, even with my eyes closed.

Pia laced her fingers together on the table but remained silent. Davide continued, his voice quieter now, more intimate.

—It was a constant struggle —trying to accept who I was while also pushing myself to become someone else… someone better. Someone worthy of… — He stopped, unable to say her name aloud. Worthy of everything I dreamed of building.

—And did you? —Pia asked in a whisper, breaking the silence that had filled the room.

Davide exhaled softly, as if her question weighed on his soul.

—I found myself standing at a crossroads, Pia. Every day, I had to choose whether to stay and face myself or let nostalgia and regret consume me. It was exhausting. A constant dance between my love for you, my desire to become better… — He paused again, staring down at his hands, as if they might reveal the strength he needed to go on. And that ever-present fear of failure.

Pia blinked, her expression unreadable. Davide raised his eyes and continued, this time with a vulnerability he hadn't shown before.

—There were nights…—his voice cracked slightly— nights when I asked myself if I'd made the right choice by leaving. If walking away had protected you… or just protected me. Protected me from you seeing who I really was.

The silence between them stretched, thick with everything that had been left unsaid for years. Finally, Davide added, his tone firmer now but no less sincere:

—But at the same time, there were moments of clarity, Pia. Fleeting, but real. Moments when I understood that this path, painful as it was, had to be mine. I needed to find myself, to face my fears… to decide if I could be more than the boy who ran away.

Davide looked up, and his eyes met Pia's.

—This is the moment that shaped my life. That turning point where I had to choose who I wanted to become. That's why I'm here. To tell you that my leaving… it wasn't for lack of love, Pia. It was the desperate act of someone who didn't know how to face who he was or who he wanted to be.

At that moment, Umberto entered the semi-private dining room with the grace and assurance of someone who knows his craft intimately. In his hands was a dish, exquisitely presented, which he placed gently at the center of the table.

—A carpaccio of veal, sliced thin as a sigh —he announced, as the fresh aroma of the plate began to fill the air. It's dressed with a lemon and olive oil emulsion, topped with wild arugula, 36-month-aged Parmigiano Reggiano shavings, and a hint of freshly grated black truffle.

The dish was a visual poem: the delicate veal slices arranged like petals on a white porcelain canvas, the arugula lending a vibrant green, and the cheese catching the light in golden flecks. The black truffle, earthy and intense, hovered in the air like a secret waiting to be tasted.

Before leaving, Umberto placed a decanter on the table, filled with a red wine that shimmered like a ruby under the room's soft lighting.

—I've chosen for you a 2016 Barolo, he said, with a knowing smile. That vintage was exceptional in Piedmont —one of the best of the last decade. You'll find notes of ripe cherries, tobacco, and a trace of rose petals. The tannins are round, and the finish is long and elegant. I've let it breathe so it can show its full character.

The decanter was simple yet elegant, and the wine it held gleamed like liquid treasure. Umberto poured with expert precision, offering Davide a small taste. With a subtle nod of approval, Davide signaled for him to serve Pia as well. The wine's bouquet complemented the subtle complexity of the carpaccio perfectly, creating a harmonious balance between the intensity of the flavors and the depth of the vintage.

—I hope you enjoy the pairing —Umberto added, bowing his head slightly before leaving the room with the same discretion with which he had entered.

Pia took a silent sip from her glass. The Barolo, with its full body and elegant character, seemed to mirror the day she was sharing with Davide: intense, brimming with emotion, and with an ending still uncertain.

She turned her attention back to the letters, but the words no longer held the same weight. Her eyes scanned the pages, but her mind remained caught in the conversation they had just begun. Silence settled at the table like a third guest, and the aromas of carpaccio and wine mingled with the dense thoughts floating between them. From afar, Umberto watched them discreetly from the bar, his movements slower than usual. He had never seen Davide so serious; he had always been the soul of any conversation. But today, he was a shadow of the smiling young man Umberto once knew.

Pia laid the letters down and raised her eyes. Still glistening with tears, they met Davide's.

—Why did my father want to speak with you?—she asked, her voice steady but thick with disbelief. Her words carried the weight of anger and sorrow.

Davide took a sip of his wine, as if the time it took to drink would help him find the right words. His gaze drifted toward the window, searching the warm hues of autumn for a foothold.

—He called me a few months ago, he finally said, his voice deep but composed. He wanted us to have dinner — just the two of us. When I arrived, he didn't waste time. He got right to it, just like he always did. He told me he was terminally ill.

Pia stared at him, lips pressed tightly together, holding back a surge of emotions. Davide went on:

—He apologized, Pia. He told me he never intended things to end the way they did. He confessed he hadn't realized the damage he could cause by pushing me away. He explained his intentions —that he just wanted you to have a bright future, a successful career. But then he told me it was a mistake. That I was just a boy back then, and that he never should have interfered in what we had.

Pia leaned back in her chair, overwhelmed. Davide lowered his eyes, tracing the rim of his glass with a fingertip.

—He told me clearly —Davide continued—. I protected my daughter from something that ended up hurting her more than I imagined. He confessed that when he saw you fully absorbed in your career but without the light you used to carry when you were with me… that's when he realized he had made a mistake. But by then, he thought it was too late.

Pia exhaled slowly, folding her arms across her chest.

—You mcn… she said, her voice laced with fury and disdain—. How could my father not tell me? How could he make such a monumental decision without even asking me? I was the one in love, Davide! I was the one looking for you in every corner, the one who saw your shadow at every turn. And he decided for me?

Her voice cracked, but she quickly recovered, hardening her expression.

Davide didn't respond right away. He knew this was her moment, not his. He waited, letting her speak, though every word struck him like a hammer.

—Ten years, Davide…—Pia said, her voice now softer, almost a murmur—. Ten years of unanswered questions, of sleepless nights, of wondering what I had done wrong. Do you know how many times I dreamed you'd come back? That you'd show up out of nowhere and explain everything to me? And now you tell me it was because of my father…

She paused, letting the weight of her words settle into the space between them.

—I'm so confused, Davide. Ten years…—she repeated, and this time, the tears in her eyes spilled freely, and she didn't try to stop them.

Davide leaned forward, setting his glass aside.

—I know, Pia —he said gently, his voice heavy with remorse. I know, and there are no words that can undo what happened. But I'm here now because I don't want another day to pass without giving you the answers you deserve. I don't want you to live with those questions —neither about you nor about me.

Pia looked at him closely, as if weighing whether his words could begin to mend something long broken. But ten years of pain couldn't be erased in a single conversation—and they both knew it.

Pia let her fingers idly trace the edge of one of the letters, her eyes fixed on Davide. Her expression was a blend of disbelief and resignation. Across the table, Davide sipped from his glass of Barolo, the deep crimson of the wine catching the light like a reflection of everything unspoken between them.

—You know, Davide began, his voice softer now, as if he feared the weight of his words might shatter something fragile between them, there are three phrases that have stayed with me all these years. Not just in my mind, but here —he gently tapped his chest— etched into my heart like a refrain of everything I lost and everything I still needed to understand.

Pia held her breath. It was as if each word Davide spoke tugged at an invisible thread, slowly unraveling the knot she had carried for ten years.

—If you truly love Pia, Davide —he said, pausing to let the memory settle over him— let her go and let her be. His voice wavered slightly as he recalled those words. Then, inhaling deeply, he continued—. You must work on your future, Davide. That was the next thing he said, in that quieter, almost fatherly tone he had.

He hesitated, searching for the exact phrasing of the final memory.

—Adolescence — he finally added— that age that forgives all mistakes and poor decisions is coming to an end.

Davide breathed in again, speaking now with a slower cadence, as if each word was a fragile piece of truth.

—Pia, I don't want you to misunderstand what I'm about to say. But I believe your father was right —about something important.

He lowered his gaze, avoiding her eyes for a moment, his fingers nervously circling the rim of his wineglass. Then he looked up, directly into her, with an honesty that cut through the heavy air.

—With the mindset I had back then, with that short-sighted view of the world I carried through high school... we wouldn't have made it, Pia.

He paused, letting the words breathe before going on.

—I lived one day at a time, without a clue what it meant to build something lasting or real. My life was just waking up, killing time, and falling back into bed —no purpose, no plan. He leaned slightly toward her, his gaze steady and intent. How could I offer you any kind of stability when I didn't even have it myself? We would have failed, Pia. Not because I didn't love you —because I did— but because I wasn't equipped to hold something as precious as what we had.

His voice softened into a whisper, raw with emotion.

—Your father saw it. And even if the way he intervened was harsh, even if it was unfair to you... I understand now that he wasn't entirely wrong. I needed to find myself before I could be someone worthy of you. But the price of that lesson…—he trailed off, his face shadowed by the weight of all those lost years— was losing you.

The room fell silent, save for the soft flicker of candlelight. Pia couldn't help but notice the vulnerability in his voice —something she had never associated with Davide during the time they were together. For a moment, it felt as if past and present had collapsed into one fragile, irreversible truth —suspended here in this quiet corner of Agordo.

—Two years ago —Davide said, his voice low again— I asked Armando about you. He told me you were seeing someone —seriously— a professor at the University of Florence. When I heard that, I felt a deep emptiness. Not because I didn't want you to be happy, but because I realized I had no place in your life anymore. I thought I'd lost my chance, that returning would be selfish... intrusive. You deserved someone who could be there for you in ways I never was. Someone stable. Someone with vision. All the things it took me years to find.

Pia didn't speak. She watched him, unmoving, though her hands trembled slightly as they rested on the folder of letters. The quiet clinking of Umberto's footsteps signaled his approach. He set down the next course gently before them: a risotto with black truffle and aged Parmigiano. The fragrance was warm, deep, and earthy —an aroma that wrapped around them like a comfort long withheld. He paired it with a younger Barolo, rich with notes of ripe cherry and spice. After a subtle nod, Umberto disappeared again, leaving them in the quiet intimacy of their unraveling.

It was Pia who broke the silence.

—And now, Davide? After ten years... why now?

Davide offered a faint, melancholic smile, his eyes reflecting the weight of a decade's regret.

—Because I couldn't keep living with this weight, Pia. I couldn't move forward without explaining, without telling you the truth. I don't know if I'm here to ask you for anything or simply to free us both from this ghost that's been following us. But what I do know… is that I needed to see you, even if only to tell you how sorry I am.

Pia didn't respond right away. Instead, she reached into the folder and pulled out one of the letters. She began to read. Tears rolled silently down her cheeks as her eyes moved across the words Davide had written years ago but never had the courage to send. He watched in silence, knowing that every line was a reflection of his truth, his fears —a fragment of his soul he had never dared to show her.

After several minutes, Pia looked up. Her voice trembled but held steady.

—Davide… why? Why did you leave me? Why didn't you come back?

Davide lowered his head. When he spoke, his voice was barely above a whisper.

—There was a time, Pia, when I truly believed that disappearing was the best thing I could do for you. But what you don't know… is what happened afterward —when I tried to redeem myself for that decision.

He paused for a moment, gathering the weight of memory.

—I enlisted in the military. Not because it was my dream, but because I thought a strict regime might help me face my insecurities and help me rebuild myself.

Then, with a heaviness in his tone that could only be born of lived pain, he added:

—But everything changed in an instant.

Pia frowned, surprise crossing her face.

—What do you mean?

Davide drew a deep breath before continuing.

—During an advanced training exercise, there was an accident. We were running drills with live ammunition. My team was ambushed by mistake during a poorly coordinated simulation. A bullet went through my abdomen, damaging vital organs. I lost so much blood before reaching the military hospital that I fell into a coma that lasted more than three months. The trauma led to severe infections, and the doctors fought to stabilize me. My liver suffered serious damage, which made recovery even more complicated. At one point, they didn't even know if I would survive.

Pia stared at him, horrified, as he instinctively placed a hand over his abdomen, as if the memory still ached there.

—I didn't just come out of that hospital after months of intensive care and rehabilitation, Pia. I was discharged from the military too. My body was no longer fit for service. And during that time, lying in bed, unable to move, I thought about you. A lot. I thought about everything I had left behind. I promised myself that if I made it through, I would try to make things right… But it took me years to gather the courage to come back.

The silence that followed was as heavy as the words Davide had just spoken.

Pia, tears now welling in her eyes, held the folder of letters tightly against her chest, as if trying to absorb everything he had said through the touch of paper and ink.

Finally, she murmured, her voice barely a whisper:

—Ten years, Davide… Ten years…

And with those words, the weight of the decade that had separated them fell heavy between them, as the twilight began to paint the sky over Agordo in warm, melancholic hues —turning the evening into a canvas of amber, gold, and longing.

Pia, without replying, reached once more for the folder of letters and began to read. Her tears slipped silently down her cheeks as Davide watched her, knowing that each word on those pages held a truth he had never dared to give her when it mattered most.

Umberto, moving with the quiet grace of someone who understands the rhythm of intimate conversations, cleared the empty dinner plates. His movements were fluid, almost imperceptible, as if not to disturb the delicate air thick with words unsaid.

He returned shortly with a carefully arranged tray — a selection of cheeses that spanned from the delicate creaminess of Taleggio to the sharp, umami-rich bite of aged Parmigiano Reggiano, paired with fresh figs, candied walnuts, and a drizzle of golden acacia honey.

On a smaller tray, he placed two glasses filled with the same Barolo he had poured earlier, ensuring every detail harmonized with the evolving atmosphere. Then, gently, he set a slender bottle of artisanal grappa from the Trentino region on the table, beside two petite glasses that seemed to wait, quietly, for the moment to arrive.

To finish, Umberto presented Pia with a handwritten card —a simple, elegant menu with two choices of house-made dessert: a creamy tiramisù, perfectly balanced between the bitterness of espresso and the silkiness of mascarpone, and a panna cotta infused with Madagascar vanilla, delicately topped with wild berries and a raspberry reduction, shimmering like a memory you're afraid to revisit.

Pia lifted her gaze toward Umberto, moved by his attention to detail. Her voice, though soft, carried the curiosity that had taken hold of her.

—Thank you, Umberto. Everything has been exquisite, she said with a gentle smile, her fingers brushing the rim of her wine glass. I'm curious... how do you know Davide? She paused, as if weighing the importance of what she was about to ask next. And… how would you describe him?

Umberto, who until then had maintained a respectful distance, offered a warm smile. He stepped just close enough, his hands folded in front of him like someone preparing to speak from the heart.

—Signorina, Davide is one of those guests who always leave a lasting impression. He's well-loved here. A true gentleman —friendly, thoughtful, and kind. He often comes with his employees, and I can tell you, they hold him in great esteem. There's always a kind word, a generous gesture, something about him that sets him apart.

Umberto paused for a moment, searching for the right words.

—But to be honest, I only know him as a customer. Still, when you see as many people pass through a place like this as I do, you develop a sense for reading faces, for listening to silence. And I assure you, signorina, Davide is a good man. One of those people who seem to carry more than they ever say.

—In other words —he said softly— Davide is one of those water people. As my mother would say, *"Transparent,"* flowing wherever they go, leaving behind either a lesson or that unshakable urge to live and explore.

She listened attentively, nodding now and then. She didn't add anything more. Instead, she offered Umberto a grateful smile and reached for a piece of Parmigiano Reggiano, pairing it with a touch of honey, while Umberto excused himself with the quiet grace of someone who knows exactly when to leave people alone with their thoughts.

Night was beginning to fall, and the private dining room filled with soft shadows that mingled with the warm glow of candlelight.

Pia took the folder of letters into her lap and began to read, one by one, as Davide, maintaining a forced calm, turned his attention to the cheeses and the wine. Each word on the page seemed to reach across time, echoing from the past to fill the hollow spaces of the years lost between them.

Pia, though she tried to maintain her composure, couldn't stop a few tears from sliding silently down her cheeks.

—They're beautiful, Davide —Pia said at last, breaking the silence that had only been interrupted by the occasional clink of glasses. But I wonder… why did you never send them to me?

Davide, who had been slowly rotating the glass of grappa between his hands, looked at her with a mixture of melancholy and regret.

—Because I didn't think they were enough —he replied, with a sincerity that seemed to ache within him.

Pia said nothing more. She dove back into the letters, accompanying each line with small sips of wine, while the grappa remained untouched in her glass, waiting for the moment when both of them might feel ready to face the ghosts still lingering between them.

The night moved slowly, wrapping them in an intimacy that not even time or distance had managed to break. Outside, the mountains of Agordo were covered in stars, as if they, too, wanted to witness what, in that small corner of the restaurant, was beginning to write itself between two souls that had never stopped searching for each other.

After a few moments, Pia called out:

—Umberto, would you come here for a moment, please?—she said, lifting her hand slightly. Her voice, though soft, carried a note of resolve.

Umberto, who had been adjusting some glasses at a nearby table, approached with that warm smile that seemed woven into his very being.

—Yes, signorina, how can I help you?—he asked, his tone courteous and light.

—I've eaten and drunk so much I'm not even sure I can walk after this —Pia said, with a fleeting smile that, for an instant, lit up her entire face. So I'd rather just keep eating. Could you bring me a panna cotta and a tiramisù?

Umberto let out a soft laugh, nodding with a kind complicity that suited him well.

—An excellent choice, signorina. The finest desserts to end an evening like this. I'll bring them right away.

As Umberto turned and headed back toward the kitchen, Davide stopped him briefly with a quiet request:

—Umberto, could you speak with Hildegarde and ask her to reserve a double room for me?—he said, in a low, almost confidential tone. Then, with a faint but tired smile, he added—. And I'll need you to drive me. Honestly, I'm in no condition to be behind the wheel. When we're ready to leave, I'll let you know.

—Of course, Davide. No problem. I'll talk to Hildegarde right away. Just let me know when you're ready, Umberto said, giving him a light pat on the shoulder before walking away with the same effortless grace with which he had arrived.

Once they were alone again, Pia turned toward Davide with a look that blended exhaustion with brutal honesty.

—Don't get your hopes up tonight, Davide —she said, her tone firm, though not unkind. Besides, I'm in no condition to make any decisions right now.

Davide met her gaze calmly, showing no surprise or discomfort. Then, with the poise of a gentleman, he replied:

—Pia, I'm not here to ask for anything, nor to expect anything from you. I just want tonight to be what it must be —a conversation between two people who share a long history and many wounds. Nothing more. Whatever else comes… will come when it's meant to, or it won't come at all.

For a long moment, silence fell over them once again. But this time, it wasn't an uncomfortable silence —it was meaningful, profound, full of everything that still pulsed quietly between them without the need for words.

Shadows of Jealousy Beneath the Dolomites Peaks III

Hidden in the shadows, Giacomo watched as Pia and Davide prepared to leave the restaurant. Anxiety took hold as he remembered that his Fiat 500 barely had enough gas to keep up the pursuit. Heart pounding, he slipped back to his car—only to see the couple, accompanied by Umberto, stepping into a black BMW X6. He tried to start the engine, but it didn't respond with the speed he needed, and soon the taillights of the BMW vanished into the distance.

Frustration consumed him. He slammed the steering wheel with both palms, his breath forming clouds in the freezing air. His reddened eyes and dripping nose bore witness to the harsh cold. A wave of abandonment and despair washed over him, bringing him to the brink of tears.

Minutes later, to his surprise, Umberto returned alone to the restaurant, parking the BMW in the same spot. Seizing the opportunity, Giacomo approached with determination and confronted him, demanding to know Pia and Davide's whereabouts. Umberto, taken aback by Giacomo's disheveled appearance, mistook him for a gypsy and chose to ignore him, turning away and hastening his steps.

Umberto's indifference lit a fuse inside Giacomo. Without a word, he attacked him from behind; Umberto fell to the ground with a dull thud as Giacomo threw himself on top of him, knocking the air out of his lungs and keeping him from crying out for help. With trembling hands, Giacomo pulled a knife from his trench coat and pressed the blade to Umberto's neck, leaving a thin cut that was beaded with blood. He held him tightly, demanding answers that the stunned and dazed Umberto couldn't give. Giacomo's frustration culminated in a brutal blow to the head with his elbow, leaving Umberto's face buried in the cold pavement, while the starry night of Agordo bore silent witness to the unraveling of a man consumed by jealousy.

Some diners exiting the restaurant screamed at the sight, while others, hands shaking, pulled out their phones to record the scene. Realizing he had been seen, Giacomo fled in haste, his footsteps echoing in the quiet night. Tourists and restaurant staff rushed to Umberto's side, who lay wounded on the ground. Minutes later, the Carabinieri arrived, but no one could identify Giacomo—he had vanished into the shadows, like a specter fading into the dusk.

With the little strength he had left, Umberto began to question the influence Pia might have had over Davide. For a moment, doubt took root in his mind, wondering if she might somehow be a bad influence on his friend. He tried to reach for his phone, but the screen was completely shattered, and just as he attempted to call the hotel to warn Davide, darkness overtook him and he lost consciousness.

Since the victim could not give a statement, the police initially assumed it was an armed robbery. However, the restaurant employees informed the Carabinieri that the area was extremely safe and had never seen a similar incident. Outside the major cities, the Dolomites region was known for its tranquility; most court cases were civil, not criminal.

As an ambulance transported Umberto to the emergency room at Agordo Hospital, about twenty minutes from the restaurant, Giacomo resolved the fuel issue and drove aimlessly until he reached Santa Giustina, a small town in Veneto. There, he found the Piazza dell'Angelo, a picturesque square surrounded by historic buildings with warm-colored facades and balconies blooming with flowers. At its center stood a carved stone fountain depicting an angel, the symbol of the town, and wooden benches invited passersby to rest under the shade of leafy trees.

In one corner of the square, a rustic pizzeria was about to close. Warmly lit, the space featured a dark wood counter and walls adorned with old photographs of the region. Few patrons remained inside—some drinking beer, others absorbed in electronic gambling machines flickering with intermittent lights.

Giacomo's entrance did not go unnoticed; all eyes turned toward him, instantly recognizing him as an outsider. Without stopping, he headed straight to the bathroom to freshen up. In the mirror, his reflection revealed the toll of the day: a haggard face, wrinkled clothes, and sweat stains. He hadn't eaten all day. He felt dehydrated, and a sharp headache throbbed in his skull. An inner voice whispered that he was losing control.

Determined to regain his strength, Giacomo ordered a spicy gorgonzola and speck pizza. It arrived steaming, with a golden, crispy crust, generously topped with melted gorgonzola whose bold, slightly spicy flavor was perfectly balanced by thin slices of speck—a smoked and cured ham from Alto Adige that lent smoky, salty notes. To accompany the meal, he chose a Hefeweizen—a cloudy, golden German wheat beer with a thick, creamy head and aromas of banana and clove, the product of special yeast fermentation.

As he ate, Giacomo began running mental calculations. Considering the time elapsed and speed limits, he deduced that Umberto could not have taken Pia and Davide more than 50 kilometers from the restaurant. This realization led him to plan a return to Agordo, hoping to find Pia again and resolve the torment gnawing at him.

Immersed in introspection, Giacomo barely acknowledged the waitress's attempts at conversation, remaining withdrawn. His drawn face reflected in his phone screen as he booked a room at a nearby hotel. He knew he faced a twenty-minute drive to the establishment on Via Don Minzoni in Belluno.

As he drove along the SP1 road, the imposing silhouette of a moose emerged from the shadows, forcing him to brake sharply. The majestic animal, its antlers branching like roots toward the sky, stared at him—or so Giacomo believed. In that instant, he remembered Franco and Professor Sequera; the voices of his conscience took form: Franco's temptation in his tone, and Sequera's reason in his words. With his heart still racing, he resumed the drive to Belluno.

Upon arriving at the hotel—a chalet-style building with wooden balconies adorned with geraniums—he was greeted by a soft glow that gave the place a welcoming atmosphere.

The assigned room was simple yet comfortable: a polished wooden bed with pristine white sheets, a nightstand with a beige-shaded lamp, and a window that offered a view of the surrounding mountains, their snow-capped peaks glistening under the moonlight. The bathroom, lined with cream-colored tiles, featured a transparent glass shower, a white porcelain sink, and a wide mirror that reflected the warm light from the fixture above.

After freshening up and changing his clothes, Giacomo let himself fall onto the bed, lost in thoughts that drifted between guilt and hope, while the silence of the night wrapped itself around the hotel.

Under the Shadows of the Dolomites Towers IV

Upon arriving at the hotel, Pia held the folder with the letters firmly, as if they were an anchor in the midst of the emotional storm she was going through. At the reception, Hildegarde awaited them, an Austrian woman with blonde hair and light-colored eyes, whose warm smile contrasted with the cold, starry night.

The hotel, nestled in the heart of the Dolomites, combined Alpine elegance with modern comfort. Its dark wood facade and balconies adorned with seasonal flowers evoked Tyrolean tradition, while inside, the minimalist decor and large windows allowed the majesty of the mountain landscape to integrate with the common areas.

Hildegarde led them to the main suite, known for offering the best views of the valley. Upon entering, a cozy atmosphere enveloped them: light wood-paneled walls, a lit stone fireplace casting dancing shadows, and a king-size bed covered with feather duvets. But the most impressive feature was the picture window that occupied the entire front wall, revealing a private balcony from where one could contemplate the night sky, dotted with stars that shone with unusual intensity, thanks to the purity of the mountain air.

Davide, anticipating Pia's needs, had prepared a suitcase with clothes for her: silk pajamas in pastel shades, plush slippers, delicate lace underwear, a new toothbrush, and a couple of lipsticks in the colors he knew she preferred. Each item and object reflected his attention to detail and his desire to provide her comfort.

Furthermore, Umberto, always attentive, had prepared a selection of delicacies for the evening. In a wicker basket, carefully wrapped, he had placed a freshly baked baguette, crispy grissini, thin slices of cured ham, and a generous piece of Piave Vecchio cheese, known for its intense and slightly fruity flavor. Alongside these delicacies, a bottle of red wine stood out: a Pinot Nero from the Alto Adige region, 2015 vintage. This wine, recognized for its elegance and complexity, offered notes of ripe cherry, raspberry, and a subtle spicy touch, perfectly complementing the selection of cheeses and cold cuts. Umberto did not forget to include a cheese knife, two porcelain plates, and a pair of fine crystal glasses, ensuring everything was ready for an intimate and memorable evening.

The combination of Hildegarde's warm hospitality, Davide's meticulous preparation, and Umberto's generosity created a conducive atmosphere for Pia and Davide to share, reflect, and perhaps find a path towards reconciliation under the starry mantle of the Dolomites.

The night advanced with its starry mantle, while Pia, absorbed in reading the letters, deciphered every word Davide had poured into them. Their voices, previously laden with reproaches and silences, now flowed in a conversation tinged with understanding and nostalgia. The red wine filled the glasses, and the delicacies prepared by Umberto became silent accomplices to that reunion.

As the hours slipped by, the light of dawn began to creep over the horizon, tinting the sky with soft hues. Tiredness, inevitable, overcame them. Without a word, their bodies sought refuge in an embrace that seemed to defy time and distance. In that instant, the universe seemed to conspire to reunite them once more, and, surrendering to sleep, they let themselves be carried away by the magic of that reunion, sleeping for several hours in the serenity of each other's company.

The Name Written in Water

Giacomo, consumed by anxiety and insomnia, rose long before dawn broke the sky. With trembling hands, he dressed and took the wheel, driving toward Agordo. Yet in his chest weighed a silent call, and as he crossed the center of Belluno, something stopped him. He advanced along Via Monte Grappa until the Ponte della Vittoria caught him in its spell of stone and water. There, where the Piave River whispered secrets of the moon and stars, Giacomo stepped out of the car and walked to the edge, as if led by a fever dream. The railing, standing like a geometric chant, carved crosses and Xs between its stone blocks, guardians of the abyss.

The river danced in its bed, reflecting the firmament with silver glimmers, while Belluno slept in the distance under the starry veil. Possessed by a fierce impulse, Giacomo climbed halfway up the railing, planting his feet on the horizontal crosses like a tightrope walker of fate. He pivoted his feet precisely, forming angles that defied logic, and with his body leaning toward the abyss, opened his arms in a triumphant gesture. Then, with a cry that shattered the night's stillness, he proclaimed: —Pia, you are mine!—

The echo of his words merged with the murmur of the river, traveling toward the city like an eternal oath, while the stars seemed to flicker in disapproval from an unfathomable sky.

Energized by the autumn's icy winds, Giacomo resumed his course toward Agordo with the irrational idea of rescuing Pia. Upon arrival, he found the town cloaked in mist, as if the earth itself tried to hide its secrets. At one of the roundabouts, he spotted a police car on the opposite side of the bridge that crossed the Cordévole stream. Driven by instinct, he veered off course; instead of continuing along the SP347, he left the roundabout and took Via Campagna, heading toward Taibon Agordino, planning to rejoin his original route later.

Upon reaching Canale d'Agordo, he saw Davide's car parked along Via XX Agosto. At that instant, the fog began to slowly retreat, as if responding to the solemn march of the sun. It was almost theatrical: the mist dissolved in slow motion, like the red curtains of La Scala rising, unveiling the bare edges of the road and the unmistakable signs of the season. Nature, indifferent to human drama, seemed to fall silent before what was about to unfold.

Noting that the white Porsche remained unmoved, Giacomo parked his Fiat at a prudent distance. With measured steps, he approached Davide's sports car, circling it with a knife in hand, carving a deep gouge into the paint. Through the glass, his gaze landed on a winter hat he recognized as Pia's—and that vision ignited an uncontrollable rage in him.

In the misaligned labyrinth of the universe, Giacomo is a man who has lost the thread of Ariadne that once gave meaning to his existence. Without Pia, his life unfurls like a map without north, a blank scroll where neither time nor space offers an anchor. The absence of Pia is not just the absence of a love, but the loss of a mirror in which to recognize himself, of a cardinal point that once ordered his days.

Giacomo walks among shadows cast by his own uncertainty, trapped in the mirage of a past that refuses to die, like a ghost whispering his name down the corridors of memory.

In his obstinate denial, Giacomo defies the logic of the cosmos—that endless river that flows toward nothingness and yet contains everything. But Giacomo does not know how to flow. He clings to the riverbanks of memory, to the scattered fragments of a happiness that, like ancient Gnostic manuscripts, seems to contain the key to a truth he can no longer decipher.

The loss of Pia is not just an event; it is a labyrinth he cannot escape, a defeat that, in its complexity, resembles eternity.

To Giacomo, the universe is no longer the infinite game spoken of by the ancients, but a vacant board, a battlefield where movement has ceased and victory is impossible. The idea of accepting absence, of finding meaning in the relentless flow of days, is intolerable. Instead of becoming the wise man who embraces the current, Giacomo has become the man who tries to stop the river with his hands—who refuses to accept that permanence is an illusion, and that Pia is now a name written in water.

Giacomo is the creator of his own labyrinth, an expert in mirages who has lost sight of the fact that the core of the labyrinth is not the answer, but the silence. In resisting change, he has fused pain with truth, longing with destiny, and lost love with the entire universe.

In that constant displacement, Giacomo does not understand that the labyrinth has no walls, that its entrances are infinite as the stars, and that the river of life, regardless of his suffering, continues its course toward forgetfulness.

Perhaps, one day, Pia and he will never again meet in a dream. And if they do, time may wash it all away.

Trilogy of the Soul: Accept, Adapt, Advance

Davide opened his eyes around noon, when the sun's rays pierced forcefully through the curtains, bathing the room in a golden glow that seemed to want to wrest secrets from the shadows. He sat up in silence, as if afraid to disturb the stillness of the moment, and settled into an armchair in the corner of the room. It was a discreet piece of furniture, with a cushion embroidered with a melancholic phrase: — Love never fails.— From there, his gaze rested on Pia, still asleep, wearing that deceptive calm that only the exhaustion from an emotional storm can bring. He observed her with the intensity of a scanner, but his thoughts went beyond the visible: Pia is trapped in the syndrome of the passage of time, he told himself. Beautiful, yes, but carrying the weight of the days in every line whispered by her skin.

Driven by the urge to freeze that moment, he picked up his phone to capture her in a photograph, but the device was completely dead, as useless as his intention to hold onto something so fleeting. Resigned, he got up and went to the shower, letting the water wash away the last remnants of sleep. When he came out, ready and refreshed, he met Pia's half-open eyes, who greeted him with a sweet gaze, heavy with fragility, and a smile that seemed at once a refuge and a plea.

—Good morning, Pia,— Davide said, breaking the silence.

—Morning...— she replied, her voice a broken whisper. —Tell me this has all been a bad dream, Davide. I feel... swollen from crying so much.—

Her words, a mixture of vulnerability and exhaustion, slipped between them like an echo. Before Davide could respond, she added with a slight gesture of tenderness:

—Please, I need a cappuccino... and a painkiller.—

Davide nodded without hesitation.

—I'll go get them right away,— he said, with that mixture of decisiveness and care that characterized him.

Davide returned shortly after, carrying a cappuccino that gave off a warm aroma, a glass of crystal-clear water, and a couple of pills that he carefully placed on the nightstand. While Pia was getting ready in the bathroom, the muffled sounds of water and drawers sketched the quiet ritual of someone trying to piece themselves together after a storm. From the other side of the door, his voice crossed the space with calm:

—I'm going down to talk to Hildegarde. Have her charge the phones and arrange transport for us back to Umberto's restaurant.—

Pia answered with a barely audible murmur, but Davide no longer expected confirmation. He had learned that, in moments like these, gestures mattered more than words, and that caring for Pia was his way of fighting against the shadows that still surrounded them.

Davide returned to the room shortly after, but this time he knocked softly on the door, as if afraid of shattering the fragile equilibrium of the moment. When Pia opened it, she found him standing there, arms outstretched, holding a small bouquet of half a dozen red roses, fresh and radiant, as if they had been plucked from a dream. Pia, still distant, accepted them with a faint smile that concealed the echo of sadness lingering in her heart. She approached Davide, hugging him with a slow, tender sweetness, and left a light kiss on his cheek.

—Thank you, my Davide. You haven't lost the details that make you unique,— she said, her voice carrying a melancholic gratitude.

He offered a discreet smile and replied with serenity:

—Some things should never be lost.—

Davide broke the brief silence with a practical tone that contrasted with the tenderness of the moment:

—A chauffeur will come for us in a couple of hours. I think we can pack calmly and eat something before leaving. What do you think?—

Pia nodded, playing with the petals of one of the roses.

—Sounds good to me. That gives me time to write a little before we go. I'm almost ready; I'll gather my things and we'll go down right away.—

The hotel restaurant welcomed them like a warm refuge on an autumn midday. It was an elegant yet discreet space, with large windows that let in natural light, illuminating the tables covered with impeccable linen tablecloths. The high ceilings, adorned with dark wood beams, and the wrought iron lamps evoked a cozy atmosphere, almost like a scene taken from an old book. The walls were decorated with paintings of Alpine landscapes, and in the background, a lit fireplace added a touch of intimacy that seemed to contradict the vastness of the space.

Salvatore, the chef, an old acquaintance of Davide's, greeted them at the entrance with a warm smile and an energetic handshake. He assigned them a table next to one of the windows, from where they could admire a view that looked as if it had been plucked from a postcard. The mountains in the distance, imposing and majestic, were covered with the first autumn snows, while the valley shimmered with the golden and coppery hues of the trees in transition. Closer to them, a stream meandered among the stones, reflecting flashes of sunlight that danced as if they had a life of their own.

—What can I offer you today?— Salvatore asked, his voice laden with the familiarity of old friends.

Davide, still recovering from the excesses of the night before, answered with a smile:

—Something light, Salvatore. Yesterday we ate and drank more than enough.—

The chef tilted his head slightly, thoughtful, and after a moment proposed:

—How about a roast chicken with rosemary potatoes, accompanied by a fresh lettuce salad with olive oil and a touch of lemon? As a starter, I could prepare some grilled eggplants and peppers, dressed with a drizzle of extra virgin olive oil and fresh herbs.—

Davide's eyes shone with approval, but it was Pia who, with a contagious smile, suddenly interrupted:

—Perfect. But we also want two bottles of San Pellegrino, please.—

Salvatore nodded, amused, and added:

—To drink, I'll bring you half a liter of our house wine. It's a young red with fruity notes that balance its acidity—perfect to accompany something light.—

While they waited for the food, Pia took out her diary and began to write with the calm of someone who finds refuge in words. She headed the page with the date: — Saturday, October 29.— Davide, sitting across from her, watched her in silence, amused by the way she slightly frowned whenever something made her hesitate. Nothing had been mentioned about what had happened the day before; it seemed that, without needing words, they had sealed a tacit pact of truce.

The silence between them wasn't awkward, but laden with meanings. In each pause, in every slight rustle of the pen on the paper, there seemed to be a promise: that of a new beginning that still dared not speak its name.

Salvatore returned to the table with a satisfied gesture, carrying a plate that looked like a work of culinary art. The roast chicken, golden with a perfection that could only be achieved through patience and mastery, gave off an enveloping aroma of fresh herbs and rosemary, mingling with subtle notes of garlic and lemon. The skin was crispy, a perfect contrast to the tender and juicy meat, which promised to melt in the mouth at the first bite. The potatoes, arranged alongside it as if part of a naturalistic painting, had a golden and crispy exterior, while the inside was a creamy purée that melted upon contact with the palate.

Salvatore placed the plate on the table with the ceremony of an artisan displaying his masterpiece.

—I hope you enjoy it. It's a simple dish, but simplicity is also an art, don't you think?— he said with a smile as he served the house wine into their glasses.

Pia put down her pen and closed the diary with an elegant movement. She looked up toward Davide and then toward Salvatore.

—Perfect timing,— Pia said with a smile that lit up her face. —I just finished writing.—

Davide nodded with a discreet smile as he picked up his wine glass.

—Enjoy your meal, Pia. May this dish be as memorable as this day,— he said, lightly raising the glass toward her.

Pia followed suit, with a slight gesture of gratitude in her eyes.

—Salvatore, this aroma is wonderful. I can already tell it will be one of those unforgettable dishes,— Pia commented as she cut the first piece of chicken. Upon tasting it, she closed her eyes and let the flavors flood her senses.

—It's magnificent. The crispy skin, the meat so juicy... and the potatoes... are the perfect combination,— she added, turning her gaze back to Salvatore with a gesture of genuine admiration.

Salvatore, pleased, bowed his head in a humble gesture.

—The secret, signorina, is not in complicating the ingredients, but in treating them with respect. Now, enjoy yourselves, and I will return later to make sure everything is to your liking.—

As Salvatore walked away, Pia and Davide immersed themselves in the feast, letting the moment fill with flavors, shared silences, and the promise that, at least for an instant, the world seemed to be in perfect balance.

Pia's Journal

Saturday, October 29, 2022.

Ah, the triple A, that triptych that whispers into our ears the wisdom of navigating the labyrinths of destiny. Accept, adapt, advance: three verbs that are conjugated within the infinite verb of being.

In the universe, where time flows like a river and reality unfolds into a thousand and one stories, suffering is nothing more than the imprint of our stubborn refusal to accept fate, to dance to the rhythm of life with its joys and sorrows. Wisdom, on the other hand, is the secret kept in the hearts of the elders, the magic recipe that allows us to sail through the turbulent waters of existence with the serenity of a boatman who knows the tides and the whims of the wind.

To accept *is like letting oneself be carried away by the current of the Po River, trusting that its waters will lead us toward the Adriatic, even if along the way we encounter whirlpools and waterfalls. It is understanding that life is a one-way journey, a carnival of dreams and disappointments, and that only those who dare to dance in the rain will discover the hidden beauty in every moment.*

To adapt *is like the chameleon that changes its color to blend into the jungle; it is the ability to transform oneself to survive in a world full of dangers and wonders. It is learning to read the secret language of nature, to decipher the messages sent to us by the birds and the stars. It is letting oneself be carried by the wind like a cotton seed, without resisting the whims of fate.*

To advance *is like the journey of a hero. General Armando Díaz walked a path full of battles in the Veneto* *and broken dreams, but also of unattainable affections and moments of grace. It is to keep moving forward despite adversities, with the hope of finding meaning in our existence amidst the chaos. It is understanding that life is a story written with invisible ink, and that only at the end of the road will we be able to read its true meaning.*

Umberto

The chauffeur picked them up at the threshold of the hotel, and as the vehicle advanced along the winding mountain roads, silence filled the space between them, broken only by the whisper of the engine and the murmur of the wind caressing the dry leaves.

Davide, with his phone in hand, tried to listen to the voicemails piling up in his inbox, but the signal, weak and capricious, refused to cooperate. With a resigned sigh, he set the device aside and turned his gaze back to Pia.

She sat absorbed, lost in the landscape unfurling beyond the window: rocky mountains rising like sentinels of time, cliffs seemingly carved by the patient hand of eternity, streams and waterfalls dancing to the rhythm of their own murmur, winding brooks reflecting the sky, and crags scattered with scorched autumn leaves, flung at random by the wind. Above it all stretched an intense blue sky, while the sun gained ground against the snow that stubbornly resisted, a last vestige of winter refusing to die.

Davide broke the silence, his voice soft, as if afraid to disturb Pia's thoughts.

—Are you okay, Pia?—

She didn't take her eyes off the landscape, but her answer came clear and serene.

—Yes,— she said, almost in a whisper, her gaze continuing to roam every corner of the world before them. —I'm remembering our first trip to the Dolomites.—

After a pause, Pia turned her head toward him. Her glasses, now holding back her hair, gave her an air of spontaneity that contrasted with the depth in her eyes. She observed Davide intently, as if searching for something within him, and offered a smile that ended with a barely audible sigh. Then she pressed her lips together, as if holding back words she didn't dare to speak.

In that moment, tenderness filled the air like a warm breeze in the midst of autumn. Pia raised her hand and slid it beneath Davide's, intertwining their fingers in a gesture that spoke louder than any words. Davide, feeling the warmth of her touch, needed no words. Between them, the landscape became a mere backdrop; the true journey was happening there, in the shared silence, in the touch of their hands, in the weight of memories, and in the unspoken promise of what was yet to come.

When they arrived at the restaurant, the car braked gently by the curb. Davide noticed a disheveled man sitting on the sidewalk, his gaze lost at some invisible point on the horizon. For an instant, their eyes met, and something about that face struck a vague chord, like an image trapped in a half-forgotten dream. Yet before he could search his memory further, the chauffeur interrupted.

—Here, sir?—the driver asked, turning his head toward Davide.

—A little farther ahead, please, where the white car is— Davide replied, signaling briefly as he refocused on the present moment.

The car rolled forward a few more meters and stopped. Pia was the first to step out, and her gaze immediately fell upon the vehicle parked in front of them.

Something about the paintwork caught her attention. She walked toward it, her brow slightly furrowed, examining the scratches that scored the bodywork like scars on wounded skin.

—Could they have already been there when he picked me up in Padua?— she wondered, tracing the marks with her fingers. But when she looked at the hood, her thoughts froze. Rough, aggressive letters screamed from the white paint: "*DIE.*"

—Davide!— she exclaimed, her voice ringing out with a mixture of alarm and confusion.

Davide, busy at that moment paying the chauffeur, quickly looked up. On his arm hung the basket Umberto had prepared for them, and in his other hand he held his briefcase and carry-on. Hearing Pia's tone, he dropped everything and looked over the roof of the car. What he saw made him stop short: the word scrawled across the hood and Pia's face — a mixture of fear and confusion that pierced his heart.

Before he could react, the restaurant doors burst open, and two women — Giuseppina and Lucia — hurried out toward him. Their steps were firm, almost aggressive, and their gazes were loaded with reproach. Even the chauffeur, intrigued, stepped out of the car and cautiously observed the scene.

—Davide, this is a disgrace,— Giuseppina said, her voice tight with suppressed anger.

Lucia, younger but just as furious, looked him up and down before whispering:

—It's Umberto… They found him beaten last night, nearby. He's in the hospital, under observation. Davide blinked, incredulous.

—Umberto? Beaten?— he repeated, as if the words made no sense at all. Giuseppina leaned in closer, lowering her voice even further.

—Some think it has to do with… her,— she said, casting a quick glance toward Pia, who still stood by the car, motionless, absorbed by the words slashed into the hood.

The air grew heavy with tension. Davide felt the tourists and locals beginning to stop, drawn by the low murmur of the scene. He knew he had to react quickly.

—Giuseppina, don't drag Pia into this,— he said firmly, even though his mind was still racing to grasp the gravity of what he had just heard. — Tell me exactly what happened.

But before the woman could respond, Davide turned toward Pia, who remained rooted to the spot, staring at the letters. Her face mirrored conflicting emotions: fear, confusion, and a growing doubt that seemed to fracture the invisible connection between them.

—Davide…— she murmured, her voice barely audible. —Why would someone want to do this to you?— He tried to approach, but she stepped back, as if she needed distance to process what was happening.

—Pia, I don't know who did this, but I swear to you — it has nothing to do with me, Davide said, his voice urgent, as if trying to smother a fire before it consumed them.

She stared at him, searching his eyes for a truth that his words couldn't guarantee.

—What kind of person are you, Davide?— she finally asked, her voice trembling, thick with a suspicion he had never seen in her before. —What kind of life are you leading that someone would want you... gone?—

Davide felt the weight of her words hit him like a blow to the chest. He knew this wasn't the time or place for lengthy explanations, but he also knew he couldn't let Pia's doubts grow.

—Pia, trust me. This isn't what it looks like. I have nothing to do with what you're imagining, he replied, but even he could hear the uncertainty in his own voice.

Meanwhile, the murmurs of the curious crowd grew louder. Giuseppina and Lucia stepped back, leaving Davide alone to face the brewing storm. In Pia's mind, unanswered questions and unfounded suspicions began to weave a veil of uncertainty, pushing her farther and farther from the trust she had once placed in him.

The murmurs mixed with the growing roar of an engine that seemed to tear through the air. People scattered toward the edges of the street like leaves swept by a violent gust of wind. The sound was chaotic, furious, approaching with an intensity that chilled the blood.

Davide, still at the center of it all, felt time stretch out — every second becoming an endless echo. He turned toward the source of the noise, and in that instant, he saw it: the red car was speeding toward them, and behind the wheel was the disheveled man he had seen moments before.

Everything seemed to unfold in slow motion. Pia, knocked down by the panic of the crowd, struggled to get up, unable to decipher the shouting around her. Giuseppina and Lucia, frozen in the doorway, stood paralyzed as Davide and a small boy, no older than six, stood stranded in the middle of the street — motionless, trapped as if in a painting.

Davide's eyes locked onto the driver's. This time, the man's face was partially hidden behind dark sunglasses and a black beret. When the car was only a few meters away, Davide sprang into action. In one instinctive, precise movement, he grabbed the child by the waist, lifted him, and dove sideways, twisting his body in the air so the impact against the pavement would fall on him, not the boy.

The car accelerated and vanished among the streets of the town, leaving behind a brief silence, broken only by gasps and murmurs from the witnesses.

Pia scrambled to her feet and ran toward Davide, her heart frozen with terror.

—Davide! Davide!— she cried, tears streaming down her face.

The child's mother — a young blonde woman with American features — rushed over almost simultaneously, kneeling beside her son and inspecting him frantically.

—Sam! Are you okay?— she asked, hugging him tightly and checking him from head to toe. —Say something, baby!—

The boy, still trembling, looked at her and nodded, his voice broken but firm.

—I'm okay, Mom… he saved me.

The mother, her eyes brimming with tears, turned to Davide, who still lay on the ground.

—Thank you… Thank you for saving him, she said in heavily accented English, her words soaked in emotion.

Meanwhile, Pia knelt beside Davide, placing a hand on his neck to check if he was breathing.

—Davide, please… Say something,— she pleaded, tears falling onto him.

Davide opened his eyes slowly, then shut them again. Pia, desperate, leaned closer, hugging him and pressing a trembling kiss to his lips.

That was when Davide smiled — a mischievous, boyish smile that lit up his face.

—Pia… it hurts a lot,— he whispered, weak but playful. —I think another kiss would help.—

Pia, laughing through her tears, shook her head in relief.

—You fool… You scared me so much,— she whispered, brushing away her tears with the back of her hand.

Still lying on the ground, Davide lifted a hand weakly.

—We have to go see Umberto…— he said, now serious.

Pia nodded, helping him to his feet as the curious crowd slowly dispersed. Giuseppina and Lucia returned, crossing their arms as they watched Davide with concern.

—Davide, this can't be a coincidence,— Giuseppina said in a conspiratorial tone. —Maybe it was the same guy who attacked Umberto.— Lucia nodded.

—Yeah, too many coincidences… you need to be careful, Davide.—

The boy's mother, still clutching her son, turned to Davide once again.

—Thank you… again. I don't know how to repay you. Sam is alive because of you.— Davide, with effort, smiled and nodded.

—Just make sure he's okay. That's enough.—

With Pia's help, Davide got back into the car, while the golden autumn sunlight bathed the village in a warm, deceptive peace. He settled into the passenger seat and looked at Pia.

—Let's go to the hospital… We need to know how Umberto's doing. Pia nodded, took the wheel, and without a word, drove off toward Agordo Hospital, leaving behind the chaos of the village and carrying with them more questions than answers.

At the hospital, Umberto wasn't allowed visitors and was under observation in the ICU. He was responding well, but the doctors wanted to rule out any possible brain injury from the blow. Davide asked Umberto's wife to keep him informed of any developments.

Via Tito Livio Burattini

The fall had left its mark on Davide. His pants and jacket, torn, now bore the stains of earth and asphalt. As they climbed into the car, Davide glanced at the dirt on his clothes and sighed, his tone tired but resolute.

—Pia, I need to change. Let's go to my apartment in Belluno before we head to file the report.

Pia nodded silently and started the car. The journey, usually serene, was wrapped in an uncomfortable silence that seemed to stretch with every kilometer. The events of the day had shattered the spell of the morning, and both were trapped in their thoughts. Finally, Davide broke the silence, his voice firm, as if he had unearthed something lost deep in his memory.

—Basilica of Saint Anthony of Padua.—

Pia glanced at him sideways, puzzled.

—What a fright, Davide. What about the basilica?—

Davide took a deep breath before answering.

—That's where I saw the man who tried to run us over. I also saw him when we were getting to the car this morning, sitting nearby, but I didn't pay him any attention between paying the chauffeur and handling the bags.

Pia frowned, and her mind drifted back to a day she had tried to bury deep in her memory.

—Are you talking about Dad's funeral?—

—Yes, exactly,— Davide answered, his tone heavy with unsettling certainty. —He was there, among the crowd. I don't know who he is, but I remember his face perfectly.

Pia, visibly shaken, remained silent while the GPS guided them through the streets from the SP203 toward Belluno.

Belluno, with its history seemingly written in stone and air, welcomed them with its usual discreet splendor. Its streets wound between ochre-toned buildings and terracotta rooftops that glowed under the soft light of the streetlamps. They passed through Piazza dei Martiri, where time seemed to have come to a halt, and turned onto Via Mezzaterra, a picturesque street lined with small shops and balconies adorned with flowers now withered by autumn. Finally, the GPS led them to Via Tito Livio Burattini, where Davide's apartment was located.

Upon arriving, they climbed to the top floor, and Pia was struck by the spaciousness of the place. Davide's apartment was a blend of modernity and warmth, with polished wooden floors and large windows that offered a spectacular view of the mountains they had left behind. The kitchen, impeccably outfitted, looked like something from a design catalog: stainless steel appliances, white marble countertops, and soft lighting that highlighted its functionality. Every corner spoke of meticulous order, a life carefully built.

Exhausted but determined, Davide dropped his things to the side and headed for the bathroom. —Make yourself at home, Pia,— he said before closing the door behind him.

Pia took the half-dozen roses they had brought and began searching for a vase. As she wandered through the apartment, something in the living room caught her attention: a framed photograph of her and Davide, taken at the Eiffel Tower. The image made her pause. She took it into her hands and, with the photo still in hand, stepped out onto the balcony.

The universe seemed to dance before her. The waning crescent moon and the stars sparkled in a clear sky. In the distance, the mountains seemed to whisper stories, their snowcapped peaks standing firm against the sun's fading battle. Pia let the cold wind envelop her for a moment before returning inside.

As she moved through the apartment, she was surprised to notice that pictures of her still occupied visible places. There was something strange about it, something that made her think Davide didn't share his space with anyone else, despite how organized and comfortable everything looked.

One particular photo captured her attention. It was a recent image, perhaps taken a couple of years ago, where Lucien, Nicoletta, herself, and Giacomo appeared — though Giacomo, on closer inspection, seemed not to have been an active participant in the picture.

—Why does he have a recent photo of me?— she murmured to herself.

Driven by curiosity, she began to open the drawers of the cabinet in the living room. Everything was meticulously arranged, without a speck of dust, every object perfectly placed. It was then that Davide appeared behind her, a playful smile on his face.

—Everything okay, Pia?—he asked, startling her slightly. —Yes, sorry. I was... well, just snooping,— she replied, embarrassed, quickly closing a drawer.

Davide chuckled softly. —This is your home, Pia. You can open whatever you like.— She looked at him and, changing the subject quickly, pointed at his shirt. —You're wearing your T-shirt inside out.—

Davide glanced down and laughed.

—I wanted to get dressed quickly; I didn't even notice.— He straightened his shirt in front of her, and that's when Pia noticed something that took her breath away. — My God!—she exclaimed, her hand flying to her mouth. — Have you seen your back?— Davide raised an eyebrow, puzzled. —No, not really. Why?—

Pia stepped closer, concerned, and gently touched the large bruise spreading across his back. —You have a huge bruise... and...— she hesitated for a moment before continuing, —you also have scars.—

Davide, noticing her expression as he turned around, softened his voice. —They're from the past, Pia. Stories that aren't worth telling now—

But Pia couldn't tear her gaze away, her fingers brushing gently over the marks that seemed to speak of ancient pains. In her mind, questions about Davide, his life, and his past multiplied like stars across an endless sky.

The Photograph and Portrait of Giacomo

Pia, worry still reflected on her face, crossed her arms as she watched Davide fix his shirt.

—Davide, before going to file the report, we should stop by the emergency room. That bruise is huge, and we don't know if there could be something more serious.

He shook his head, with a faint smile that tried to reassure her.

—It's not necessary, Pia. My neighbor, Teresa, is an internist. I'll call her on the way and ask her what I should do. If she thinks she needs to see me, we'll stop by here on the way back.

Pia sighed but nodded, realizing she wouldn't get him to change his mind.

—Alright, but make sure you call her. I don't want you to let this go.— Davide placed a hand on her shoulder with a reassuring gesture.

—I will. I promise I won't neglect it.—

With that, they both gathered what they needed and left the apartment, leaving behind the moment of temporary calm as they prepared to face the chaos that awaited them.

On the way to the police station, the initial silence between them was broken by Pia, her voice laden with a mix of curiosity and confusion.

—Davide...— she began, without taking her eyes off the landscape rushing past the window. — In your apartment, I saw a recent photo of me with my parents… and Giacomo. I'd like to know why you have that photo.

Davide kept his hands firm on the steering wheel, but his expression hardened slightly, as if preparing an answer he had rehearsed many times in his mind.

—I always wanted to know about you, Pia,— he finally said, with a sincerity that cut the air. —When Armando moved to Padua, I would occasionally ask him if he had seen you.—

Pia looked at him intently, waiting for him to continue.

—One day, Armando called me and told me he had run into you by chance. I asked him to take a picture of you; I wanted to see you, I wanted to know how you had grown up, what kind of woman you had become. The last time I saw you, you were a teenager, and… I wanted to see that smile I carried with me so much.

Pia smiled softly, although there was a hint of sadness in her eyes.

—I always thought that photo was of you with your parents. I didn't know someone else was there. I never would have kept it if I had known someone else was with you.

The silence between them was filled for a moment with the sound of the engine and the echo of Davide's words. Finally, Pia spoke.

—Yesterday you mentioned that Armando had told you I was in love with a university professor…

Davide nodded slowly, without looking at her.

—Yes. I never thought of interfering in your life. I just wanted to know you were happy, even if you weren't by my side. Seeing you happy comforted me… If it bothered you, I apologize. It wasn't ill-intentioned.—

Pia remained silent for a moment, weighing his words. Finally, she took the photo out of her wallet and held it in her hands as the car stopped in front of the police station.

—He's no longer part of my life, Davide,— she said, her tone firm but gentle. —Giacomo and I… we didn't work out.—

Davide turned his face towards her, but before he could respond, Pia continued.

—Look, here he is,— she said, trying to show him the photo while pointing to Giacomo in the background. — This is Giacomo.—

Davide quickly raised a hand, covering his eyes.

—No. I don't want to see that photo anymore. Pia looked at him in surprise.

—Why not?—

Davide took a deep breath, his voice laden with a mix of sadness and resolve.

—I wouldn't have kept that photo if I had known someone else was by your side. I prefer to remember it as what I always thought it was: an image of you with your parents, nothing more.

Pia put the photo back in her wallet, her fingers nervously playing with the edge of the paper as she spoke.

—Actually, that was Giacomo. Always scattered, always on the margins. He never figured in the important things. My mistake was wanting him to be someone he's not...—

Davide looked at her gently, a contained sadness reflecting in his eyes.

—We all make mistakes, Pia. Sometimes, we simply expect people to fill spaces that aren't made for them.—

Silence filled the car again, but this time it wasn't uncomfortable. It was a moment of mutual understanding, of shared wounds that, although not fully healed, were beginning to scar over.

Finally, Davide turned off the engine and gestured towards the police station.

—Are you ready?—

Pia nodded, adjusting her bag on her shoulder as she got out of the car. They both knew there were things left unsaid, but they also knew that, for now, silence was enough.

The carabinieri station was located in a gray stone building, with a small bronze plaque next to the door inscribed —Stazione dei Carabinieri—. Despite its sober and functional facade, the interior possessed an unexpected warmth, with dark wood furniture contrasting against the light walls. In a corner, a coffee machine emitted a welcoming aroma that competed with the smell of paper and ink pervading the atmosphere. Small Italian flags decorated the main counter, alongside a framed photograph of the President of the Republic and a crucifix hanging discreetly on the wall.

Davide calmly filed the report, describing the damage to the vehicle and the attempted assault with meticulous precision. The officers took notes in silence, with the characteristic efficiency of those who have seen all kinds of incidents. When it came time to give the description of the alleged assailant, one of the carabinieri, a middle-aged man with a well-groomed mustache and an affable demeanor, turned to Pia.

—Signorina, would you like a coffee or tea while you wait?—

Pia, who until that moment had been silent, nodded with a slight smile.

—Tea would be nice, thank you.—

The officer gestured for her to follow him. They walked down a narrow corridor, lit by fluorescent lamps, until they reached a small room with a coffee machine and a tea dispenser. While they waited for the water to boil, the officer started a casual conversation.

—Is he your husband?—he asked, gesturing vaguely towards the area where Davide was still talking with the other officers.

Pia smiled softly, as if the question had taken her by surprise.

—No, he's not… But we've shared many things.— The officer nodded, noticing the tone in her voice.

—It's good to have someone you can trust in times like these. These incidents can be quite difficult.—

—Yes, it is,— Pia replied, looking out the window towards the cobblestone street, as if searching for words to continue.

The whistle of boiling water interrupted the moment, and the officer hurried to prepare the tea.

—Here you go, signorina. I hope this helps you relax a bit.—

—Thank you,— Pia said, accepting the cup with a gesture of gratitude.

When they returned to the main counter, Davide had already finished giving his statement. He turned towards them upon hearing the sound of footsteps and noticed the tea in Pia's hands.

—Everything alright?—he asked, his tone calm but attentive. Pia nodded, taking a sip of tea before answering.

—Yes, everything's fine.—

The officers closed the file with a firm stamp on the documents, and one of them handed a copy to Davide.

—Thank you for your cooperation, sir. If there's anything else we can do, don't hesitate to call us.

Davide nodded and, with a slight nod of thanks, took the copy before heading towards the exit with Pia at his side. As they left the station behind, the cold night air enveloped them, bringing with it a silence heavy with unexpressed thoughts.

Teresa

Upon leaving the police station, Davide dialed Teresa's number from his phone. The call was brief and direct, but carried a warmth that denoted trust. Teresa had insisted he stop by her house so she could check him over before the day ended.

Teresa was a stunning woman, one of those who seemed crafted to draw attention. Her luminous white skin contrasted with her jet-black hair, perfectly straight and tied back in a low ponytail. Her green eyes, intense and almost hypnotic, seemed to capture every detail with a mischievous glint. Her features were fine and delicate, but her bearing conveyed a confidence—and a certain superiority—that did not go unnoticed.

When Davide and Pia arrived, Teresa greeted them at the door with a wide smile that faded slightly upon noticing Pia.

—Davide, darling, come in. And who is…?—she asked, her tone aiming for casual but barely masking a disinterest toward Pia.

Davide didn't let the moment linger.

—Teresa, this is Pia —he said, his voice calm but firm. Meet my eyes, the love of my life.

For a moment, the air in the room seemed to stop. Teresa, who had always suspected Davide spoke of someone special, now had it confirmed. The intensity of his words was irrefutable. However, her expression only softened briefly before returning to her habitual mask.

—Pleasure to meet you, Pia —Teresa said, her smile never quite reaching her eyes.

Pia, though courteous, couldn't ignore the aura of silent competition Teresa seemed to project.

—Thank you for taking care of Davide —she replied, her voice calm, but laden with meaning.

In the small clinic Teresa had set up at home, Davide removed his shirt so she could examine him. Pia watched from a corner, trying not to be affected by what she perceived as blatant flirting.

—Let's have a look at that torso —said Teresa, her hands cold but skillful as they moved over Davide's skin. No fractures, but that bruise is impressive.

As she examined him, Teresa chuckled softly, her hands lingering longer than necessary, at least from Pia's point of view.

—Davide, always so strong, but you really must take better care of yourself. How do you always manage to get into trouble?

Pia pressed her lips together, forcing herself not to react. Finally, Teresa straightened up, removing her gloves.

—I don't believe there's any internal damage. Take some painkillers for the soreness, and keep an eye out for any signs of fever. If anything changes, call me immediately.

Davide nodded, thanking her with a gesture as he got dressed. Pia, for her part, couldn't wait to leave.

Aglio, Olio e Peperoncino

Back at home, they fulfilled what they had agreed upon: cooking together. Davide opened a bottle of Brunello di Montalcino, its robust aroma filling the air as he let it breathe.

The preparation of the spaghetti *aglio, olio e peperoncino* began with almost choreographic precision. Davide took a sharp knife and started slicing the garlic into thin slivers, each one nearly transparent.

—The secret is not to let the garlic burn, just to brown it perfectly —he said, as he moved the slices in a pan with olive oil that shimmered under the warm kitchen light.

Pia, by his side, chopped the parsley into small pieces, her hands working deftly.

—It's amazing how something so simple can be so perfect —she commented as she grated fresh Parmesan over a plate.

The aroma of golden garlic mixed with the subtle spice of the *peperoncino* that Davide added to the pan. Meanwhile, the pasta boiled in a large pot, its al dente texture checked with precision.

Once drained, Davide tossed it into the pan, mixing it with fluid motions so that it absorbed every flavor. Pia sprinkled the freshly chopped parsley over the top, and together they served the plates, adding a final touch of grated cheese.

The spaghetti gleamed under the soft kitchen light, its aromas filling every corner. The first bite was a symphony of flavors: the mellow, caramelized garlic; the perfect hint of heat from the *peperoncino*; the freshness of the parsley; and the depth of the Parmesan cheese.

The wine, a special vintage Brunello di Montalcino, paired perfectly with the dish. Its intense flavor, with notes of dark cherries, leather, and spices, seemed to wrap each sip in a warm and comforting embrace.

Aglio, Olio e Peperoncino

Song to the Earth, to Time, and to the Mystery of Moments That Do Not Return

Although Pia was enjoying the moment, she couldn't ignore how quickly her heart seemed to be opening to Davide —so fast it scared her. Every shared laugh, every synchronized movement in the kitchen, made her feel as if time had never passed, as if they had never been apart.

When they finished eating, Davide, without saying a word, took it upon himself to clean the kitchen and wash the dishes. He did it with a naturalness that seemed to minimize everything that had happened that day.

—Go to the balcony, Pia. Finish your glass out there. I'll join you in a moment —he said as he dried the last plate.

A few minutes later, he appeared with thick blankets draped over his forearm and, in his right hand, a pair of crystal glasses and a bottle of red wine —a Pinero Ca' del Bosco, a liquid poem that wore a light red, like the faint veil of a sunset dissolving into nostalgia. From the glass arose an aroma that burst into a song of red fruits —raspberries and blackberries— like a chorus of tiny hearts beating in the forest, while its perfume was a sweet whisper, a murmur of fallen leaves evoking forgotten stories.

—Let's toast to today —said Davide, filling their glasses and looking into her eyes.

Pia lifted her glass, her heart pounding, while the night's chill and the warmth of the moment seemed to fuse into an instant neither wanted to break.

Tasting it, Davide felt the wine unfold in his mouth like a cautious lover: balanced, serene, with tannins that caressed like the hands of the dawn. For Pia, the finish of the first sip was a long, enveloping embrace —one she didn't want to release. That wine sang to the earth, to time, and to the mystery of moments that never return. A great Pinot Nero, worthy of verses born between the roots and the sky.

Davide invited her to sit on a comfortable sofa placed out on the balcony. From there, the universe unfolded before them. The stars twinkled in the clear sky, and the moon bathed the mountains in a silver light. The snow on the peaks glistened like diamonds, resisting the approaching winter.

Pia leaned gently against Davide's chest, letting his steady breathing set the rhythm of a moment that seemed suspended in time. The faint groan from Davide broke the stillness —barely a murmur of discomfort from the pressure of the sofa's back, from the blow, and from the delicate weight of Pia. She shifted slightly, willing to move away, but Davide's warm, firm hand rested on her arm, stopping her with a gesture that said more than a thousand words.

—Don't move —he whispered, his voice barely a breath that melted into the cold balcony air—. It was just a moment… And even if it hurts, I don't care. I've never felt so alive… nor so grateful.

Pia slowly lifted her head, her gaze seeking his, as if she could decipher some eternal riddle in his eyes. Davide's eyes, dark as a moonless night, received her with a glimmer that seemed to contain all the words they dared not say. He leaned closer, and the universe itself seemed to pause, as if the cosmos wished to witness what was about to happen.

Their faces met halfway, and in that instant, their lips touched —first with the timidity of a sunrise just peeking over the mountains, then with the intensity of a storm that had waited centuries to break free. It was more than a kiss; it was the union of two souls that, after wandering through deserts of absence, finally found their lost homeland —that corner where love becomes absolute and time ceases to exist.

The world around them seemed to vanish. The stars sparkled in the heavens as silent witnesses, and the night wind carried the whisper of distant leaves dancing in the trees. It was as if nature and the entire universe had conspired so that this fragile and perfect moment could exist.

Between their lips, there was not only love but a silent pact —a vow of two hearts promising to keep beating as one, no matter what destiny might have in store.

The Unexpected Visitor

The phone began to ring insistently, shattering the spell that had wrapped them. At first, Davide and Pia ignored it, as if the outside world had no right to intrude on such an intimate moment. But the ringing persisted so relentlessly that, at last, their lips parted, and they looked into each other's eyes. It was a brief instant, enough to be sure that it had not been a dream, that the kiss had been as real as the hearts beating in unison within them.

—Forgive me, Pia —Davide said, caressing her cheek with a tenderness that made her tremble—. This must be important. Let me see who it is.

Pia, still lost in the moment, nodded with a faint smile.

—Of course, go, love.

Davide smiled at the sweetness of her words and, for a moment, hugged her, as if he wanted to capture that moment and keep it forever. As the phone continued to ring, he rose quickly and walked toward the kitchen, followed closely by Pia, who couldn't hide her curiosity.

The phone, lying on the countertop of the kitchen island, displayed an unknown number. Davide frowned, but decided to answer.

—Pronto?

The voice on the other end responded quickly.

—Davide, it's Umberto. Ciao.

Davide put the phone on speaker so Pia could listen too.

—Are you okay? Giuseppina and Lucia told me what happened. I'm sure it's the same person who attacked me. He kept asking insistently about the signorina. Idiot... —Where did you take the signorina?— Now I can't remember her name.

Davide tightened his jaw, and his response was direct.

—Pia. Her name is Pia. Are you telling me he's looking for her?

Umberto paused before speaking again, his tone now tinged with worry.

—Yes, he's looking for her. Take care, boy. I don't know what mess this Pia is involved in, but you're in danger.

Before Davide could reply, a female voice interrupted the call.

—Sorry, Davide. This is Aurora, Umberto's wife. When he woke up, he got very agitated and started shouting that he had to talk to you. Now the nurses are coming in to give him a sedative. I didn't know what else to do, but I wanted to thank you for answering our call at this hour of the night.

Davide, with his usual calmness, answered courteously.

—You have nothing to thank me for, Aurora. It's I who should thank you for the warning. Take good care of him. Goodbye.

When he hung up, the silence in the kitchen was thick, heavy with questions neither of them knew how to form. It was Pia who finally broke the silence, her voice trembling and her eyes glassy.

—Davide... I'm sorry. I swear I don't know what to say to you or where all of this is coming from. I'm ashamed that I doubted you, and I realize I am the creator of all this turmoil.

Davide, with that virtue of his —of maintaining serenity in the midst of chaos— approached her and took her hands in his.

—Just breathe, Pia. We'll figure it out together. Let's think clearly.

Pia nodded, closing her eyes for a moment to catch her breath.

—The man who tried to attack me was at Lucien's funeral —Davide said, thinking aloud—. Now that I think about it, I remember that while I was rushing toward the front row of the Basilica, I bumped into someone. He reacted aggressively, I think he said something to me, but I don't recall exactly. I know I looked at him and made a gesture of apology by putting my hands together.

Pia opened her eyes wide, as if something in her memory had suddenly ignited.

—Several weeks ago... I felt like someone was following me. But I didn't think much of it.

Davide turned toward her, his eyes calm, but inquisitive.

—Do you have photos of the friends or acquaintances who were at the Basilica?

Pia took her phone and began scrolling through the images in her gallery. For several minutes, she showed— the faces of friends and classmates from the faculty. But none of the faces sparked recognition in Davide.

Finally, he asked, almost in a whisper:

—Which of these photos is of your ex-boyfriend, boyfriend, or the friend you just met?

Pia put the phone aside and sighed with frustration.

—I've deleted them all… even the ones from social media.

Suddenly, her face lit up with an idea.

—Wait.

She jumped up and searched her purse. She took out the photo she had saved, the same one that included Lucien, Nicoletta, Giacomo, and herself.

—It can't be Giacomo —she murmured, as if trying to convince herself. But when she took out the photo and showed it to Davide, his expression said it all.

—Yes, it's him —Davide said, with a slow, grave nod.

Pia fell silent, looking at the photo in disbelief. Giacomo: thin, 1.70 meters tall, slightly disheveled light brown hair, and brown eyes that seemed devoid of emotion.

He had always had an elusive presence, almost like a shadow moving among people without drawing attention.

An instinct ignited in Pia, and without hesitation, she dialed Nicoletta's number.

—Mom, has Giacomo called you lately?

Nicoletta's voice sounded confused on the other end of the line.

—No, dear. Why do you ask?

—Listen, Mom. If Giacomo calls you or tries to come to the house, don't open the door. Please, promise me.

—Pia, you're making me nervous. What's going on? Are you okay?

—Yes, Mom, we're fine. But we think Giacomo has lost his mind… I'll explain everything later.

An uncomfortable silence settled on the line, until Nicoletta spoke again, her voice trembling.

—Dear… Giacomo is here.

Pia's heart stopped for an instant.

—What?

—He just arrived. He's here, at the door.

Pia felt the ground disappear beneath her feet, while Davide approached, his alert expression reflecting that he had grasped the gravity of the situation.

Silence Resounded

Giacomo gripped the steering wheel tightly, his hands trembling — not from fear, but from pure rage. He slammed his fists against the dashboard and screamed, sending tiny flecks of dry saliva flying in an uncontrollable burst of fury.

—Damn you! Damn you, Davide! —he shouted, his voice echoing in the cramped space of the car—. I'm going to kill you! You'll pay for this! You don't understand, no one understands. Pia is mine, she has always been mine! She always will be!

His breathing was erratic, and his heartbeat pounded like war drums. Giacomo, completely unhinged, imagined every possible scenario in which Davide and Pia had uncovered the truth. In his distorted mind, every second that passed was a new conspiracy against him. But no — he still had time. If Pia had recognized him, he had to act fast. He struck the steering wheel again and started the engine, leaving Belluno behind with a metallic roar.

The road to Padua stretched out like a labyrinth of secondary roads and narrow highways. Giacomo avoided the toll roads at all costs, afraid of leaving any trace that could betray him. He took the SS51 toward Ponte nelle Alpi, where the mountains began to give way to open fields. The lights of small towns flashed by like indifferent sparks against the storm raging inside him.

The landscape, under the cloak of night, looked like a somber painting. The shadows of bare trees stretched into the gloom, and his car's headlights barely managed to light the winding paths. Giacomo no longer saw the outside world; his mind was trapped in a single thought: Pia. There was no room for reason or fear, only for a deranged impulse that pushed him onward.

He reached Padua deep into the night, parking about three kilometers from Pia's parents' house. He walked the rest of the way quickly under the cover of darkness, pausing to watch every corner, every street.

Finally, he reached the house. From the sidewalk, he saw that a few lights were on downstairs. The curtains were not fully closed, allowing him a glimpse of the dim light from the television and the silhouette of Nicoletta.

He approached quietly, peeking through the windows. Nicoletta was alone. There was no sign of anyone else in the house. He breathed deeply, trying to recover some composure. He ran his hand through his hair and adjusted his jacket, attempting to look as normal as possible. Then he rang the bell.

The sound of the doorbell echoed through the house like an unexpected intrusion. Nicoletta, comfortably seated in front of the television, startled. Her first reaction was surprise at seeing Giacomo at the door, but soon unease settled into her chest.

—Giacomo, what a surprise —she said as she opened the door and greeted him with a kiss on each cheek, as courtesy dictated—. What are you doing here at this hour?

—I'm sorry for coming so late, Nicoletta — Giacomo replied with a smile that didn't reach his eyes—. I needed to talk to you. It's something important about Pia.

Before he could continue, Nicoletta's phone rang from the living room.

—Wait a moment, Giacomo —she said, motioning him inside—. Let me see who it is.

Nicoletta picked up the phone.

—Hello, dear.

Pia's voice was quick, urgent.

—Mom, has Giacomo called you lately?

Nicoletta frowned, confused.

—No, dear. Why are you asking me that?

Pia's tone grew more urgent.

—Mom, you're making me nervous. What's happening? Are you okay?

At that moment, Giacomo, who had been observing her carefully, realized Pia was talking about him. His gaze changed; the eyes that had tried to maintain a facade of calm now filled with contained fury. Slowly, he closed the door behind him and turned the lock with a click that echoed in the silence of the house.

Nicoletta felt a shiver run down her spine. Something in the atmosphere turned oppressive, and Giacomo's expression, dark and menacing, left her paralyzed.

—Dear... Giacomo is here —she said into the phone, her voice trembling.

Pia reacted immediately.

—I'm going there right now!

Nicoletta couldn't respond. Giacomo had already approached and, with a swift movement, snatched the phone from her hand.

—Don't worry —he said, his voice a chilling blend of calm and threat—. You won't be needing this anymore.

He turned off the phone and let it fall to the floor. Then, he pulled a knife from his pocket and held it up to his face.

—Listen carefully, Nicoletta. If you do exactly what I say, you won't get hurt.

The look in Giacomo's eyes —filled with a fire Nicoletta had never seen before— left her completely frozen. In that moment, she understood that her life, and perhaps her daughter's, hung by a thread far too fragile to survive.

The Edge of Night

Davide and Pia rushed out of the house, leaving behind any trace of calm the day might have offered them. The night was thick, a shroud of shadows and doubts covering the city as Davide started the dark blue BMW X5, the roar of the engine resonating in the silence. As they accelerated, the lights of Belluno faded in the rearview mirror, and the highway unfolded before them like an endless tunnel into uncertainty.

—I've already alerted the Belluno police, said Davide, his eyes fixed on the road. They are notifying Padua. They'll get there before we do.

Pia nodded, breathing deeply, trying to contain the whirlwind of emotions that threatened to consume her. Yet something inside her told her it would not be enough. She pulled out her phone and dialed hurriedly.

—Alessia? —her voice, strained with the effort to sound calm, echoed through the speaker.

—Friend! What a surprise!—Alessia answered cheerfully on the other end of the line. What's up?

—Are you in Padua? Alessia had stepped away from the table to hear better.

—Of course. I went to your house this morning and had a coffee with your mom. Didn't she tell you? She told me about Davide. I can't wait to meet him.

—Alessia!— Pia interrupted sharply, cutting through her enthusiasm. I need you to go back to the house immediately. Mom is in danger.

Pia's authoritative tone surprised Alessia, who, sensing the gravity of the situation, set aside her usual joviality.

—What's happening, Pia? Are you okay?

—There's no time for explanations. Please, do as I say. Go back to the house and stay close to Mom. I'm on my way.

—Okay. I'm at a bar in Arcella. I'm leaving right now.

Alessia hurried back to the table, her face reflecting concern.

—Tomasso, I have to go —she said, grabbing her purse with clumsy movements.

—What's going on? —asked Tomasso, raising an eyebrow.

—A friend. Something's happening with her mother. Until now, she had hidden, out of jealousy, that the friend's name was Pia.

Tomasso looked at her carefully, trying to understand the urgency in her words.

—I'm going with you.

—No —Alessia stopped him with a firm, almost authoritative tone. You stay here.

—What? I'm not just going to sit here and do nothing.

—You wait for me here —repeated Alessia, locking eyes with him.

Tomasso, confused but obedient, sank back into his chair like a soldier who had just received a direct order. Alessia left the bar without looking back, while Tomasso, after a few seconds of hesitation, stood up, pulled out a fifty-euro bill —more than he owed— handed it to the bartender, and slipped out discreetly after her, keeping a cautious distance.

After walking several blocks, Giacomo's red Fiat appeared parked by the side of the street. As Alessia passed by the car, she placed her palm on the hood. It was warm. Her heart began to race, starting to grasp the seriousness of what might be happening.

—My God —she whispered, quickly pulling away.

A few meters away, Tomasso watched from the shadows. He did not know what was going on, but something in the air warned him to stay back. A patrol car sped by with its sirens blaring, and Tomasso muttered a curse under his breath.

—Shiiit —he drawled, stretching the 'sh' for a couple of seconds and elongating the vowel sound—. What the hell am I doing here? —he asked himself, but his steps did not falter.

In the distance, Alessia turned a corner and disappeared from Tomasso's sight. Faintly, he saw the shadows of two people walking in his direction. Tomasso quickened his pace, trying to reach her without drawing attention. When he finally spotted her, she was only a few meters away. She almost caught him following her, but he saw how she hid behind a car, seeming to whisper into her phone, while Tomasso pressed his body against the trunk of a tree to stay hidden.

At Nicoletta's house, the police arrived swiftly but silently. Two patrol cars pulled up in front of the entrance. The officers found the front door ajar and the television still on. They checked every corner of the house, weapons drawn and on high alert, but everything was in order. There were no signs of robbery or violence, except for a cell phone lying on the floor.

Meanwhile, out on the street, Tomasso, hidden behind the tree, watched as a male figure and an older woman walked in the distance. The woman seemed to walk with difficulty, while the man behind her spoke aggressively, almost pushing her.

Suddenly, Alessia emerged from her hiding place like a predator ready to strike. Her only weapon was her phone; she had shared her location with Pia and had the line open.

—Let her go, Giacomo! —she shouted, her voice ringing out with an unexpected authority that shattered the calm of the night.

Giacomo froze, visibly startled. Nicoletta, trembling, could barcly stay on her feet.

—What the hell are you doing here?—asked Giacomo, his voice tinged with rage and confusion.

—Let her go —repeated Alessia, slowly advancing towards him. You don't have to do this.

Giacomo, desperation painted across his face, grabbed Nicoletta by the neck and placed the blade right against her skin.

—Don't take another step!—he yelled, his eyes gleaming with uncontrollable madness. Stay out of this, Alessia!

—Calm down, Giacomo. This is between you and me. Let her go, and we'll resolve this however you want.

Alessia raised her hands, showing the phone still in her grip. Giacomo stared at her with distrust, tightening his grip on Nicoletta.

From a distance, Tomasso watched the scene, his heart pounding in his chest, hoping the tree would shield him. Just then, the dark blue BMW rounded the corner and advanced slowly down the street.

Inside the car, Pia spotted a figure crouched next to a tree. Although she couldn't identify him, something in her heart told her he wasn't a stranger.

—Davide, stop here —she said with a trembling voice.

The car stopped in the middle of the street, and both braced themselves for whatever the night had in store.

Under the Crimson Light

The screech of tires breaking the night's stillness tore through the silence like a scream awakening the neighborhood. Davide disappeared momentarily between the houses, while Pia ran desperately, following Alessia's steps.

The scene that unfolded before her eyes was a mixture of terror and despair: Giacomo was holding Nicoletta tightly, the knife gripped firmly in his hand.

—Giacomo, please!—cried Pia, approaching slowly. Let her go. She has nothing to do with this! Take me instead, but let my mother go.

Giacomo looked at her with a twisted smile, his eyes burning with a fury he could barely contain.

—Take you? —he spat, his voice dripping with sarcasm—. And what guarantees that you won't abandon me again, like you always have?

Pia felt the air grow heavier; each of Giacomo's words was a poisoned dart. Alessia, terrified by what Giacomo might reveal, advanced with slow, calculated steps. Tomasso, still hidden behind a nearby tree, gathered enough courage to leave his shelter. But his movement did not go unnoticed.

Giacomo turned his head toward him, his lips curling into a sneer.

—Are you sleeping with him too now?—he shouted at Alessia, his voice full of venom.

Pia turned her face toward Tomasso, utterly bewildered, then looked at Alessia, seeking answers.

—Shut up, Giacomo!— Alessia screamed desperately, trying to calm the situation. What the hell are you saying?

Giacomo let out a bitter laugh.

—Alessia... the great Alessia. She's slept with all of us, Pia. She's a bitch, a real traitorous whore.

He couldn't finish the sentence. Alessia, with a cry of pure fury, hurled herself at him. Giacomo, startled, violently shoved Nicoletta, who fell hard onto the cold pavement with a sickening, terrifying thud.

—Mom!—screamed Pia as she ran toward her, tears filling her eyes at the sound of Nicoletta's body hitting the ground.

Giacomo drew back his arm, waiting for Alessia to get closer, and drove the knife into her abdomen. Alessia hadn't expected it; the expression on her face was one of terror. She placed her hand over the wound, feeling the warm blood quickly soaking her hands.

At that instant, Davide appeared behind Giacomo. With a swift move, he grabbed him by the neck, trying to subdue him. But Giacomo, like a cornered animal, swung his arm again and plunged the knife into Alessia's chest.

—This is for being a bitch!—he bellowed as the blood began to stain the pavement.

Before he could strike again, Davide tightened his grip, struggling to maintain control. However, Giacomo twisted the knife and buried it into Davide's thigh.

—Bastard!—shouted Davide, his voice thick with pain, but he didn't let go. He squeezed even harder, drawing strength from somewhere beyond the pain.

Alessia, wounded but fighting to remain conscious, tried to get up, supporting herself on her hands and knees. But Giacomo, in a burst of cruelty, kicked her squarely in the face, sending her crashing back down to the pavement.

—Help!—screamed Pia, holding her mother and watching Tomasso, frozen in place, his face a mask of terror.

Despite the pain, Davide made a calculated move with his body. He twisted sharply, causing Giacomo to lose balance and fall on top of him. The knife snapped in the process, leaving the blade buried in Davide's thigh.

In the distance, the police sirens shattered the silence. The blue and red lights began to reflect off the nearby houses' windows, heralding the arrival of the carabinieri. The patrol cars blocked the street, one by the BMW and another arriving from the opposite end.

The officers quickly jumped out of their vehicles, weapons drawn, as they advanced toward the scene.

—Drop the weapon!—shouted one of the officers, aiming directly at Giacomo, who, after the struggle with Davide, could barely remain standing, clutching the broken handle of the knife.

With clumsy movements, Giacomo raised his hands, letting the shattered knife handle fall to the ground. The officers grabbed him and cuffed him forcefully, while another team rushed toward Davide.

—Sir, put your hands down. You are in custody.

Pia, with tears streaming down her face, stepped between Davide and the officers.

—No! He hasn't done anything wrong!—she cried out desperately. He saved my mother's life... and maybe Alessia's too. One of the policemen, with a serious expression, slightly lowered his weapon.

—Can you confirm that?—he asked, addressing both Pia and Nicoletta, who was just beginning to regain consciousness. The officer shot a firm glance at Tomasso, and he nodded silently.

—Yes, —Nicoletta said, her voice weak but firm—. Davide saved us.

The officers exchanged glances and nodded. One of them approached Davide to examine the wound in his thigh.

—Sir, you need immediate medical attention.

Davide, grimacing in pain, tried to stand as Pia supported him.

—I'm fine. Help Alessia first, he said in a hoarse voice, his left pant leg soaked in blood, his gaze fixed on Alessia's fallen figure, who was struggling to move on the ground.

The Wound of the Soul

Tomasso finally broke the spell of fear that had kept him paralyzed and rushed toward Alessia. She lay sprawled on the pavement, fighting to stay conscious as blood continued to gush from her abdomen. Her face, pale and covered in cold sweat, reflected the intensity of the pain coursing through her. Tomasso, his hands trembling, pressed against the wound to try to stop the bleeding, his words a mixture of pleading and desperation.

—Alessia! Stay with me, please. Don't close your eyes; look at me. Look at me!—his voice cracked as his eyes searched hers for any sign of response.

Alessia, breathing in ragged gasps, looked at him weakly, her lips barely moving as she tried to speak, but only a faint whimper escaped her throat. Pia, her heart pounding wildly, approached from the other side, placing a hand on Alessia's arm.

—Alessia!—she called out, her voice firm yet tender. The paramedics are here; they're coming. Please, hold on a little longer.

The beams of the ambulances lit up the scene like a lighthouse in the darkness. The paramedics jumped out quickly and professionally, carrying stretchers and medical equipment. With precise movements, they pushed Tomasso and Pia aside as they began to work on Alessia.

—Please, give us space —one of them said in an authoritative but kind tone.

Pia and Tomasso stepped back, watching helplessly as they placed Alessia on the stretcher. The sound of the heart monitor and the quick, sharp instructions between the paramedics created a frantic rhythm. They inserted an IV line while one of them pressed firmly on her abdominal wound to control the hemorrhage.

Tomasso, watching as they loaded Aloooia into the ambulance, approached Pia with eyes full of guilt and regret. He said nothing, but his gaze spoke volumes. Pressing his lips together, he tried to convey what words could not express. Pia returned the look, understanding the message, though the weight of everything that had happened made it impossible for her to respond.

—Go with her, Tomasso —she finally said, her voice barely a whisper. Stay by her side.

Tomasso nodded quickly before jumping into the ambulance, which sped away, vanishing among the blue flashes of the patrol cars.

Meanwhile, another medical team was tending to Nicoletta and Davide at the edge of the second ambulance. One paramedic, his expression focused, examined the wound on Davide's thigh.

—He needs stitches and a procedure to remove the knife fragment, but it doesn't seem like any major arteries were hit —he told the ambulance driver.

Nicoletta, though conscious, had her vital signs checked and was given oxygen as a precaution. Despite the pain in her body, she insisted on remaining calm for Pia's sake, while Pia, nerves frayed, watched everything unfold with anxious eyes.

A carabiniere approached Davide and Pia with a notepad in hand.

—We need your identification and a brief statement of what happened. Please cooperate —he said with a formal but not unfriendly tone.

Davide handed over his ID and, between pained breaths, recounted the essential details. Pia did the same with another officer, although her mind was still trapped with Alessia and the horror she had just witnessed. The officers asked them to remain available for any further clarification during the investigation.

Finally, Nicoletta and Davide were placed in the same ambulance, a break from protocol, but the paramedics understood the emotional urgency of keeping them together. Nicoletta was laid out on a stretcher for observation, while Davide, his thigh soaked with blood, sat in the companion seat, enduring the pain with stoic silence.

Pia, watching the ambulance drive off, climbed into the BMW and slid into the driver's seat. With trembling hands, she started the engine and followed at a distance. Through the rearview mirror, she saw Giacomo, handcuffed and his face darkened with defeat, being led by the carabinieri into a police vehicle. The blue and red lights flashed in his eyes, marking the end of a night that had left deep scars in everyone.

As she drove, Pia took a deep breath, trying to calm herself. But the silence inside the car was deafening, and the weight of what had happened pressed on her chest like a heavy stone. She looked ahead, watching the ambulances carve a path through the darkness, and she knew the battle wasn't over.

The deepest wound wasn't of the body—it was of the soul.

Alessia

Alessia died on the operating table at Sant'Antonio Hospital in Padua, her life extinguished by the severity of her wounds and the irreparable loss of blood. The machines ceased their constant beeping, and the operating room fell silent, broken only by the murmured voices of the doctors confirming the inevitable. The news fell like a weight on the shoulders of everyone present at the hospital. Tomasso, motionless in the waiting room, refused to accept what had happened, his gaze fixed on the floor, as if searching among the tiles for some answer that could bring Alessia back. His breathing was slow, and heavy, as if each breath cost too much.

Nicoletta, though physically fine, was in the throes of an evident nervous crisis. Her hands trembled as she clutched the glass of water she had been given, her fingers marked by abrasions from the fall. Her bruised knees were a physical reminder of the horror she had lived through. Pia remained at her side, holding her hand, trying to find the right words to offer comfort.

Meanwhile, Davide had come out of surgery after a minor procedure to remove the knife blade embedded in his thigh. He walked slowly, supported by a crutch, but his face carried a dim smile and showed signs of deeper emotional exhaustion than physical pain. The night had been endless, and dawn was beginning to unfold on the horizon in shades of purple and orange, as if the day itself wished to return some hope after so much darkness.

Pia, exhausted both physically and emotionally, asked Nicoletta for a few minutes to speak with Davide. She approached him as he sat down in one of the lobby chairs.

The morning light streamed in through the large windows, enveloping them both in a melancholic warmth.

—Davide —Pia began, her voice barely a whisper— I need you to listen. It's important for me to tell you that I love you. With you, I've known what true love is. But... after everything that's happened —Giacomo, Alessia, and you— I feel I need time. I don't know how to process it all, and I know I must go through this process alone. Besides, my mother needs me now more than ever.

Davide looked at her, his eyes wavering between understanding and pain. He took a moment before responding, as if searching deep for the right words.

—Pia, I understand. And I love you. I don't want to pressure you or rush you. Take all the time you need. I'll be here... ready whenever you are.

Pia gave him a sad smile, her eyes glistening with tears that dared not fall. They embraced, and in that hug they said everything words could not express. It was a hug full of unspoken promises, of hope, and of a silent certainty: both wished for a future together, but they knew the present demanded separate paths.

Davide, unable to drive because of his wound, handed Pia the keys to his BMW.

—Take the car. I don't need it right now. Keep it as long as you need.

Pia tried to protest, but he had already signaled to a taxi driver waiting outside the hospital.

—Take care of your mother, Pia. And take care of yourself. We'll see each other soon —Davide said, offering a faint smile.

The taxi's horn interrupted the moment. They embraced once more, this time shorter but just as intense. Pia watched him walk toward the taxi, each step slow yet steady. Before getting in, Davide turned his gaze toward Tomasso, who remained seated in the waiting room, his face buried in his hands.

—And him? —Davide asked, signaling with a nod of his head. Pia sighed and replied coldly:

—That's Tomasso. He doesn't matter. I don't want to get involved—I already have enough.

Davide nodded, not insisting, and got into the taxi.

As the vehicle pulled away, Pia and Davide exchanged one last look, their gazes intertwined with hope and the promise of a better, albeit uncertain, future.

Pia returned to the lobby, where Tomasso still sat, unmoving. She allowed herself a moment to take a deep breath and look at the dawn through the windows. The light was beginning to illuminate the streets, and with it, a new opportunity to heal and rebuild everything that had been broken.

Pia's Journal

Tuesday, November 1, 2022,

I have arrived at the threshold of a moment that could be called crucial but that is nothing more than the inevitable reflection of a destiny that had always been awaiting me. These recent days, laden with an intensity I can scarcely name, have been like mirrors multiplying the shadows and reflections of my own existence. Giacomo, with his overflowing violence; Alessia, with the betrayal that tore apart the threads of trust; and Davide, the echo of a love that never fully extinguished, have been pieces on a board I thought I knew but which now reveals itself as infinitely vaster and more complex.

Giacomo showed me not only his own ruin but also mine. His violence was nothing more than a mirror forcing me to see the blurry boundaries I have allowed in my life, the concessions made at the cost of my own essence. Alessia, for her part, was a reminder of how fragile human connections are and how illusory it is to believe we truly know those around us. In her betrayal, I have also seen the times I betrayed my own needs and desires, seeking an ideal that never existed. And then there is Davide, whose return is like a line written in a forgotten book, a sign that refuses to fade, an anchor inviting me to remain in the present while I attempt to decipher the past.

What I have learned is as vast as time itself, as elusive as sand slipping through fingers. I have lived under the illusion of expectations, believing I could mold others, forging them into the image of my desires and needs. But the truth, cruel and luminous, is that I did not love Giacomo for who he was but for who I wanted him to be. I did not see Alessia as she was, but as I needed to see her. I have lived inside a hall of mirrors, where the reflected images were not of them, but of my own longings.

With Davide, however, I feel the possibility of something different. Not because he is perfect, nor because I am, but because together we could build something without the lies of the past, without the masks of idealization. But for that to happen, I must first reconcile with my own story; with the wounds and mistakes, and find in them not a burden, but a lesson.

It is not about forgetting, because forgetting would be denying the map of my existence. It is about understanding, about accepting that the shadows are also part of the light. Giacomo, Alessia, and even Davide are chapters of a narrative that is still being written. I am not the victim of this story, I am its author. I must learn to love from authenticity, not from the desire to fill voids, but from the ability to share what I already am.

This is the beginning of my rewriting—not to erase what was, but to chart a new path. I know that love is not a perfect refuge but an honest mirror that returns to us what we are, with all our imperfections. And I know that, alongside Davide, I have the possibility of being not a half seeking completion, but a whole choosing to share its light. In the end, perhaps, I will discover that there is no beginning or end—only an endless road—and that the true destination is, finally, to arrive at myself.

Alessia

249

The Big Apple

The morning of Friday, November 18, dawned under a sky tinged with gray, and the Italian autumn trees were shedding their last golden leaves. Pia, her heart beating to the rhythm of a mixture of nostalgia and hope, grabbed the keys to Davide's BMW and set off toward Belluno. The road wound through mountains that seemed to bid her farewell with their melancholic beauty, as if they understood the importance of this journey. Upon arriving, Davide was waiting for her at the entrance to his building, wearing a serene smile that seemed to contain a world of emotions.

They embraced, and in that instant, time seemed to stop. It was a hug laden with unspoken promises and restrained goodbyes. Their lips met briefly, as if that kiss would have to sustain them until they met again.

—Thank you for coming to get me, Pia —Davide said, breaking the silence as they climbed into the car. You have no idea how much it means to me.

Pia smiled, her hands steady on the wheel as they drove out of Belluno heading toward Padua.

—I had to return the car, didn't I?—she joked, although the truth was evident in her eyes. Besides, I wanted to see you. I couldn't leave without saying goodbye.

During the drive, they talked about everything and nothing. The recent days had felt like a hurricane, and now that the air was clearer, they could afford to dream again.

—Davide —Pia said, breaking a comfortable silence as the highway stretched out before them— I need you to know something. This trip is important to me, not just because I need time to heal, but because I need to find myself. But I want you to know that what I most wish for in this world is that, when I'm ready, you'll be there for me.

Davide looked at her, his eyes shining with that mix of love and patience that so defined him.

—Pia, I'll wait for you as long as it takes. I'll always be here, no matter how long it is. The only thing I want is for you to find what you're looking for and be happy.

They arrived at Nicoletta and Antonella's house in Padua, where the two women awaited them with a table full of delights: brioche, cornetti, and cappuccino that filled the home with a warm, welcoming aroma. Pia and Davide sat together, holding hands, as laughter filled the room.

—Davide —said Nicoletta, serving him a cappuccino—, I hope you'll take good care of my daughter when she decides to come back. I'll accept nothing less.

—You can count on it, signora —Davide replied with a smile, giving Pia's hand a gentle squeeze.

Antonella, always cheerful, couldn't resist teasing.

—Well, Davide, if you make her suffer, you'll have to answer to me first.

Her words brought a nervous laugh from Pia, who struggled to maintain her composure amid so much emotion.

Finally, the moment to leave arrived. They loaded the luggage into the car, and while Antonella and Nicoletta waved them off from the doorway, Davide and Pia set off toward Marco Polo Airport. The day, with its partially cloudy sky and the crisp autumn air, seemed to mirror Pia's emotions: a balance between the uncertain and the promising. The journey passed in a comfortable silence, broken only by the soft murmur of the radio and the looks they exchanged at each stoplight.

Upon arriving at the airport, Davide parked the car and took the suitcases, making sure to carry them all the way to the check-in counter. Taking advantage of a moment when Pia was distracted, he slid his credit card to the airline agent.

—Please upgrade her ticket to first class, he said in a low voice.

The agent discreetly returned the card, and Davide went back to Pia, who looked at him with tenderness.

—Thank you for everything, Davide. Not just for bringing me, but... for everything. For being you.

He smiled, leaning down to kiss her forehead.

—I just want you to come back when you're ready. I'll be here, waiting for you.

In the boarding lounge, time seemed to speed up. They said goodbye with a hug that lasted longer than necessary, as if they were trying to absorb each other's energy for the days ahead.

When the final call for the flight was announced, Pia gathered her things and looked at Davide one last time before disappearing behind the security doors.

Once on board, Pia handed over her boarding pass, unaware that something had changed.

It was when a flight attendant guided her to seat 5D that she understood what had happened.

The warm welcome, the glass of Prosecco offered before takeoff, and the spacious seat were clear proof of Davide's gesture.

She smiled to herself and moved.

—Is there anything else we can bring you before takeoff?—asked the flight attendant with a smile.

—No, thank you. I'm fine —Pia answered, as a tear slid down her cheek—not from sadness, but from hope.

As the plane ascended, Pia gazed out the window, watching as Italy became a tapestry of autumnal colors. In her heart, she carried the certainty that this was not a goodbye, but a new beginning.

The Roman Emperor

Upon arriving in New York, Pia found herself immersed in a vibrant city that seemed alive, a metropolis pulsing to the rhythm of millions of intertwined stories. Antonella's apartment, located on Fifth Avenue with views of Central Park, was a reflection of the elegance and good taste that characterized its owner.

At the entrance, a uniformed doorman, whose seriousness seemed chiseled in marble, opened the door with a slight nod. No sooner had Pia crossed the threshold than Mike, the butler, greeted her with the precision of a Swiss clock.

—Miss Pia, I presume —said Mike, offering a bow so slight it was almost imperceptible. Mrs. Antonella asked me to ensure everything is perfect for your stay.

He took Pia's suitcases and, while accompanying her to the elevator, handed her an envelope containing the apartment instructions and the contact number of the neighbor who was taking care of Piccolo, the little Maltese dog.

—If you need anything, don't hesitate to call me — he added with a discreet smile before disappearing behind the elevator doors.

The apartment was an oasis of sophistication. High ceilings and massive windows framed a privileged view of Central Park. Inside, classic furnishings were combined with modern touches, and every corner exuded a calm that contrasted with the bustle of the city that never sleeps.

Pia soon met Piccolo, Antonella's Maltese. With his dignified bearing and commanding nature, he seemed lost in the geometry of the cosmos, believing he lived in the body of a Saint Bernard. He was more like a Roman emperor demanding attention and veneration at every moment than a simple companion dog. Piccolo let out a low growl, as if establishing who was in charge in that territory.

—Piccolo, we're going to have to learn to live together, Pia said with a smile as she stroked his silky fur.

After settling in, Pia decided to fulfill one of her dreams: to eat an authentic American hamburger. She hailed a yellow cab whose driver, with a Caribbean accent and a mischievous smile, skillfully wove through traffic.

—First time in New York, huh?—he asked as he navigated the bustling streets.

—Yes, and I hope it won't be the last —Pia answered with a smile.

The cab dropped her off at the corner of Sixth Avenue and 36th Street. Pia lingered on the sidewalk for a moment, taking in the ceaseless movement of the city. The energy of New York amazed her, but hunger soon pulled her from her reverie and led her into the restaurant.

The place was not just a restaurant —it was a journey back in time. Crossing its doors, Pia felt transported to the New York of the late nineteenth century, to an era of elegance and bohemia. The establishment, with its dark wood-paneled walls and high ceilings, breathed history in every corner. Gas lamps, still illuminating parts of the rooms, cast dancing shadows across the tables draped with white linens.

The walls displayed hundreds of clay pipes, relics from a time when smoking was a social ritual. Antique photographs and caricatures of celebrated figures decorated the wood-paneled spaces, creating an atmosphere of a private club and a refuge for intellectuals.

The environment was warm and welcoming, tinged with nostalgia. The scent of grilled meat mingled with the aroma of old wood and leather armchairs. The murmur of conversations blended with the clinking of glasses and the sizzle of meat on the grill. In the midst of that gentle commotion, the bar rose like an oasis, a refuge for loners and conversationalists alike. It was an imposing structure of solid wood, polished by the passage of countless elbows and a silent witness to innumerable stories. Behind it, bartenders in rolled-up white shirts and black vests prepared classic cocktails and served craft beers and wines from the world's best vineyards. The atmosphere was relaxed and friendly, perfect for striking up a conversation with the bartender or other patrons. Pia sat on one of the red leather stools, feeling as though she had been transported to a time when elegance and conversation were an art.

—Table for one?—asked the hostess kindly.

—Yes, I just arrived from Italy, and I've always dreamed of eating a real hamburger in America.

—Would you mind sitting at the bar?—the hostess offered.

—Not at all —Pia replied, excited for the adventure.

At the bar, Tom, a burly and affable bartender, welcomed her.

—Welcome to New York! What can I get you?

—An American IPA beer. I've heard they're famous here.

Tom nodded enthusiastically.

—I've got a Lagunitas IPA on tap. It's a gem, with citrus aromas and a refreshing bitterness.

—Perfect —Pia said, mimicking the thumbs-up gesture she had seen Americans use so often.

When the Miss Keen's burger arrived, Pia couldn't help but smile. The juicy beef, the melted cheddar cheese, the crispy bacon, and the secret sauce turned it into a sublime experience. The golden, crispy fries were the ideal accompaniment.

—How is it? —Tom asked, watching her with curiosity.

—It's... perfect. Worth the trip just for this —Pia answered between laughs.

Satisfied and amazed by the feast, she decided to walk back to the apartment. The lights of New York, the skyscrapers touching the sky, and the blend of cultures wrapped her in a feeling of belonging and freedom. It was as if the city itself invited her to reinvent herself, to write a new chapter of her life.

Pia knew that this trip was not just an exploration of the city but of herself. New York presented itself as a blank canvas, and she was ready to fill it with new colors and shapes.

A Winter in New York

Pia woke up each morning to the soft light filtering through the curtains of Antonella's apartment, reflecting the silvery shimmer of snow gathered on the windowsill. New York, with its vibrant energy and ever-awake streets, had become her refuge—her space for rediscovery. Her days began with a walk through Central Park, a morning ritual in which Piccolo, the Maltese, accompanied her with his proud gait, as though he were the true master of the park.

On one of those walks, Pia ventured into the Metropolitan Museum of Art. The grandeur of its neoclassical facade impressed her, but what truly captivated her was the serenity she found within its galleries. In front of a Turner painting, she stood transfixed, feeling how the colors and forms spoke of emotions she couldn't express in words. There, amid the hushed buzz of visitors, she felt a spark of peace for the first time. She allowed herself to wander aimlessly through the halls, stopping in front of pieces that seemed to whisper secrets to her.

After the museum, she walked to a small café in the Upper East Side, where she found shelter from the winter cold. The scent of freshly ground coffee mixed with the soft murmur of conversations in different languages. She sat by the window, cappuccino in hand and a book she had picked up from an independent bookstore in the West Village resting in her lap. Each page invited her to dive into other lives, but her thoughts often circled back to Davide, to Nicoletta, to everything she had left behind.

Days passed, and Pia explored the city's most iconic and hidden corners. One afternoon, she wandered into Chinatown, where the exotic aromas of spices and dumplings enveloped her. In Little Italy, she found a tiny trattoria that reminded her of the flavors of home. As she left, she bought a small amulet from an antique shop that promised protection and good fortune.

The city's relentless rhythm soon swept her away completely. She took the train to Brooklyn to visit DUMBO, where she stood in awe at the view of the Manhattan Bridge framed by brick buildings. She walked along the High Line, a park that seemed to float between skyscrapers, and allowed herself to get lost in Chelsea Market, where the buzz of diners and the smell of fresh bread filled the air.

As December wore on, the city transformed into a spectacle of lights and holiday decorations. Rockefeller Center lit up with its towering tree, and Pia watched as couples and families skated across the ice rink. She bought a hot chocolate from a street vendor and let herself be carried away by the magic of the moment, feeling that, for the first time in a long while, she was learning how to enjoy the present.

On Christmas Eve, Antonella's apartment was wrapped in a warm atmosphere. Piccolo slept peacefully beside the radiator while Pia decorated a small tree she had bought at a market in Greenwich Village. The lights twinkled gently, casting golden reflections on the walls. She sat on the sofa, holding a glass of wine Antonella had left for her, and gazed out at the city through the window. The streets were blanketed in snow, and the lights from the buildings glowed like fallen stars.

She picked up the phone with determination. She dialed Davide's number and waited, listening to the dial tone as her heart pounded in her chest. On the other end, the familiar voice of Davide answered, warm and slightly groggy —Pronto, amore.

—Davide, I'm so sorry to call you this early —Pia began, her voice trembling slightly, almost a whisper—. I know it's the middle of the night there, and I didn't want to disturb you, but I needed to hear your voice.

Davide paused, his tone suddenly alert, filled with concern and tenderness.

—Pia, you don't have to apologize. Are you alright? Has something happened?

—No, no, Davide… nothing bad —Pia took a breath, trying to calm her nerves. It's just… I've been thinking a lot about us, about everything we've been through, and I couldn't wait any longer to say this.

On the other end of the line, Davide remained silent, listening with the attentiveness of someone who knew something important was about to be said.

—Davide… I'm ready —she continued, her voice now steadier, though laden with emotion. I'm ready to come back. I want to build a future with you. And if you'll have me, I'd love for you to be here with me so we can start again.

The silence that followed was brief but full of meaning, like the moment just before the sun rises on the horizon. Finally, Davide spoke, his voice warm and full of relief.

—Pia… you have no idea how long I've waited to hear those words. I'm here, ready for you. I always have been. And if you want me there, I'll be by your side— anywhere, anytime.

In that moment, the distance between New York and Belluno vanished, and both of them felt they were exactly where they belonged: in each other's hearts.

Pia closed her eyes, letting the tears fall gently down her cheeks. For the first time in months, she felt she had found her place, that the chaos of her life was beginning to take shape. Outside, the snow kept falling, blanketing the city in purity, as if everything she had lived through had only been a prelude to this new beginning.

The Phantom of the Opera

It was already Christmas in Italy. December 25, 2022. As soon as Davide hung up the phone, the clock struck 2:30 in the morning. With emotion pounding in his chest, he quickly packed a small suitcase. He didn't forget to place the engagement ring, carefully wrapped in a handkerchief, inside his briefcase. Then he left his apartment in Belluno and headed for Marco Polo Airport in Venice.

After weighing his options, he found a KLM flight that would arrive at JFK in New York at 1:37 PM. He knew he had no time to waste; this time, Pia wouldn't have to wait.

Hours later, in New York, Antonella, with her usual energy, convinced Pia that she couldn't spend all of Christmas locked inside with Piccolo. She persuaded her to attend a special performance of The Phantom of the Opera at the Majestic Theater. —It's a classic, Pia. It'll do you good to see something so magical, Antonella insisted, casually mentioning that the tickets were a gift from an influential friend.

Pia agreed, though somewhat reluctantly. Christmas in New York, surrounded by lights and bustle, clashed with her craving for peace. But Antonella's insistence, as always, was impossible to resist.

At 8:00 PM, Pia arrived at the Majestic Theater, a jewel of architecture in the heart of Broadway. The theater, with its Art Deco design and sparkling chandeliers, seemed to envelop attendees in a halo of glamour. The atmosphere buzzed with anticipation. Pia, in her black coat and red scarf, entered and was guided to her central seat, strategically placed with a perfect view of the stage.

What Pia didn't know was that, just minutes before, Davide had arrived straight from the airport to the theater. Antonella, with her connections and talent for orchestrating surprises, had arranged everything to perfection. Davide changed quickly in one of the dressing rooms, adjusted his dark suit, and took a deep breath as he finalized details with the show's director.

The performance began with the splendor only Broadway can offer: a dazzling display of lights, music, and talent that left Pia captivated. Davide, seated a few rows behind her, watched her with a blend of love and nerves. He waited for the right moment to take the stage.

When the show reached its second act, just after intermission, the orchestra began to play something unexpected. "La Vie en Rose" filled the theater with its melancholic sweetness. Pia, surprised, tensed slightly in her seat. What was that song doing here? It wasn't part of The Phantom of the Opera's regular repertoire.

Suddenly, the stage lights focused on a male figure walking toward center stage. Impeccably dressed, Davide stepped into the spotlight, his presence radiating confidence and love. The entire theater fell into a stunned silence. The audience, unsure whether this was part of the show, watched in awe.

—Pia —Davide said, his voice strong, projecting across the crowd—. I've crossed an ocean to tell you something that cannot wait.

The stage lights slowly turned to illuminate Pia in her seat. The audience turned to look at her as she, completely stunned, brought a hand to her chest, unsure if this was a dream.

—I've loved you from the first day, and I will always love you. Today, here, in this place full of magic, I want to ask you something I've carried in my heart for years.

Davide knelt at center stage and pulled out a small black velvet box.

—Pia, will you marry me?

A wave of murmurs ran through the audience, followed by applause and delighted gasps. Pia, eyes brimming with tears, stood up. With her heart racing, she walked toward the stage, followed by the spotlight, never taking her eyes off Davide.

When she reached him, silence once again filled the theater. With a trembling but full-hearted voice, she replied:

—Yes, Davide. Yes, I'll marry you!

The theater erupted in applause as Davide stood to embrace and kiss her. The orchestra resumed La Vie en Rose, and the actors, crew, and audience rose in a standing ovation that seemed to never end.

That night, the Majestic Theatre witnessed not only an unforgettable performance but the rebirth of a love that crossed continents to be rekindled in the heart of Broadway.

While Pia was still at the theater, Mike—with the precision and devotion that defined him—made sure Antonella's apartment was immaculate and perfectly decorated for the couple's return. The red flowers, meticulously chosen by Antonella, were the centerpiece of the décor: scarlet roses, oriental lilies, and crimson peonies adorned every corner of the space. The arrangements, placed strategically, filled the home with a sweet, enveloping fragrance.

On the dining table, a spectacular bouquet stood tall in a cut-crystal vase, the flowers arranged like a work of art that seemed to defy gravity. On the piano, a smaller bouquet of tulips and vibrant ranunculus lent a romantic air to the corner where Pia often sat to gaze out at the park. Even in the kitchen, a small cluster of red carnations in a white vase completed the feeling of harmony and care.

Because it was Christmas, food options were limited, but Antonella—with her excellent taste and attention to detail—had suggested a well-known Chinese restaurant nearby. Following instructions, Mike placed the order, ensuring each dish was a delight for the senses. When the perfectly sealed containers arrived, the aroma of spices filled the apartment.

The feast was worthy of a celebration for six. There was Peking Duck, its golden crispy skin served with delicate flour crepes, scallions, and an exquisitely sweet and salty hoisin sauce. The Dim Sum came in a variety of fillings: pork, shrimp, vegetables, and a crabmeat specialty touched with ginger.

A large bowl held Mapo Tofu—silken tofu with minced pork, bathed in a vibrant, spicy sauce of fermented chilies. Beside it, Cantonese-style prawns, perfectly browned and sautéed with garlic and spices, gave off an irresistible aroma. To complete the spread, a steaming plate of Singapore Noodles—stir-fried with curry, shrimp, chunks of chicken, and crisp vegetables.

The table was set with white and gold china, and at the center rested a bottle of prosecco, elegantly chilled in a silver bucket. The sparkle of crystal glasses reflected the apartment's soft lighting, creating a warm and sophisticated atmosphere.

When Pia returned to the apartment with Davide, still glowing from the events at the theater, she opened the door and stood completely amazed. Her eyes lit up at the sight of flowers adorning every corner. She walked slowly through the living room, one hand on her chest, lips curved in a smile of gratitude and wonder.

—It's… perfect —she whispered, looking at Davide, who watched her reaction with tenderness. Mike, with his characteristic discretion, stepped forward.

—Miss Pia, Mr. Davide, I hope everything is to your liking. Mrs. Antonella insisted tonight must be special.

Pia turned to Davide, her eyes full of emotion.

—Did you plan this too?

Davide smiled, a knowing sparkle in his eyes.

—I had help, of course, but I wanted this night to be unforgettable. For you… for us.

Pia walked to the dining table, where the feast awaited. The warm, spicy aromas filled the room, and the prosecco shimmered under the candlelight.

—It's more than I could have imagined, said Pia, taking Davide's hand. Thank you for everything.

Davide gently squeezed her hand and, with a gesture that seemed to suspend time, said:

—All that matters is that you're happy, Pia. Tonight… and every night after.

Mike, with his usual grace, withdrew after ensuring everything was perfect.

—If you need anything, don't hesitate to call. Good night, Miss Pia. Mr. Davide. He gave a slight bow before quietly closing the door behind him.

The silence that followed was a poem unto itself, an intimate rhythm woven with invisible threads of desire and hope. Christmas night, laced with bittersweet nostalgia, seemed to pause in the instant their eyes met—as if the universe conspired to silence everything except the shared beating of their hearts.

Pia stepped toward him, slow but sure, and took his hand with the tenderness of someone who knows they are about to cross a threshold. Her smile, a reflection of all the words left unspoken, carried the weight of years apart and the promise of what was still to come.

—There's something we left unfinished on that balcony in Belluno…—she said in a whisper that trembled with the depth of an echo inside her soul.

Davide tilted his head slightly, his gaze locked on hers, as if in her green eyes was written a map to a destiny he had always known.

—That's true —he replied, his voice as soft as snow falling in silence beyond the windowpane.

The room became a stage of light and shadow, a space where time fractured into infinite fragments of restrained longing. Between nervous laughter trembling like olive leaves in the wind and caresses that seemed to discover the texture of the universe for the first time, they walked together toward the bedroom, each step a verse in an eternal poem.

At the doorway, they paused, the air thick with the breath of something sacred. Pia, with the grace of someone shedding not only clothes but also fears and doubts, began unfastening the buttons of her blouse, one by one, as if each movement carried the reverence of an ancient ritual. Davide, eyes never leaving her, unbuttoned his shirt with hands that trembled slightly—not from hesitation, but from the weight of so many emotions held in for so long.

When their bodies met, it was as if love, long asleep, had awoken in a burst of light and flame. Every touch was a melody, every kiss a shooting star across the firmament of the night. Their sighs were wordless verses, their caresses the notes of a symphony only they could hear. In the meeting of their skin, the entire universe seemed to converge—and in that instant, time ceased to exist.

The shadows of the room danced to the rhythm of their passion, and every corner bore silent witness to a love reborn through surrender. In barely audible whispers, the names they spoke became prayers, and their movements, the language of two souls finally recognizing themselves in one another. There, beneath the cloak of night and the mantle of Christmas, Davide and Pia became one body, one spirit—as if in that act, they sealed a secret pact with the stars watching from the frozen sky.

At last, when their breathing slowed and silence wrapped around them again, Pia rested her head on Davide's chest, listening to the drumming of his heart as if it were the heartbeat of the entire world. Outside, the snow kept falling—silent and eternal—blanketing their shadows and leaving only the light of what they had just created.

Past midnight, after a moment of shared stillness in each other's arms, they decided to move to the dining room, where the feast Mike had prepared still waited. The prosecco had lost its chill in the ice bucket, but it didn't matter. Pia uncorked the bottle while Davide served the plates.

Seated by the window, with New York City as their backdrop, they shared laughter and memories. The lights of the skyscrapers twinkled in the distance, reflecting in their glasses like an echo of stars in the sky.

—Do you realize how far we've come?—asked Pia, breaking the silence as she raised her glass to Davide.

—I do. And I still can't believe I'm here with you — he replied, his gaze full of a tenderness that said everything.

They toasted—not to the past nor the future, but to the present that now held them. In that moment, the world felt perfect, a place where wounds had begun to heal and where love finally found its true meaning. And so, between shared bites and knowing glances, Davide and Pia began a new chapter in their story—one that promised second chances and the love they had always deserved.

Pia's Journal

Monday, December 26, 2022

New York was a mirror. In every bustling street, in every silent museum, and in every café where I sat watching the comings and goings of strangers, I saw all the fragments of myself reflected. I saw myself as I truly was—without filters, without idealizations. I was not only the woman who had loved and lost but also the woman who survived, who learned, who was reborn. In this place, where the lights never go out and the voices never fall silent, I found refuge in my own solitude. I learned that being alone does not mean being lost. On the contrary, it means being at home, within oneself.

I walked through the streets carrying the weight of my decisions and my mistakes. Giacomo was a shadow, a specter of the past that I refused to see, but now I understand. It was not he who was lost—it was me, clinging to an idealized version of a love that never truly existed. I tried to mold him, I waited for him to become something he never could be, and in doing so, I lost myself. But now I know that to love is not to demand, not to condition, not to shape. To love is to accept, to allow, and to let go.

Alessia's betrayal wounded me deeply, not because of what it meant for her, but because of what it meant for me. It was irrefutable proof that even those we love can fail us. But I also realized that betrayal does not define the other—it forces us to look at ourselves, to ask if we can forgive. And I did. I forgive Alessia because her mistake taught me something invaluable: that forgiveness is a gift we give ourselves.

In my conversations with Davide, I felt something I had not felt in a long time: peace. It was not an escape; it was not a solution. It was simply the echo of a love that never stopped being—a love that does not ask, that does not demand, that simply waits. In those late-night calls, while the city sparkled and the winter wind brushed my face, I understood that Davide was not my savior. He was my witness. My witness in this process of rediscovery, of reconstruction.

Today I am someone else. I am the woman who has left guilt behind, who has embraced her scars, and who has learned to love herself in her entirety. I am the woman who sits to write this, not from pain, but from hope. Because in the end, the wound that hurt the most was not the one others inflicted, but the one I inflicted upon myself by not accepting who I was. Today, I close that chapter. Today, I accept myself. Today, I love myself.

And that is why, on the eve of Christmas, I called Davide. I told him that I am ready—not because I want him to complete me, but because I want to share this new chapter with him. I told him that I love him, that I want to build a future by his side. And what fills me with the greatest peace is knowing that it will not be a happy ending. It will not be an ending at all. It will be a beginning. A story that we will write together, with all that we are, with our shadows and our lights, but above all, with our truths.

Today is Christmas, and I feel that I am being reborn. Not as someone new, but as someone who finally recognizes herself. And that, perhaps, is the true miracle.

The End.

References and Credits

In the Echoes of Pia, I have incorporated quotes and references from various works and authors that have profoundly inspired this narrative:

1. Erich Fromm, The Art of Loving. The quote appears on page 13.

2. Joseph Campbell, phrase: "The treasure you seek is not in someone else, but in yourself." This quote, taken from The Hero with a Thousand Faces, is found on page 29.

3. Jean-Paul Sartre, for his philosophy of existentialism. Inspiration is taken from Being and Nothingness, cited on page 41.

4. Albert Camus, The Plague. The reference to this work is found in the context: "You challenged the apparent meaninglessness of existence and, in that challenge, turned shadows into light," cited on page 49.

5. Carl Jung, phrase: "The privilege of a lifetime is to become who you truly are." Cited on page 49.

6. Charles Chaplin, phrase: "Sing, laugh, dance, cry, and live every moment of your life before the curtain falls and the play ends without applause." Cited on page 49.

7. Jorge Luis Borges, references to his philosophy on reflection and labyrinths. Inspiration is taken from his works The Mirrors and The Library of Babel, cited on page 49.

8. Edmond Rostand, for his work Cyrano de Bergerac. Cited on page 53.

9. Jovanotti, song "Baciami Ancora". This song, part of the soundtrack for the homonymous film released in 2010, is cited on page 57.